LAST ONE TO DIE

BOOKS BY DANA PERRY

DETECTIVE NIKKI CASSIDY BOOK 2

LAST ONE TO DIE

DANA PERRY

bookouture

Published by Bookouture in 2024

An imprint of Storyfire Ltd.
Carmelite House
50 Victoria Embankment
London EC4Y 0DZ

www.bookouture.com

ISBN: 978-1-83790-960-5
eBook ISBN: 978-1-83790-959-9

PROLOGUE

It was important for her to always make him happy.

He was nice to her when he was happy.

But sometimes, when she disappointed him, he was not so nice.

She'd found that out in the beginning when she'd questioned one of his orders that didn't make much sense to her.

He'd punished her—punished her severely—for the slip-up.

He'd told her "never to ask why" he wanted something done.

Then he'd made her repeat that over and over again until he was convinced that she had learned her lesson.

She knew there had been other girls before her—he sometimes made references to them, always in the past tense—even though she never found out what had happened to any of them.

But that was their problem, not hers. Those girls probably didn't make him happy.

As long as she kept him happy, she kept telling herself, everything would be all right. You see, she was special. He told her that. And he promised he would never really hurt anyone as special as her.

But today she was scared.

More scared than she'd ever been in her life.

She had made him unhappy, and she didn't even want to think about what he might do to her now.

ONE

It all started with Becky Benedict.

Becky's mother came to the FBI office in Washington, D.C., where I work, to ask me to find out who murdered her daughter. That was unusual. Not many people show up in person to ask me to investigate a case. But Eleanor Benedict was an unusual woman. And this was an unusual case.

"You are Nikki Cassidy, right?" she said.

"Yes, I am."

"And you solve cases involving abductions and murders of young women?"

"We're the FBI's Washington field office for the Crimes Against Children Squad," I said. "That's our job."

"My name is Eleanor Benedict, Agent Cassidy. I want you to find out who killed my daughter, Becky." She reached into her handbag and took out a picture for me to see.

The teenage girl in the photo was smiling sweetly for the camera. She was pretty, in that innocent way a girl is at that age. Long blonde hair, big blue eyes. Her face looked full of energy, full of hope and full of life. Except, as Eleanor Benedict

explained, someone took that life away from young Becky—
violently and tragically—at the age of fifteen.

"Becky was the shining angel of my life," she said to me.
"Beautiful. Smart. Just a wonderful girl. She was my only child,
so I suppose I doted on her quite a bit. But she deserved it. Only
fifteen years old, but already had figured out her life's dream.
She wanted to be a doctor. She told everyone she wanted to
devote her life to helping others. That was the kind of girl
Becky was.

"Until someone murdered her. It happened on her way
home from school one day. In broad daylight, in a nice neighborhood. They just took her off the street. I knew something was
wrong when she didn't come home at her normal time. Becky
was always so responsible and punctual. That night I called the
police. They spent days looking for her. Then they finally found
her. They found... they found my Becky dead.

"My husband died of a heart attack not long after that. No
matter what the doctors say about him having heart disease, I'm
convinced it was the stress and the anguish of losing Becky that
killed him. I've been alone since then. No husband. No daughter. Just me. And all I care about now is catching the person
who took the life of my darling girl."

Mrs. Benedict didn't resemble her daughter at all. In fact, it
was kind of difficult to believe she was the young girl's mother.
She seemed much older, almost like she could be the grand-
mother. Gray hair, a frail body, and a weary look on her face.
Maybe she'd had Becky later in life. Or else she'd simply been
beaten down by the tragic events that had occurred to her
family.

But why come to the FBI, instead of going to her local
police?

I asked her that question.

"I read about you," she said. "The things you did with your

sister's case. So I decided to come to you to help me find justice for Becky. Just like you did with your sister."

I sighed. I'd made national headlines and gotten voluminous TV coverage not long ago when I solved the years-old murder of my little sister Caitlin in the small southern Ohio town of Huntsdale where I grew up.

That's how this woman knew me.

They'd arrested someone for Caitlin's murder right after it happened, but it turned out that the man in jail all these years wasn't the one who did it. Oh, he'd been involved, but the actual murder was carried out by a top official in Huntsdale—a seemingly respectable citizen—and others like him who turned out to also be responsible for the abduction and murder of other young girls.

I was happy about cracking that long-ago—and very personal—case, of course. But it had taken a lot out of me, forced me to relive moments of my past that I'd spent a lifetime trying to forget.

You see, I carried a lot of guilt about my sister's death because I was supposed to be watching her at a summer carnival —she was only twelve and I was eighteen—on that terrible day when she disappeared for good. But I had let her run off at the fairground and she was found dead in a wooded area of the town with a bouquet of roses bizarrely placed on top of her body. The roses turned out to be the calling card of the killer of Caitlin and other young girls.

My guilt over Caitlin's death—how I allowed something like this to happen—had haunted me for most of my adult life, pushing me to seek some kind of closure by finding out the answers about what really happened to my sister. In the end, I'd gotten the answers to a lot of those questions, but the ordeal had drained me emotionally and left me frustrated over the answers I couldn't get. Or didn't like.

Sure, catching the person responsible should have finally provided a sense of closure for me. And it did, no question about that. But, well... not as much closure as I thought it might. I still felt empty sometimes when I thought about everything that had happened to Caitlin.

Maybe because I had spent my whole life dreaming about getting the answers to her death, and the reality—as satisfying as it might be to find the man who did it—could never quite match the dream. Or maybe because I still had some unanswered questions about Caitlin's death. Questions that now would likely never be answered. The only person who might have been able to do so was my father, who was the police chief at the time in Huntsdale. And he was long dead.

That's what happens when you dig into the past. You can never be sure what you're going to find back there.

"When did this happen, Mrs. Benedict?" I asked the woman now. "When did your daughter disappear?"

"Twenty years ago."

"Twenty years?"

"Almost twenty-one years now."

Well, that explained why she looked so much older than I expected.

"And the police never caught anyone?"

"Oh, they arrested a man. Sent him to jail for life."

I was confused. "Then what do you want from me? From us here at the FBI?"

"I want you to find out who killed my daughter."

"But you said someone has been in jail for twenty years for the murder."

"That's right. He confessed. He confessed to murdering my Becky. And so for twenty years I've at least had the peace of mind from knowing that he was behind bars and justice was done for my daughter. But that's all changed now. There's new evidence the man in jail couldn't have done it. And he's admitted that his original confession was false."

"Then..."

"The police got the wrong man," she said. "The person who really killed Becky is still out there. Just like what happened with your sister."

TWO

The facts of the Becky Benedict murder went like this:

On May 8, 2003, fifteen-year-old Becky disappeared on her way home from school. She lived in Dorchester, a small town not far from Philadelphia. She was a freshman in high school, and was finishing up her first year as a straight-A honor student. She also was a junior varsity cheerleader, a class officer and belonged to the chess and the science clubs too.

And Dorchester? Well, Dorchester is a friendly, rustic place with very little crime, where people move to get away from the problems in the big cities like New York and Philadelphia.

But it all changed that afternoon more than two decades ago.

When Becky didn't come home from school at her normal time, her mother very quickly became worried. Becky was always punctual, trustworthy and reliable, not the type who would go off spontaneously with friends without telling her parents where she was. But Mrs. Benedict held off calling the police for a while, trying to convince herself there was some sort of reasonable explanation. Finally, when Becky still hadn't returned home by that evening, the police were contacted.

A search—growing in scope and intensity—was launched for the missing girl. The only lead to her whereabouts came from someone who saw Becky getting into a car in a neighborhood not far away from her school that afternoon—but no one knew why she would do that or who was driving the car. Friends were contacted. Hospitals checked. Anyone with a criminal record involving young girls in the area was investigated. But it all came up empty.

Until the moment everyone dreaded finally happened.

Several days after she disappeared, Becky Benedict's body was found inside a dumpster on a road outside of Dorchester.

"He threw my baby away like a piece of trash," Mrs. Benedict would say when she got the news.

The girl had been badly beaten and then stabbed. There was no sign of sexual abuse. Whoever did this had apparently not been motivated by obvious sexual desires, they had seemingly abducted and killed her for no apparent reason—other than, possibly, the thrill of it.

It was a shocking thing for the people of Dorchester back then. And there were sighs of relief when—very soon after the discovery of the body—there was a break in the case. Someone had used Becky's ATM card to try to withdraw money from her bank. The transaction was caught on a security video, including the face of the person using Becky's card. They were identified as a forty-six-year-old ex-con named Daniel Gary Leighton who was on parole from a Maryland state prison.

When he was found and arrested, Leighton at first tried to claim he'd found the girl's bank card near a trash bin and didn't know anything about her murder. But he eventually confessed to abducting her in his car, torturing and beating her for several days, and then killing her when she tried to escape.

He had no real motive for the crime. Just said that he saw her on the street, that he hated pretty young girls like that because they never paid any attention to him, and decided on the spur of the moment to grab her.

As bizarre as this all sounded, what happened next was an even weirder part of his confession. After he admitted to killing Becky Benedict, he stunned the authorities questioning him when he blurted out: "Now do you want to hear about all the other women I killed?" He then proceeded to talk in some detail about the murders of other women—as many as twenty-five— that he had committed, many of them unsolved cases across the U.S. over a period of years. He bragged about being one of the most prolific serial killers in U.S. history. He seemed proud of it.

For local authorities where these murders had occurred, it was a way to clear many cases in their unsolved files, which was certainly a welcome development. Everyone was happy and relieved Daniel Gary Leighton had confessed to all that.

He never backed down either. Not as he was sentenced to death—which was later commuted to life in prison without the possibility of parole—and not during all those years in jail. In fact, as the cases he had confessed to moved from the unsolved files to closure in many places around the country, he added even more. The number of murders he said he'd committed first doubled, and then tripled to close to one hundred. According to Leighton's accounts, he had traveled the country for years— killing women of all ages and types and demographics in whatever state he was in.

There was no consistent means of death either. He murdered them using everything from a gun to a knife to a pair of scissors to running them over with a car or—several times— strangling them. He said he especially liked strangling women. It made him feel the pain and the anguish that came with their death, he told authorities.

As the cops listened to his confessions, more law enforcement officials came to him with unsolved cases to see if he might be responsible. Some provided him with details of murders in their jurisdictions, and Leighton then willingly added more information to his confession until the case was officially closed.

For the victim's families and loved ones—as well as law enforcement authorities—Leighton's multiple confessions provided a sense of closure they thought they would never see.

And it all started with Becky Benedict.

Her murder was what led them to this horrendous serial killer of women.

Justice was finally going to be done.

And for a long time everyone believed that was what had happened.

Until everything suddenly changed.

An investigative journalist making a documentary about Daniel Gary Leighton's crimes had recently discovered a discrepancy in one of his accounts. The journalist found out that Leighton had gotten a traffic ticket in a town several hundred miles away the night before the girl in question was killed, and had worked out that it would have been almost impossible for him to have been at the crime scene in time to kill her.

The reporter began analyzing the facts of some of his other crimes and found more discrepancies in Leighton's accounts of the murders. Confronted with this, Leighton eventually admitted the truth. He wasn't really a prolific serial killer; he was simply a prolific—and convincing—liar. He had made up most of it.

Yes, he had killed a few people. A landlord who had demanded his back rent. A waitress in a diner where he went to eat. And even his mother and sister. But the rest were all lies. Lies he told to make him seem like an epic legendary criminal figure.

In the end, Leighton—once he was telling the truth about everything—said he'd never seen Becky that day. He'd made up the story about abducting and killing her. He really had found her ATM card, and was simply trying to cash in on it when he was arrested. Every other detail about Becky Benedict's murder was from his imagination.

So after years of believing the killer of their loved ones had been caught and was in jail, hundreds of people were now suddenly faced with this awful truth: the real killer had somehow escaped justice and was still out there somewhere.

People like Eleanor Benedict.

She still wanted, she still needed, she still demanded answers about what had happened to her daughter.

And she wanted me to find those answers for her.

THREE

"Twenty-five cases?" Alex Del Vecchio said to me.

"Probably more. Maybe two or three or even four times as many as everyone thought was solved by this guy's confession years ago—but are now open cases again."

"And you and I are going to solve them all?" she asked.

"I thought we'd just start with this one. Becky Benedict."

Alex and I were partners. We were eating lunch at a cafeteria type place on the first floor of the FBI office building in Washington. She and I had worked a lot of cases together over the past few years. Not on all my assignments for the bureau, but most of them. I liked Alex. And, even more importantly, I trusted her. So she was the first person I told about my conversation with Eleanor Benedict.

"Are you going to ask Dave if we can be assigned to the Benedict case?"

"As soon as we finish eating lunch here."

"What are you going to say?"

"Well, I'm going to start by not calling him Dave."

David Blanton was our new boss at the bureau. He was okay, I guess, but a bit too hung up on office protocol. He called us Agent Cassidy and Agent Del Vecchio. He wanted us to call him Chief Blanton. Or just "Chief" was okay too. It seemed silly to me, but it was a small price to pay for getting along with him.

"Do we even have jurisdiction for the Benedict girl's murder?" Alex asked.

"I think so."

The FBI works under some pretty specific rules and regulations when it comes to what it's allowed to investigate. Especially with murder cases. Generally those are handled by local police. But it changes if kidnapping is involved or state lines are crossed—which puts it under federal, i.e. FBI, jurisdiction, as well as local.

"Becky Benedict was abducted," I said, digging in hungrily to my lunch. "And her death may still be connected to some of these other deaths in numerous states over a long period of time. I think we can figure out a way to get jurisdiction."

I liked eating in cafeterias. Not many of them around anymore, but the ones that were—like this one—gave you a big selection of food to choose from. You could even try a few different things, if you wanted. Me, I had a macaroni salad, a bowl of tomato soup and a roast beef sandwich. The roast beef was a bit chewy, but the macaroni salad and soup were okay. I figured two out of three was good. Hey, I'm a glass half full kind of gal. Alex was eating some kind of a salad filled with vegetables and fruit. She was always eating—and doing—healthy stuff. She was a few years older than me, but she didn't look it. She had a terrific figure, although she was a mother with a young son. She hardly seemed to have put on any weight when she returned to work after giving birth. I hoped I was the same when it was time for me to have children. Although, given my current track record when it came to relationships, that might not happen for a while.

I finished off my macaroni salad and tomato soup, then tried the roast beef one more time, hoping it might have gotten tenderer sitting out there on the plate. It had not. Oh, well, you can't win them all.

"How are you and our new chief getting along?" Alex asked.

"Chief Blanton and I are fine."

"Good to hear."

"I miss Les Polk though."

Polk had been our boss until recently. I'd liked working for him a lot. But one of the reasons he was gone, ironically, was because of me. He'd gotten promoted to a big job upstairs among the FBI brass after I'd cracked the serial killer case involving my sister.

"You know, I saw something not long ago on Netflix or one of those channels about a similar case to this Leighton guy," Alex was saying. "It was a true story about a supposed serial killer who it turned out made up most of it."

"It makes you wonder how they got away with it."

"In the other case the answer was pretty simple. A lot of the law enforcement authorities, especially the local ones, were eager to clear long-unsolved cases off their records. So when someone was doing it for them by confessing to these crimes they were happy to take it out of the unsolved category and move on."

I nodded. "It was a gift to get a confession so no one bothered to look too hard to make sure the facts fit the confession details."

"Exactly."

I thought about my sister's case. The wrong man had confessed there too. And I—along with everyone else—never questioned his guilt. I'd questioned why he did it and I'd questioned the details of how, but I'd never doubted he was guilty. Until I found out he wasn't the one who actually murdered my sister.

"When someone confesses to a horrific crime you simply assume they're telling the truth," I said. "I mean, why would someone make up a confession like that?"

"In this other case, it was worse. Some of the authorities then tried to cover their own asses. They were more concerned about keeping quiet that they'd been conned by a false confession, than they were in worrying about the fact that the people who had actually committed these murders were allowed to go free."

"They covered it up?"

"Some of them did. They tried to stay with the guy's confession as long as they could make it seem viable, ignoring any new evidence that pointed them in a different direction. Like I said, they were covering their asses. Makes you proud, huh?"

"You and I would never do anything like that, Alex."

"I'm with you there, sister."

I finished off my meal and carried the remains to a trash can. Then I went over to check out the dessert selection. There was the choice of a fruit cup, Jell-O and chocolate eclairs. I agonized over my decision for a while. Finally, I bought all three. I ate the chocolate eclair in line while I was waiting to pay. Then I took the fruit cup and the Jell-O back to the table where Alex was waiting.

"Really?" she said, looking at what I'd brought back with me.

"What?"

"I don't think I've ever seen you eat fruit before."

"C'mon, I always like to make healthy food choices."

"Yeah, well, you still have some chocolate on your face from whatever you ate before."

I wiped my face clean.

"So, assuming Blanton gives you the okay, all we have to do is close twenty-five or thirty open cases, huh, Nikki?"

"It could be as many as a hundred."

"Damn!"

"Like I said, all I want to do right now is solve the first one."

"Becky Benedict?"

"Yes. We have to find out who really murdered this teenage girl twenty years ago."

"And then?"

"Then we begin trying to crack the other ninety-nine unsolved cases still out there."

"Ninety-nine cases," Alex repeated.

"There are killers running free because everyone believed the phony confessions from Leighton. These killers got away with murder. They've probably killed a lot more victims while Leighton has been sitting in that jail cell claiming to be the perpetrator. And they'll very likely kill even more victims unless we stop them."

"We can't crack a hundred unsolved murder cases after all this time, Nikki."

"We sure can try."

FOUR

Alex and I flew out the next morning to investigate the Becky Benedict case. Dorchester, Pennsylvania was a small town, but not the kind of small town where I grew up in Ohio. It was more of a bedroom community to Philadelphia.

I decided to start at the local police station. It was always good to check in with the town's law enforcement authorities and let them know you were working there. It helped avoid unpleasant confrontations and mix-ups later. And, who knows? Maybe the local cops would even have some leads that could help me. Sure, they hadn't solved Becky Benedict's murder— not really solved it, anyway—in twenty-plus years. But that didn't mean they couldn't get lucky with it now.

Alex and I had split up after we landed in Philadelphia. She drove to the prison about a hundred miles away where Daniel Gary Leighton was being held to try to talk to him. We figured that was probably a lost cause, since if he didn't kill Becky he likely couldn't tell us who might have done it. But it was important to check out everything. So Alex went to the prison to see Leighton, while I got the job of introducing myself to the Dorchester police chief.

We almost didn't do either one.

Dave Blanton, my new boss at the FBI Crimes Against Children Squad, wasn't as easy to convince to let us handle the case as I'd hoped he would be. Not that he didn't think the FBI should investigate the long-ago Becky Benedict case now that it was an ongoing, open murder file again. He just wasn't sure I was the one who should be doing it.

"Nikki, this case you did involving your sister took a lot out of you. Yes, you did a great job on it. But, no matter how much you try to ignore the facts, it affected you deeply. You know that, and so do I. Jumping back into another cold case murder of a girl not much older than your sister was might not be the best thing for you. We can find you something else to work on besides a murdered teenage girl. Not forever, but until you get over the trauma you've been through solving your sister's murder."

Blanton had said things like this to me before. At first, he'd wanted me to take some time off. Then he'd kept trying to assign me less stressful assignments, like he wanted to do now. He had even suggested I seek psychological counseling from the department's medical resources—i.e. see a psychiatrist—to talk about my feelings about Caitlin and the rest of the things that had happened to me back in Huntsdale.

I had rejected all of that though and I rejected his latest attempt.

I knew what I needed. I needed to get back to work.

And Becky Benedict's suddenly unsolved murder was the best way for me to do that.

"Be sure you don't make this personal," Blanton said before finally giving me approval to go to Dorchester.

"Caitlin was personal," I said. "This isn't."

"You make everything personal, Nikki."

"Chief, this is just another case."

It turned out that Blanton was right, and I was wrong.

There's always a delicate dance you have to do with local authorities when you come to their town as an FBI agent. Lots of local police resent the intrusion—what they think of as 'big footing'—by an FBI agent like me and do their best to avoid cooperating very much. That's what had happened to me in Huntsdale. The police chief there—an older, by the book, insecure guy named Frank Earnshaw—did everything possible to keep me out of the investigation. He and I clashed repeatedly over my jurisdiction, my authority, and pretty much everything else.

The one good thing on the Huntsdale police force had been a young officer named Billy Weller. I'd worked closely with him, and we even had the beginnings of a romantic relationship —even though we never got to the physical stage. Tragically he died in a shoot-out during the capture of the man who murdered my sister. He died in my arms. And he died saving my life.

I still feel sad and empty and in a state of shock over Billy's death. Why, I sometimes ask myself, does the world lose a good man like Billy Weller while life goes on as normal for a jerk like Huntsdale Police Chief Frank Earnshaw?

The police chief of Dorchester was a man named Connor Nolan, and he was a lot different to Earnshaw. Younger for one thing. Much younger than I imagined he would be. Maybe in his early thirties, about the same age as me. He was a husky, good-looking guy with curly blond hair who greeted me with a big smile and a friendly handshake. I liked that. I liked Chief Nolan right off.

I mentioned to him that he seemed awfully young to be a police chief, and he smiled and said, "Family tradition. I started early."

"Huh?"

"My father was on the police force in Philadelphia for many years. I always knew I wanted to be a cop."

"No kidding? My father was a police chief in our town in Ohio."

"I know."

"How do you know that?"

"I know all about you. You're pretty famous. You were all over TV and newspapers and websites when you tracked down the killer of your sister and all those other young girls. I remember one interview where you talked about how you hoped your father would have been proud of you for what you did. It was very eloquent."

"My father died a long time ago," I said.

"My father died too."

"I guess we have a few things in common."

"Including catching a killer who's gone free—without anyone realizing it until now—for more than twenty years."

Nolan told me everything he and his department had been doing since it was discovered that Leighton wasn't really Becky Benedict's killer. He talked about how cold the trail was after all this time.

"Except for the mother, there really aren't very many people still around who were here when it happened," he said. "And the few we tracked down who remembered the girl—well, they forgot or never knew much about her and the murder. Plus, I have a small force here, and we have to work on crimes that are happening now—not twenty years ago. We're stretched very thin and not prepared for something like this. That's why I'm glad you're here, Agent Cassidy."

Yep, this sure was a much warmer reception than I got from the local police in Huntsdale. And I definitely liked Chief Nolan better than I liked Chief Earnshaw.

A lot better.

"Maybe you'll find something we haven't," he said.

"Maybe so."

"Do you really think you can catch the killer after twenty-plus years?"

"The FBI always gets their man."

"Really?"

"That's our slogan."

"I thought that was the slogan for the Royal Canadian Police."

"We stole it from them." I smiled.

I told him I'd be in touch soon. He seemed happy about that. So was I. Before I left, he shook my hand again. I looked down and saw that he didn't have any kind of a wedding ring on his hand. Not that it really mattered, of course. But I'm a professional investigator, and I notice stuff like that.

FIVE

There was a pounding on the door of my hotel room the next morning. It was Alex.

"When did you get here?" I asked when I let her in.

"Never mind that. Have you seen what's online?"

Alex called up a website on her phone. There was a big picture of me and above it was a headline that said: BACK ON THE MURDER TRAIL: STAR FEMALE FBI AGENT CHASES ANOTHER KILLER FROM THE PAST.

"What is this?"

"TMZ."

"TMZ," I repeated.

"The biggest gossip news site on the internet."

"Where did TMZ get this from?"

"Where does TMZ get anything? They've got a million sources."

"Jeez."

"For whatever its worth, you're trending higher than Meghan Markle, Taylor Swift or Donald Trump at the moment."

"What does that even mean?"

"It means a helluva lot of people are reading this."

I read the article too. They had a lot of information. Even about my visit to the police station yesterday. How did TMZ find out about all of it? Did it come from a leak in the FBI office back in Washington? Or did they have a source here, maybe in the Dorchester police? Well, no matter how it happened, the information about me and the Becky Benedict case was out there now. It was up to me to decide what to do about it.

My phone rang. I looked down and saw Blanton's name.

Of course.

"How did TMZ find out about you?" he asked.

"I sure didn't tell them."

"Somebody did."

"I have no idea who."

"This is terrible."

"Maybe not."

"What do you mean?"

"Chief, they've had big success covering crime stories like this. A lot of people read TMZ. Maybe one of them knows something. Maybe one of them will contact me because of this. Maybe this could give us a break in a long-ago cold case where we damn well need one. So let's spread the word even more. Let's push this idea of finding Becky Benedict's killer."

"Are you talking about—"

"A press conference."

"I don't know if that's a good idea," said the chief.

"Everyone will cover this case if I call a press conference. Newspapers. Cable news. Online media. Maybe even the network news shows. I'll make a public appeal for anyone to come forward with information. I'll tell the media that we're trying to right the injustice that was done more than twenty years ago that allowed the real killer of Becky Benedict to go free."

"And you think this might give us some useful leads?"

"What have we got to lose?"

The press conference went pretty much the way I expected. Lots of media covered it. There were questions about Becky and Leighton and how the police screwed up two decades ago. Questions too about why the FBI was involved now. I was able to answer most of them well enough.

And, of course, I made my public appeal.

"If you have any information—if you know anything at all—about what happened to this fifteen-year-old girl," I said, holding up a picture of Becky Benedict, "I urge you to come forward. It's not too late to get justice for Becky. Please contact me or any law enforcement authorities here if you have any knowledge whatever about this case."

Over the next few days, we got lots of calls and texts. Most of them worthless.

No one knew much about Becky Benedict.

No one had any information that could lead us to the killer.

And no one—at least the ones who had responded so far—even seemed to care very much about what had happened to Becky.

There were tasteless remarks and jokes about her death. Questions about why the government was wasting taxpayer money chasing after local murder cases instead of terrorists. A few callers "confessed" to Becky's murder, but their so-called confessions turned out to be as bogus as Leighton's had been. And people even made sexual innuendos about me and commented about "how hot" I looked on screen.

Okay, it had been a long shot—a real Hail Mary try—on my part to get us a break in the case. But it didn't work. Now I was going to have to answer to Blanton, who'd never liked the idea of going public in the first place.

My cell phone rang, and I looked down expecting to see it

was Blanton calling me. I wasn't looking forward to this conversation.

But the call was from Area Code 740. That wasn't Washington. It was sure familiar though. It was the area code for my hometown of Huntsdale, Ohio. Who would be calling me from there?

It turned out to be the town's mayor. A woman named Stacy Harris. We'd met—and worked together—when I was there solving my sister's murder. I liked her. And I think she liked me. But I didn't figure we were close enough for her to reach out just to have a casual conversation.

I was right about that.

"Nikki, there's been another murder in Huntsdale," Mayor Harris said. "A young girl. Only fourteen years old."

I was stunned. Huntsdale was a very small town. You didn't get many murdered teenage girls there, like you did in New York or Washington. There was my sister a long time ago, and another local girl that went missing while I was there investigating Caitlin's murder—but she was rescued and I'd caught the person responsible for both crimes. So how did another girl die?

"You've got to come back to Huntsdale right away," she said.

"I'm sorry but I'm working on a big case. Another murdered young girl—"

"Listen to me, Nikki—"

"Give it to the local police to handle, Mayor. I was only there last time because it was my sister who died. I don't have any connection to whatever is going on there now. Let the police handle it."

"You do have a connection. That's why I'm calling you."

She told me then that there was something else found with the body in Huntsdale.

A bouquet of roses.

Just like the bouquet of roses that had been with my sister's body years ago.

The mayor told me there was a note attached to the roses this time. It said:

> *Roses are red*
> *Violets are blue.*
> *You know what roses mean, Nikki Cassidy.*
> *So this one is for you.*

SIX

Her name was Jessica Staley. She was fourteen years old, and her body was found in the parking lot of a convenience store about a mile from the main Huntsdale downtown area. Jessica had been stabbed, beaten and—from the condition of the body— apparently tortured before her death.

It turned out she was not from Huntsdale. There was a wallet still with the body, almost as if it had been left there intentionally, and the ID inside told authorities her name and gave the information that she was from Elmsford—a town in the southern part of Michigan more than two hundred and fifty miles away from Huntsdale. Her family said she had run away from home and had not been seen or heard from since.

Until she was found in the parking lot of the store in Huntsdale.

Had she been killed in Michigan and then the body trans-ported to Huntsdale? If so, why?

Or had she been killed wherever she had run away to and then the body dumped in the parking lot? And, if so, why? Why Huntsdale?

Or had she traveled for some reason to Huntsdale alone and

then been killed once she arrived there? It made no logical sense to me that a fourteen-year-old girl on the run would choose Huntsdale as a destination.

Even more significant, of course, was the question of the bouquet of roses found with the body—just like the roses left with my dead sister—and the calling me out by name in the note found with them.

What was that about?

I asked Stacy Harris those questions when I arrived in Huntsdale later that day. But she had no answers. She said all her information about the case came to her from my old adversary, Huntsdale Police Chief Frank Earnshaw, who was in charge of the murder investigation. She said I'd have to find out more from him. I sure wasn't looking forward to that conversation.

I was able to look at Jessica Staley's body in the morgue with Mayor Harris, and she showed me a picture of the note and the roses found with her body. The note had been printed out so it would be virtually impossible to track. And there was no indication that the roses had been bought at any store in the Huntsdale area. All this told me that someone had bought them elsewhere and brought them here as part of a planned dumping of Jessica's body.

Finally, the mayor took me to the spot where the body had been found after I asked to see it. All that was there was a half-empty parking lot with a few cars outside the convenience store. But I always liked to visit a crime scene, just to see if I could find anything of significance there.

Except this time I didn't.

"Not many answers to all this, huh?" the mayor said.

"I think I can figure out one answer."

"What do you mean?'

"The answer to why I'm mentioned in the note with the roses."

"Tell me."

"I'm pretty well known after what happened with my sister's case. It got a lot of national attention. And then I had a big press conference the other day that was picked up on cable news and plenty of media on another young girl's murder in Dorchester, Pennsylvania. It would have been easy for all that to catch the attention of whoever killed this girl. If a killer wanted publicity, and this one seems like he does, I'd be the perfect choice to target so he got the most attention."

"That makes sense," she said.

"It's the most logical explanation I can think of. Kill the girl, bring her to Huntsdale and connect me to it with the note and roses. More logical than imagining there's another killer roaming around Huntsdale like Tommy Thompson."

"And Thompson is dead."

Tommy Thompson had killed my sister Caitlin fifteen years earlier. He was a respected citizen in Huntsdale. In fact, he was the district attorney who had prosecuted the murder case against the man originally jailed for her killing. But it turned out that man he put in prison was only peripherally involved in Caitlin's disappearance and death, and that Thompson was the one who really did it. He was part of a shadowy group known as The Nowhere Men who had also murdered other girls over the years for thrills.

But, like the mayor said, Thompson was dead now. Killed during a shoot-out when he was being captured. It was possible, of course, that other members of The Nowhere Men group could still be active out there and could be responsible for Jessica Staley's death.

Or it could be someone else. Someone who got a thrill out of killing young girls and then bragging about it to the world, just like Daniel Gary Leighton claimed to have done.

Except this time it was for real.

As for me, I was still trying to decide whether to focus on this murder—because of my name being involved in it—or return to Dorchester to hunt for the long-ago killer of Becky Benedict.

Which one did I make my priority? Did I stay here and try to unravel the mystery of the Staley girl and a killer who had dragged me into it? Or did I go back to Dorchester and work with Alex on my original assignment, the two decades old murder of Becky Benedict?

I'd discussed this on the phone with my boss, Dave Blanton, before traveling to Huntsdale, but he hadn't made a final decision. He'd just said we'd deal with that based on what I found out. I already had a bad feeling about what was happening here. And it wasn't just Jessica Staley's murder. This little town—my hometown—had now seen multiple murders and abductions of teenage girls, starting with my sister. Why? Was all of this just a coincidence or was there something else going on that I was missing?

And—the biggest question of all—were more teenage girls in Huntsdale going to die?

SEVEN

My encounter with Huntsdale Police Chief Frank Earnshaw was everything I expected it would be, and more. Or less.

"We don't need any help from the FBI on this," he said as soon as I walked into his office at the Huntsdale police station.

"Actually, you do."

"It's a Huntsdale murder case, and I'm the police chief of Huntsdale. So you can just go back to Washington or wherever it is you came here from."

"Except Jessica Staley is from Michigan, which makes it a multi-state murder case—that means it is under federal jurisdiction. And she presumably was kidnapped at some point and brought here where the body was found, and kidnap is also a federal crime. Oh, and in case you didn't notice, my name is on the note the killer left with the body. So I am very involved in this murder case, Chief Earnshaw—whether you want me to be or not."

I think he already knew he was going to have to work with me again. But he was trying to make the process as difficult and unpleasant as possible. Me, I just wanted to be brought up to speed on the evidence and to get involved in the case as quickly as possible. I told Chief Earnshaw that.

"I very recently helped you solve your last murder case here," I pointed out.

"You got lucky."

"Well, your department didn't get lucky during all those years they had the wrong man in jail for murdering my sister."

"Hey, I had nothing to do with that—it was your father who did it."

Earnshaw was right. It had been my father who originally got the case wrong. Then he died soon afterward, and took with him to the grave a lot of secrets about how he made that mistake. It wasn't a good thing for me to bring up with Earnshaw, but I admit I was a little off my game. I'd gotten shook up a bit when I got to the station and walked past the desk where Billy Weller used to sit.

Billy had... well, he was in love with me, I knew that. And maybe I was starting to fall in love with Billy. He'd died helping to save my life, so I'd never know what might have happened between us. I feel sad about that. And a bit guilty too, I suppose.

There was a long-haired, unfamiliar looking middle-aged man sitting at Billy Weller's desk now—which was a jolting reminder to me that Billy was gone.

I eventually got Earnshaw to give me a rundown on everything they'd found out so far. I had to admit he'd done a pretty decent job; touched all the bases of law enforcement basic investigation techniques for a murder like this. I couldn't fault him on any of his actions. But, despite all this, he still had no idea who killed Jessica Staley or why the killer had left the note and the roses. Still, he came up with the same theory as I had about the roses and why the note had mentioned me.

"Anybody could have gotten that information about your sister and the roses from all the media coverage you've had," Earnshaw said. "Whoever killed the Staley girl is probably trying to get attention via you and divert us from the main focus of this investigation. Which is to find out who killed Jessica Staley and left her body in Huntsdale. That's our priority."

"That's my priority too."

Earnshaw didn't say anything. He just sat there glaring at me across his desk. I was pretty sure we weren't going to have an amicable working relationship here. Any more than we had the last time I'd been here. This guy was going to make me struggle for every bit of help I was looking for from the Huntsdale police.

"Can you give me a witness list?" I asked Earnshaw. "Who found her body? Who were the people at the store when you arrived? Was there anyone else in the parking lot that might have seen something?"

"Talk to Edgar about all that."

"Who's Edgar?"

"He's at Billy Weller's old desk outside."

The middle-aged guy with long hair.

"What about contacts for the Staley girl's family and friends and school back in Michigan?"

"Check with Edgar."

"What about a security video at the store?"

"What about it?"

"Was there one?"

"Yes."

"You watched it?"

"Of course, we watched it."

"And?"

"Nothing out of the ordinary."

"Can I see it?"

"I told you there's nothing there."

"Humor me."

He shrugged. "Knock yourself out, if you want to waste your time."

"Where is it?"

"We have a copy here. And the original is still back at the store. We told them not to record over it like they normally would."

"How do I watch it?"

"Which one—the original or the copy?"

"Either one."

"Talk to Edgar."

"One more thing. The police report on Jessica Staley's murder. I want to see everything you have on record so far. Let me take a look through your murder file. I want to make sure I have all the basics down."

"You need to talk to—"

"Edgar?"

"Yes, go talk to Edgar. I don't have time to waste going over all these things again with you. I have a murder to solve."

"So I should talk to Edgar about everything?"

"Right."

I went to talk to Edgar.

EIGHT

It turned out his name was Edgar Daniels. In addition to the long hair which hung down over the back of his neck, he had a mustache and a beard. I figured him to be about fifty, and he had a bit too much weight around his middle. He looked like an aging hippie, even though he wasn't old enough for that. But he sure wasn't any Billy Weller when it came to appearance.

"So you're the one I've heard so much about," he said to me when I walked over to where he sat at Billy Weller's old desk and introduced myself.

"Yes, I guess I did get a lot of attention in the media the last time I was here."

"Nah, I meant I heard a lot about you from Chief Earnshaw."

"What was he saying about me?"

"You don't want to know."

"Chief Earnshaw's not exactly a fan of mine."

"Very perceptive. Of course, you don't have to be a celebrity FBI agent to figure that out.'

He smiled when he said it. That was a good sign. I

wondered if he might not be that enamored of his boss any more than I was.

"I hope Chief Earnshaw's opinions about me won't prevent us from working amicably together."

"I form my own opinions about people."

"How about on Chief Earnshaw?"

"Huh?"

"What is your opinion of him?"

"He's my boss."

"That's not really an answer."

He smiled again. Maybe I *could* work with this guy better than I did with Earnshaw.

There was a picture of Bruce Springsteen on Daniels' desk. I saw it was autographed to him.

"You a Springsteen fan?" I asked.

"The biggest. I've seen him more than thirty times in concert. Great shows. That picture is when he came to Columbus a few years ago, back when I was there. Got him to sign it for me. How cool is that?"

Yep, with his long hair and the beard and his Springsteen fandom, Edgar Daniels sure seemed to be a latter-day hippie guy. Didn't mean he couldn't be a good cop though.

Daniels said he'd been a police officer in Columbus for a lot of years, then lost his job there and wound up in Huntsdale after Billy Weller's death left an opening. I didn't figure that going from a big city force like Columbus to a small place like Huntsdale was a good law enforcement career move for Daniels. I wondered if there had been a reason he had to leave and take a job like this.

"Tell me what evidence or other information you need from me," he said.

I did, running through a list of questions about the case. He let me see the names and contacts of people who had been at the convenience store when Jessica Staley's body was found outside. Then the family and friends from her hometown in Michigan. There were also a few receipts found in her wallet, including one from a motel in Zanesville, Ohio, a town not far from Huntsdale. The receipt said she stayed there for three nights, which seemed unusual for a girl on the run.

The prevalent theory was that Jessica had been picked up, or more likely abducted, by the person who killed her. It was not clear when this might have happened. When she checked into the motel in Zanesville, according to the records there, she was alone. The room was for one person. But that didn't mean someone else might not have stayed with her once she took the room.

I made copies of the receipt and all the names and contacts from Daniels to check out later. After that, in an empty conference room at the station, I read through the entire official police file on Jessica Staley's murder case.

It began with the basic description of Jessica running away from her home in Elmsford, Michigan; the receipt showing she'd stopped at the motel in Zanesville, Ohio; and the discovery of her body in the parking lot of the Huntsdale convenience store by a customer who had pulled up in his car shortly after nine p.m. that evening. The customer's name was Norman Jeffries. Jeffries said he thought at first what he saw on the ground in the parking lot was a trash bag or some other kind of refuse. But when he got out of the car and looked closer, he saw the body that turned out to be Jessica Staley. He ran inside the store, where the manager quickly made a 911 call.

There was additional information for Norman Jeffries. His address, phone number and email. Which meant I could talk to him myself if I wanted. But I didn't really see the point. Jeffries was a longtime resident of Huntsdale, and there was no indication or reason to think he had played any part in Jessica Staley's death besides finding the body. He had also made it clear in interviews with the police that he had seen nothing else—no one running or driving away from Jessica's body, no other people in the area—at all. I didn't figure there was anything else Norman Jeffries could tell me. He was just a guy who happened to be there when the body showed up.

The manager of the store and the people inside at the time the body was found were also questioned extensively by police without any significant results. Nobody saw anything or knew anything about Jessica Staley until Norman Jeffries had come running into the store from the parking lot with the shocking news there was a body out there.

There was also information about Jessica's life in the file. Her father owned a construction business in Elmsford—a small town not too far away from Detroit. Her mother did volunteer work at a local hospital. She had a younger sister, who was twelve years old. Jessica attended middle school—she was in the eighth grade—and was scheduled to go to Elmsford High School the following year. She'd had her whole life in front of her, I thought to myself, and then suddenly that life was gone.

As for how she wound up in Ohio, specifically in a small town in the southern part of the state, there was no answer for that in the file. She and her family had all been born and raised in Michigan. There was no reason for her to wind up dead in Ohio unless she was taken there by someone.

There were pictures of Jessica in the file. Before and after photos. I looked at the "before" ones first. That was easier. But sad too. She was a normal appearing young girl, with a fresh-faced look, short dark hair, brown eyes, and an infectious-looking smile on her face.

I steeled myself before looking at the rest of the pictures. These were taken after she died. This was always a tragic part of the job for me, seeing someone like Jessica—who looked so full of life—after that life had been snatched away from her. The first one I looked at was from the parking lot. She was curled up in what looked like a fetal position. Almost as if she was trying to ward off blows from the killer to the very end. She was dressed in blue jeans, a white T-shirt and black boots. Then there were pictures from later at the morgue. These were the most difficult to look at. Especially the close-ups. Even in these pictures, you could see—and for me, feel too—her pain and her anguish. Her face appeared frozen in time, as if she was still reliving in death the nightmare she had experienced. All the beauty of the fourteen-year-old girl she had been was gone now, replaced by bloody bruises and by stab wounds.

There was an autopsy report from the Huntsdale Medical Examiner. His name was Michael Franze. I knew him well. He'd been ME here for years, all the way back to when my father was police chief. Big Mickey, they called him, because he weighed nearly three hundred pounds. As a kid I knew him as Uncle Mickey. I could talk to him later in person if I wanted, but right now I only needed to read his autopsy report.

It turned out to be pretty much as I expected. It said that no knife or sharp object or heavy one that might have been used to stab and beat her was found with the body. There was no DNA, hair particles, fingerprints or any other forensic evidence found by the CSI experts who examined her body looking for clues to the murder.

But it was clear from the pictures—and from the condition of the body—that this girl was not just murdered. Big Mickey Franze had concluded in his official ME's autopsy report that Jessica Staley had been beaten, stabbed, and presumably tortured for a long period, until she was finally killed, and apparently for no other reason than the killer's twisted pleasure since there was no sign of robbery or sexual assault or any other motive for her murder.

This wasn't the first time I'd seen something like this. No, this kind of horror was an all too familiar part of my job.

I've chased after killers in a lot of places since joining the bureau. Big cities like New York and Washington. Small towns like Huntsdale where I grew up. And plenty of other locations that were in between big and small.

There are no boundaries for evil.

It could be found anywhere.

And now the nightmare had started again.

I only hoped it wasn't too late to save the lives of more young victims like this poor girl.

NINE

I asked Daniels to show me the video from the security camera
at the store the night the body had been found. It used to be that
stores kept that kind of thing on videotapes, which meant there
was only one copy and it frequently got recorded on over and
over again each day. But now it was all digital. That meant
Daniels could call it up on a computer at his desk, and I was
able to download a copy onto my phone to watch again later, if I
wanted. But right now I wanted to see the video from the store
on Daniels' computer screen.

He pushed a button and it began to play. The video when it
appeared was in black and white and seemed grainy-looking.
Despite all the digital advances, the store still used an old-fashioned camera. Probably saved money that way. But it made my
job—or anyone in law enforcement if there was a crime there—a
lot tougher.

Daniels said it was the only video camera in the store. No
cameras at all outside. And all this camera showed was the cash
register and customers coming in and out at the counter. There
was nothing even close to the parking lot where Jessica's body
had been found.

"That kind of sucks, doesn't it?" Daniels said when he told me there were no other cameras.

"So nothing at all from outside ever got picked up on camera? No car? No body being left? No face of anyone that looked like they were doing anything suspicious at all? There's no possibility the killer could be on any of this video?"

"Not unless he walked into the store to buy a Slurpee or something while he disposed of the body."

"Damn."

"Did you really think we didn't check this out before you showed up, Cassidy?"

I sighed. "Earnshaw told me there was nothing on it."

"He was right about that."

I watched the video again all the way through. Jessica Staley's body had been found in the parking lot of the store at 9:08 that night, so I then watched it from before that time—first fifteen minutes before, then a half hour, then an entire hour and then as far back as the video we had went—looking for anything that seemed to be suspicious or out of the ordinary.

It was a busy night and a lot of people were going in and out of the store. Families. Some teenagers. A mother with a baby in a stroller. A group of cheerleaders coming from a game at Huntsdale High. Even a homeless-looking derelict who had somehow panhandled enough spare change to buy a sandwich showed up.

None of them looked up at the security camera and confessed to being a murderer.

None of them dragged Jessica Staley's dead body behind them.

None of them wore a big sign saying: "I am the killer."

It seemed hopeless.

I fast-forwarded the video back to the part where the body had been found. There was a lot of activity then. People running in and out of the store. Police arriving and bursting in looking for witnesses to question. Sirens wailing outside from the ambulances and other emergency vehicles.

But whoever had left Jessica Staley's body in the parking lot was apparently long gone by then.

"How much more video is there?" I asked Daniels.

"You mean after the body was found?"

"Before the body was found."

"We took like an hour's worth from the store's camera. You just watched it all."

"Okay, where's the video before that?'

"Back at the store, I guess. But why do you want to see that? That's not going to show anything either. It's still all from inside the store, not out in the parking lot or anywhere else."

"I still want to see it."

"How much?"

"All of it."

"The whole night and day?"

"Maybe even the day or so before that."

"What are you looking for, Cassidy?"

"The guy might have cased the place before he left the body. He must have known there was no security camera in the parking lot. That's why he felt safe dumping the body there. He could have gone to the store earlier and checked it out—maybe the inside too—to get some sense of their security setup. Ergo, he might be on one of the videos from inside."

"You're going to look at all that video in hopes of finding someone who looks suspicious enough that they could be a killer?"

"Uh huh."

"How will you even know that?"

"I won't until I see him. But there might be something I see that gives him away. I want to give it a try."

"That really sounds like a long shot."

"A long shot is all we've got right now."

TEN

I stood outside the convenience store again. I'd been there earlier with Mayor Harris, but I hadn't gone inside. I looked around the parking lot one more time. Especially the spot where Jessica Staley's body had been found. The crime scene tape and everything else from the police investigation was gone. It all looked completely normal. I went inside the store.

A man of about sixty—with white hair and a stooped-over posture—was standing by the cash register. He told me he was the manager. The guy looked old and tired, like he'd been doing this job for too long. He wasn't happy to see me when he found out I was from the FBI, and not a customer. He said he had already talked to a lot of cops. He'd had to close up after the girl was found and he'd lost a lot of business. He was trying to make up for that lost income now.

I looked around and saw no one else was in the store. I bought a soda and a bag of chips in hopes it would make him a bit more pleasant to me, but he was still grumpy. Especially when I told him I wanted to watch a lot of his security video.

"There's nothing from the parking lot," he said.

"I know that."

"And the police didn't find anything on the security video from in here either."

"I know that too."

"Then what are you looking for?"

"Something that might be on an earlier video. I want to check those from the past few days. Can you let me see them?'

"That's a lot of trouble."

"So take the trouble."

"Why should I?"

"It's called being a good citizen. Cooperating with law enforcement. Doing a good deed for the safety of your community. Whatever you want to call it. Just get me that earlier security video to see."

"What if I refuse?"

"Then I'll get a subpoena for it."

"C'mon, lady, I'm the only one working here right now. I'll have to close the door and lock up—which means no customers again—while I take you downstairs to my computer in the basement to watch it. That's going to cost me money."

"I'll buy another soda so we don't do too much damage to your cash flow. How about that?"

"You think this is funny, huh?"

"No, I don't. A young girl was found murdered outside your store. I'm looking to do whatever I can to help find out who did it. I think you should be too. You can bring up the video on the computer, then let me watch it downstairs while you come back up here to open the store. That will only take a few minutes. If I have to get a subpoena, that will close your place down for a lot longer than a few minutes."

I guess that's what convinced him—not any sudden burst of good conscience—to let me see the earlier security video.

The video was as grainy as the one I'd watched with Daniels at the police station. It showed me the same view of the store too. Mostly the cash register, with customers coming and going after paying for whatever they bought. There were a few different people behind the counter, but most of the time it seemed to be the manager I'd met upstairs. I got the feeling he didn't have a lot of help working for him. Maybe that's why he seemed so tired and grumpy.

I'd already watched the video for the entire day the body was found, so I started with the video of the day before that. I set it up on the computer for the time to start around nine a.m. and pushed the play button. A printed date and time appeared on the bottom of the screen—and I settled in to watch.

Of course, I still had no idea what I was looking for. But I hoped I'd know once I saw it. Or maybe I'd see something missing that should have been there which could help me, too.

I saw a lot of different kinds of customers in the store, just like I had on the video in the police station. There were also big periods where nothing happened, no customers at the counter to see. Nothing but the manager or one of the other workers looking bored and waiting for someone to buy something.

I fast-forwarded through all this stuff—and it was a lot of stuff—to try to get through it more quickly.

I kept looking for a clue.

Anything at all.

But, after twelve hours of searching the day before the body was found, I realized there was nothing there.

I went to the next video and did the same thing. Two days before the body turned up outside.

Nothing there either.

At least nothing that I could spot.

I wasn't sure how much longer I should keep going before deciding this was a lost cause. But I tried one more video. The video that showed the coming and goings three days before Jessica Staley's body was found.

What in the hell was I looking for?

Some guy who looked suspicious, I suppose. Maybe he was carrying a bloody knife or an ax or something else that would show me he was a crazed killer.

But—in the end—what I found on the video turned out to be nothing like that at all.

Not the killer, but it sure shocked the hell out of me!

It happened at 8:26 in the evening according to the time clock on the screen—three days before Jessica Staley's dead body was found outside.

That's when I saw it.

That's when I saw the customer in line.

Not a man.

A girl.

A young girl.

She smiled as she approached the counter and put what she was buying in front of the register. Then she took out a wallet from her handbag, and handed the person behind the counter—who was not the manager—some money. She took her change, put it back into her bag, and started to walk toward the door.

It was eerie watching this taking place.

Because I saw what she had bought.

It was a bouquet of roses.

And, as she walked away, I got a clear view of her face.

It was Jessica Staley.

Jessica Staley had come to the store three days before her murdered body was dumped outside.

And she'd bought the bouquet of roses found with her.

ELEVEN

I was on a Zoom call with Alex in Dorchester and Dave Blanton back in Washington.

"Did she seem to be in any kind of distress?" Alex asked me after I told them about Jessica Staley and the roses on the video.

"No, she looked perfectly calm and smiling and acting normal."

"Even though she was buying the flowers the killer would leave with her body a few days later?"

"I'm sure she had no idea about that. Like I said, she was smiling on the video."

"How did the person who killed her convince her to do something like that though? He must have made her feel like she was safe with him."

'She was fourteen years old, Alex. Trust me, fourteen-year-old girls don't always use the best judgement."

Blanton jumped in now. "I thought you said the Huntsdale police told you that there was no indication of a bouquet of roses like that being bought in the area anywhere around there prior to her body being found."

"They did."

"Pretty sloppy police work."

"Not necessarily. The police checked out the flower shops around Huntsdale and other obvious places to purchase roses. But she found them at a convenience store, not normally where someone would go for flowers. And she paid for the roses in cash, according to what I saw on the video. So there would be no record of the transaction."

"What about the manager? Didn't he remember selling the roses to her after the body was found and her picture was all over the news?"

"The manager wasn't working then. Someone else was behind the counter. A young kid. I talked to him. He said he barely looked at her when she was in the store. He's a bit of a space cadet, the manager said he's caught him smoking weed a few times and that he seems out of it a lot of the time. So this girl didn't register on the kid's radar, for one reason or another."

Blanton sighed. I could see on the Zoom screen that he didn't look happy. Blanton liked simple cases. Simple investigations that went according to plan. There was nothing simple about this. Everything I'd found out had complicated things more. I didn't like that anymore than he did, but all I could do was follow the evidence. And this was where the evidence had taken me so far.

"Theories from you two?" Blanton asked Alex and me.

"He was sending us a message," I said.

"Us?"

"Or me. Just like he chose Huntsdale, my hometown and where I solved my sister's case, as the place to leave the body. And why he included me in the note he left with it. And made a point of making sure Jessica Staley's body had the bouquet of roses on top, like with my sister a long time ago. Then, just to add an extra dramatic touch to it, he somehow gets the Staley girl to buy the roses while he's checking out the store. He then knows afterward there's a security video inside and exactly where it is, but nothing in the parking lot."

"But you didn't see anyone else on the video?" Blanton asked.

"No, she was the only one at the counter when she bought the roses."

"Do you figure he was there in the store too?"

"Maybe, but he must have made sure to stay out of range of the camera."

"But why all the games?" Blanton said. "What's he looking for?"

"Attention," Alex said. "He doesn't want to just kill the girl —he wants everyone to know he killed this girl."

"And maybe more girls too," I said.

"Do we think he's really responsible for more deaths?" Blanton asked.

"Based on what we know about Jessica Staley, I think we have to consider the possibility," I said.

We then went through what we knew so far about the long-ago murder of Becky Benedict—the case I started out investigating until Jessica Staley's body turned up.

Alex went through everything she'd been able to find out in Dorchester. "First off, the guy Leighton who'd been in prison for it all these years definitely seems like a dead end. He's a killer, but not her killer. He admitted to me pretty convincingly how he'd made up all that confession stuff about being responsible for her and other dead women. He's a nut case. I think we're wasting our time on him.

"I've been working with the local police here, a guy named Connor Nolan who's the chief. He's very bright and cooperative and has given me whatever evidence they have on the Benedict murder. But none of it has really led anywhere so far. The trail's really cold after twenty-plus years. It's like looking for a needle in a haystack, as the old saying goes. And we're talking about a very small needle.

"I did go back to some people who knew her back then—classmates, neighbors, other people in town. But no one really knew anything much about what happened to her the day she disappeared. I'll keep trying to track more of them down in the hopes we stumble onto something."

Alex's description of her successful working relationship with Connor Nolan, the Dorchester police chief, made me a little jealous. And talking about how helpful he was made me pissed off again at Chief Frank Earnshaw. It didn't help that Nolan was a charming, good-looking guy too who—as far as I could tell—was not married.

"We're gonna need more people on this," Blanton said.

I'd thought about that too. "Okay, but I want to work with Alex," I said. "She's my partner."

"Do you want her to come to Huntsdale? We can send someone else to Dorchester."

"Or I could go back to Dorchester and let someone else handle the Staley case here, Chief."

"Which do you prefer to do?"

I still had that decision to make. Did I stay here and try to unravel the mystery of the Staley girl and a killer who had dragged me into it? Or did I go back to Dorchester and work with Alex on my original assignment, the two decades old murder of Becky Benedict?

I was still thinking about that when someone else joined the call. It was Phil Girard, another agent I'd worked with in the past. He'd been assigned to work with me when I solved my sister's case. Phil Girard had helped save my life back then so I owed him something, but I didn't want to waste time talking with him or filling him in on everything right now.

"The Staley girl spent time at a motel in Zanesville, Ohio," he said. "I just talked to the motel manager."

"We already know she was there," I said impatiently. "There was a receipt with her when she was found."

"The receipt only showed that someone—presumably her—had spent three nights in the motel, right?"

"Yes."

"No name?'

"What's your point, Phil?'

"I got a name from the manager. The name the Staley girl used when she signed into the motel. You're not gonna believe this. It was—"

And then, just like that, I knew what the name was going to be even before Phil said it.

"Becky Benedict."

TWELVE

Why would Jessica Staley have registered at the motel as Becky Benedict—a girl who was murdered years before Staley was even born?

Did this mean that the two cases were connected somehow? Was it possible that the same killer was responsible for both Jessica and Becky—even though they died twenty years apart?

And what about the roses and the note to me that was found on Jessica Staley's body? Could there be some sort of bizarre link between all this and my sister Caitlin's murder too?

None of it made any sense and these were all questions I did not have answers for.

Maybe Jessica Staley's parents did. According to Daniels and Earnshaw, the parents had traveled to Huntsdale to claim their daughter's body and take her home. I was glad about that because it meant I could ask them questions about their daughter immediately.

Diane Staley, Jessica's mother, was a surprisingly youthful-looking woman. She'd been crying when I met her at the funeral home where Jessica's body had been taken. Her husband, Tim Staley, who looked older than her—maybe by as much as fifteen or twenty years—was trying his best to hold it together, but he looked shocked and dazed as well. Not that either reaction was a surprise under the tragic circumstances.

"My daughter," Mrs. Staley sobbed after I introduced myself. "Did you see what they did to my daughter? I could barely recognize her. Why? Why would someone do that to my baby?"

I remembered how shocked I had been to see Jessica Staley's shattered face and body. I could only imagine how horrible an experience it was for her parents.

The father was more able to keep his emotions in check and he asked me if we had any more information about what had happened to Jessica. I told him what we knew—including the new details about Jessica buying the roses that were later found with her and her signing in at a motel using the name of Becky Benedict, and the background about Becky's long-ago murder.

"Did your daughter ever mention the name Becky Benedict to you?" I asked.

"No, why would she?"

"No reason. Like I said, the Benedict girl was killed a long time ago in Pennsylvania."

He looked confused. "What does this all mean?" he asked. "What could she possibly have to do with our daughter?"

"That's what we're trying to figure out."

"You don't have any idea at all who did this to Jessica?"

"That's why I want to talk to both of you. I understand how difficult this is, but I need to find out everything I can from you about what Jessica was doing and who she might have been in contact with before she died."

"How can we help?" Diane Staley asked.

"Let's start with how long she'd been gone from your home and from Elmsford before she turned up here."

She looked over at her husband uncomfortably. He turned away from her gaze. I could see this was a difficult topic for them.

"How long ago was it that she ran away from home?" I asked again.

"A little over a week," Tim Staley said. "Right, Diane?"

She shook her head. "It was ten days. Exactly ten days from when she left until we found out she was dead."

"Why did she run away?"

She sighed. "Why does any fourteen-year-old girl run away?"

"There's usually some kind of reason."

"She said she hated us," Tim Staley said. He then told a story that was similar to many cases of missing teenagers I'd investigated with the FBI. Jessica had been an A-student in the past, but recently her grades had been falling off. She was also running with a crowd of girls that both he and his wife thought were trouble. He said he found cigarettes and even some marijuana in her handbag. Then, one day while she was out of the house, he searched her room and discovered pills—uppers and speed—she seemed to be taking.

"I grounded her," he said. "She was not allowed to see any of her friends or do anything but go back and forth to school every day. She was very angry with us."

"I told him he was being too harsh," Diane Staley said. "That we were going to turn her against us. I wanted to talk with her, to reason with her about all this—"

"You don't reason with a fourteen-year-old girl who's doing drugs," he snapped. "You make them stop. Whatever it takes to accomplish that, you do it. For God's sake, Diane, I wasn't trying to kill her. I wanted to save her. It wasn't my fault Jessica did what she did."

What she did was run away from home, they said. She left a note so they knew she'd disappeared voluntarily. They contacted the police, but a runaway teenager was not exactly a priority for law enforcement—even in a small town like Elmsford. The police reported that they had conducted a search for her, but turned up nothing.

The Staleys kept hoping for some word on Jessica—hoping against hope she would return on her own—until the moment they received the devastating news of her murder.

I got as much information from them as I could about her friends, her school and anything else she'd been involved with before disappearing.

"Do you have any other children?" I asked.

"Yes, Jessica's sister. Katie. She's twelve," said Tim Staley.

"Where is she now?"

"Back at the motel where we're staying," he replied.

"We didn't want her to see the way her sister looked here," Diane Staley said.

"Can I speak to her?"

"Why?" she asked.

"She may have some information about Jessica that could be useful."

"We've already told you everything," Tim Staley said.

"Sometimes sisters tell their sister things they wouldn't talk about with their parents."

I thought about my sister, Caitlin. How we sometimes did that late at night after our parents thought we were asleep. There was a six-year age difference between us, but I would tell her stuff about high school and boyfriends I was seeing and lots more that I would never discuss with my mother or father. Maybe Jessica Staley had done the same thing with her younger sister.

"I don't want Katie involved any more than she is," her mother said.

"Don't you want to catch the person who did this to your daughter?"

"Of course, but—"

"Then let me interview her. Maybe she knows something that could help. It couldn't hurt, Mrs. Staley."

"We'll take you to meet Katie at the motel now," Tim Staley said.

THIRTEEN

Katie Staley looked a lot like her sister. Or at least the pictures I'd seen of Jessica. Dark brunette hair, cute, friendly smile and with a fresh-scrubbed look to her face. Only two years younger, but they could almost have been twins.

I wondered if that was uncomfortable for Tim and Diane Staley. To still be around a daughter who looked so similar to the one they lost. Would it help them work their way through the sorrow that lay ahead? Or would Katie be a constant reminder of Jessica being gone?

Katie was playing a video game on a hand-held console, sitting on a bed with the television playing, tuned to one of those daytime reality talk shows. She didn't seem upset or in shock like her parents. But that didn't necessarily mean anything. Based on what I found out from her parents before I went to the motel with them, Katie and her sister had been very close. Sometimes youth shows grief and loss in a different way from the rest of us.

I introduced myself and showed her my FBI credentials. She seemed impressed. Impressed enough that she put down her video game and turned off the sound for the television.

"Wow, FBI!" she said.

"That's right."

"And you're a woman."

"I am."

"Are there lots of women in the FBI?"

"More than there used to be."

"That's really cool."

"I think so too."

"So what do you want to know from me?"

I told her I wanted to talk about her sister and the events leading up to her running away.

Katie Staley looked nervously at her parents when I said that, and I realized she was uncomfortable talking about it in front of them. There had clearly been a disconnect between Jessica and her parents, especially with her father. Maybe the same thing had happened with Katie. It was something I'd seen many times in cases of runaway teenagers.

I asked the Staleys if I could talk to Katie alone. They were reluctant at first, but finally agreed, and left Katie and me in the room.

I sat down on the bed next to her. "I understand that Jessica was having a lot of difficulties with your parents before she left," I said.

"Yes, the old man was really bringing the hammer down on her pretty hard."

"Your father was very strict with her?"

"With both of us."

"How about your mother?"

"She's easier to deal with. But she does whatever my father wants in the end. He runs things. They fight about it sometimes. A lot of the fights are about the best way to deal with Jessica and me. Jess and I sometimes thought they might be headed for a divorce. I wasn't sure if that would be a good thing or a bad thing though."

"How bad were the fights in your house?"

"There was a lot of yelling and screaming. Sometimes they got physical. My father hit my mother, Jessica or me, when he got really mad. Once or twice, the police came to our house. After Jessica showed up at school with bruises or neighbors complained about all the noise from the fighting at our place. But no one... no one actually did anything about it."

"Did all these arguments and fights and stress in the house cause Jessica to start doing drugs and maybe running around with the wrong crowd?"

She shrugged. "My father made more of all that than it really was. He found a couple of pills. Big deal. And the girls she was hanging around with weren't really that bad. They just liked to have fun. Jessica wanted to have fun too. And when the old man grounded her so she couldn't see anyone, well... she decided to split."

"Did she tell you she was leaving?"

Katie hesitated.

"I won't tell your parents," I said.

She nodded. "She told me."

"Do you have any idea where she went after that?"

"No, I never knew."

"Was she with anyone?"

"Not that I'm aware of."

"Did you ever hear from her?"

More hesitation.

"Katie?"

"I don't want to talk about it."

"Don't you want to find out what happened to your sister?"

"You don't understand..."

"Maybe I do."

"Do you have a sister?"

"I did. Just like you and Jessica. My sister was murdered too."

"Was your sister older or younger than you?"

"Younger. Six years younger. She was twelve when she was killed."

"The same age as me." She thought about that. It seemed to make a real impression on her. "Were you close with her?" she asked.

"Sometimes. Other times I felt I had nothing in common with her. It changed from time to time. I loved her. I loved her very much. But I'm not sure she ever knew how much I loved her. I feel sad about that now. But that's frequently what it's like with sisters. Certainly it was like that for my sister and me. But it felt better for me—like a real sense of closure—when I was able to make the person who killed her pay for the crime. What about you, Katie? Don't you want that for Jessica too?"

She looked over at the TV. A woman and man on the screen were talking to a host. There were captions running. The woman was telling how she had found her husband in bed with their babysitter. I guess immersing yourself in other people's problems—or losing yourself in the fantasy world of a video game—keep you from being overwhelmed by the reality in your own life.

But only for a while. Sooner or later, the real world catches up with you.

"Jessica called me," Katie Staley said. "A few days before... before they found her dead. She said she wanted me to know she was all right. She sounded all right. She sounded happy. Happier than I'd heard her in a long time. She made me promise I wouldn't tell my parents or anyone else about our conversation. So I never said anything. Until now. It was a promise to my sister. The last promise I would ever make to her. I kept it as long as I could, but now... well, now I guess you should know about it."

"Did she give you any more details?"

"Not really."

"Or name anyone she might have been with?"

"No."

"Did she mention the name Becky Benedict for any reason?"

"No. Who's that?"

I shrugged and kept pushing her for any bit of information that might help. "What about where she was calling from? Any location that she mentioned?"

"That's the weirdest thing. I asked her where she was. She laughed and said: 'Nowhere.'"

"Nowhere?"

"Right. I asked her what that meant. She said it was a secret, but maybe she'd tell me more the next time we talked."

"Nowhere," I repeated.

"That's all she said. I never found out what it meant."

Was she talking about The Nowhere Men? That was the sick website where men had gone to watch girls being abducted and murdered—including my sister fifteen years ago—until we discovered it online, shut it down and shot to death the man running the deadly game, former Huntsdale District Attorney Tommy Thompson. But now I wondered if The Nowhere Men were somehow behind the murder of Jessica Staley too. And—as incredible as it might sound—possibly even linked to the long-ago killing of Becky Benedict.

I made a decision then.

A decision about what to do next.

I needed to go back to the beginning to find out.

Back to Dorchester and Becky Benedict.

FOURTEEN

Dorchester Police Chief Connor Nolan was talking to another police officer when Alex and I went to see him at his office. He introduced the officer as Donald Maris. Then he said Maris and anyone else on the force were available to help us on the Benedict investigation. I definitely liked this guy a lot better than Chief Earnshaw in Huntsdale!

Maris left then, so Alex and I were alone with Chief Nolan. He looked as good as I remembered him. Also, his left hand was still sans any kind of wedding ring.

There was something I noticed there for the first time though. A picture on his desk. A picture of a young woman. A very attractive young woman. How did I miss that?

"Your wife?" I asked him, looking at the picture and trying not to appear obvious in my interest about her identity.

"Ex-wife."

"Oh," I said, doing my best to not show any relief in my voice at that answer from him.

"It's my favorite picture of her.'

Hmmm. Not too many men have pictures of their ex-wives

on their desk. "And you just keep it there to remember all the good times you had before you divorced her?"

Alex gave me a weird look. Okay, I know that came out badly, but it really did seem strange for him to keep a picture of his damn ex-wife on his desk.

"She's dead," Nolan said.

"I'm... I'm sorry."

"Lauren and I were in the process of getting together again when it happened. We'd gone through a rough period in our marriage and called it quits. But we still loved each other. So we were giving it another try right before she died."

"How did she die?" I asked.

"In a house fire. I tried my best to save her, but I couldn't. She died before anyone could get her out." He looked at me sadly. "If you don't mind, I'd really rather not talk about this."

I wasn't sure how to react to this. He clearly still had feelings for her. But she was dead.

I looked at the picture one more time, then back at Nolan and decided to return to business. Alex and I went through the details of what we knew about the most recent dead girl, Jessica Staley, including that she used Becky Benedict's name to sign into a motel in Zanesville before she died. I also told him about her buying the roses in Huntsdale that were later found on her body. And how my name was mentioned in a note left by the killer.

"I don't understand any of it," he said.

"Neither do we."

"Especially the part about signing into the motel as Becky Benedict. You said Jessica Staley was fourteen. So she wasn't even alive when Becky Benedict was killed."

"But she presumably was still alive when I held my press conference here about Becky's death."

"You think that's what gave her the idea?"

"Maybe. Or maybe it gave someone else the idea. The same

person who convinced her to buy those roses. And that person —I have to believe at this point—was the one who killed her."

"Do you think the same man could have murdered both Becky Benedict and this new girl more than twenty years apart?"

"Seems unlikely."

"But you haven't ruled out the possibility?"

"We're still investigating," Alex said.

"It's more likely that whoever did this just got the idea for all the rest from the press conference."

I shrugged. "It's all speculation at this point."

"So what do we do here?" the chief asked.

"Find out who really murdered Becky Benedict all those years ago. If we can do that, who knows what else we might be able to find out? Maybe it will help us solve the murder of Jessica Staley too."

Later, after I left the station, I went back to my hotel room, powered up my laptop and googled "Lauren Nolan" and "fire" and "death."

I was curious.

There were several articles about it. More than you would expect to find for a simple accidental fire. I soon found out why.

The first day's headline and story were pretty straight forward. The headline said: DORCHESTER WOMAN DIES IN HOUSE FIRE. This was followed up the next day by the headline: BURNING CIGARETTE BELIEVED CAUSE OF FIRE THAT KILLED DORCHESTER WOMAN.

So she was smoking and started a fire? Did she fall asleep with the lit cigarette in her hand? The article didn't give specific details about that.

But then there were further stories—and they got a lot more interesting.

Especially a headline which read: POLICE CHIEF SUSPENDED DURING PROBE INTO EX-WIFE'S DEATH.

I read the article.

Dorchester Police Chief Connor Nolan has been temporarily suspended while authorities investigate the circumstances of the death of his former wife, Lauren Nolan née Bradford.

She fatally succumbed to smoke inhalation despite efforts by rescue personnel to save her from the blaze which destroyed her home at 221 Circle Street.

Chief Nolan was in the home with her when the blaze broke out, but managed to escape unhurt.

Fire officials at first believed a lit cigarette was the cause of the blaze, but later launched a more extensive investigation. The reason for that investigation—and the details of it—have not been made public, but pending the official results of the investigation, Chief Connor Nolan was relieved of his duties as head of the force until his role in the fire that killed his former wife could be determined.

Nolan and his wife had been married for four years before divorcing six months ago. It was not clear what Nolan was doing inside the home with her when the fire broke out...

There were several more articles about it. And then finally I found the headline: POLICE CHIEF REINSTATED TO POST. The article said:

Police Chief Connor Nolan's suspension has been lifted after he was cleared of any possible wrongdoing in the death of his former wife, Lauren, who died in a house fire.

Town officials said Nolan had been reinstated as head of the police department, and they regretted any misunderstanding that led to his temporary removal from the police chief position.

"Chief Nolan has served our police department and our town well," the official statement read. "We look forward to working closely with him again as we move forward after this tragedy."

There was a statement from Nolan too which said:

"I'm extremely happy and grateful to be able to resume my duties as head of the Dorchester Police Department. As you are all no doubt aware, this has been a very trying time for me. I loved Lauren very much, even though we weren't together as man and wife anymore, and I mourn her death. But at least now I can be back doing my duty—which I'm sure Lauren would want—as police chief helping to protect the people of Dorchester."

Well, that was all very interesting, I thought to myself. Not that it had anything to do with Becky Benedict or any of the other cases I was pursuing. But it did make me take a new look at Connor Nolan.

Maybe he wasn't the great guy that I thought he was.

FIFTEEN

"So do you have the hots for the police chief guy or something?" Alex asked me.

"Why would you say something like that?"

"I was in the meeting with you and picked up on the sexual tension."

"Sexual tension?"

"Yep."

"Sexual tension on his part?"

"Mostly from you."

"I have no idea what you're talking about."

"Trust me, Nikki. I have a real knack for picking up on sexual tension. I sure picked up on it back there."

We were in a car on our way to see Eleanor Benedict. I hadn't really talked to her since that first day in the FBI office in Washington. I wanted to ask her more questions now that we had additional information about the case.

"Connor Nolan is a good-looking guy," Alex said.

"I guess."

"And his wife died, he told us. So that means he's available."

"Maybe. But there is a problem." I told her what I'd found

out about Nolan's ex-wife dying in the house fire. How Nolan was with his wife in the house when the fire happened. How there was enough suspicion about his possible role in her death that he was suspended from his job as police chief during an investigation. And about his eventual reinstatement.

"So he was cleared?" Alex said.

"Officially."

"But you're still not sure..."

"I'd like to find out a bit more detail about that fire."

"It can't have anything to do with what we're doing here."

"Not likely."

"Then all this curiosity on your part about his wife dying in the fire is personal?"

"I guess so."

"Why?"

I shrugged. "In case anything did develop between us."

"You don't want to have a relationship with a guy who might murder a woman once he's done with her."

"It makes breaking up so hard to do." I smiled.

We talked more about the Becky Benedict case. And the Jessica Staley one too. It sure seemed pretty impossible that the two cases were connected—twenty years apart. But I wasn't ruling anything out.

Alex kept her eyes on the road. We were almost to Eleanor Benedict's house now. I thought about some of the questions I wanted to ask her.

"If there was a connection between the deaths of Jessica Staley and Becky Benedict, what could it be?" I asked Alex.

"They were both young teenage girls."

"Right."

"No sexual attack in either case."

"Okay."

"And their killings were similar—they both died from

repeated beatings and stabbing, and were probably tortured over a prolonged period before they died."

I thought about all that for a minute.

"What are the differences in their murders?" I asked.

"Time. More than twenty years apart."

"Definitely a big difference. The idea that the same killer is operating twenty years apart is hard to imagine."

"Location. Different states. Elmsford isn't even close to Dorchester. Hundreds of miles and a couple of states away."

"Time and location. Check. What else is different?"

"The victims themselves," Alex said. "Jessica Staley was a troubled kid. According to what her parents told you, she was doing drugs and running around with a wild crowd and who knows what else? There was physical violence at home, according to the sister. Between the parents and involving Jessica too. She'd been grounded by the father, showed up at school with bruises from him—and finally ran away from home in an act of defiance. Whereas Becky Benedict sounds like she was the exact opposite. An A-student, well-behaved, responsible and trustworthy, according to the mother. So if we think a killer is looking for a certain type—like a messed up kid to abduct, and later kill—Jessica Staley fits the pattern. Becky Benedict doesn't. They're completely different victims in that regard."

"Or so we've been told."

"By their parents."

"That's right."

"The parents should know."

"Unless one of them is lying."

"Why would they want to do that?"

"To make the memory of their daughter seem better. To cover up any flaws in their kid. To make sure everyone thought they were good parents, and didn't help drive their child into doing something which cost them their life."

"Well, that wouldn't be the Staleys. They were pretty open when you talked with them about all the problems they had with their daughter. And so was the younger sister."

"Which leaves us with Eleanor Benedict."

"You think maybe Becky Benedict wasn't the perfect angel Mrs. Benedict claims she was?"

"That's what we need to ask her."

SIXTEEN

Eleanor Benedict looked at us hopefully when she opened the door and saw Alex and I standing on her front porch. I guess she thought we were coming to bring her news about her daughter and the search for her killer.

But that optimism faded away as soon as we told her we were only there with more questions for her.

I introduced her to Alex, and explained that she was my partner and working with me on the case. Mrs. Benedict greeted her without much enthusiasm; she seemed more focused on me.

"Haven't you found out anything at all?" she asked me.

"Nothing that tells us who killed your daughter."

"I was hoping..."

"For more?" Alex said.

"Yes."

"It's been over twenty years since your daughter's death. That's a very cold trail for us to follow."

"Someone should have to pay for Becky's death."

"Whoever killed her could be dead by now," I said.

I'm certain Mrs. Benedict must have thought about that

possibility, too. But perhaps she didn't want to consider it. She wanted closure and revenge and punishment for someone for the loss of her daughter. That was why she had come to me in the first place.

"I thought maybe you could accomplish this—get more results than the other law enforcement people I've dealt with until now. I thought it might be different with you because of what you did for your... your..."

"My sister?"

"Yes, your sister. You solved that case. You made the person who did it pay for his crime. That's what I was counting on you doing for me."

"I'll do my best. But we need your help, Mrs. Benedict."

"Let's talk a bit more about Becky," Alex said to her.

We sat in the living room of her home and talked, drinking coffee and giving her a rundown of what we knew—and what we'd done so far—on her daughter's case. There were a number of pictures of Becky around the room, looking pretty and perky and full of life. One particularly striking one was of Becky in her cheerleader outfit smiling happily for the camera. That was how she would be frozen in time. Forever fifteen.

I didn't notice any pictures of Eleanor Benedict's husband though. The one who had died not long after Becky disappeared and was found murdered. I wondered if there was any significance to that.

"There has been a development involving your daughter," I said. "It could be important. But we're not sure what it means."

I told her about the girl found dead in Huntsdale—Jessica Staley from Michigan—who had used Becky's name very recently to sign in at the motel in Zanesville prior to her own death.

"Why would she do that?" she said.

"We have no idea yet," Alex told her.

"It's possible—very likely actually—that she simply knew your daughter's name from the press conference," I said.

"That makes the most logical sense, we think," Alex said. "What other connection could there be between this dead girl today and your daughter twenty years ago?"

"Unless the same person killed them both twenty years apart," Mrs. Benedict said.

"We're still looking into that possibility," I said, and went on to explain that one of the reasons we didn't think there could be a connection between the two girls was that they didn't seem very much alike, either in their personalities or the circumstances of their disappearances. Jessica Staley had been in constant trouble in Michigan and ran away from home after a fight with her parents. Nothing like her Becky.

She talked some more about her daughter in glowing terms —making it clear that she was nothing like Jessica Staley.

"Do you still have any of Becky's belongings that we could look through?" Alex asked. "Maybe it would help us find out something more about her and her life in the days before she was abducted."

"Yes, I still have everything of hers," Mrs. Benedict said.

"Everything?" I asked.

"I've never thrown anything of Becky's away."

She was telling the truth about that. Everything of Becky's —all her belongings—were still in this house. Her clothes. Her schoolbooks. Her cheerleader outfit. Even some of Becky's favorite foods were still stored in the kitchen, according to her mother. As if she was waiting for her daughter to walk back into the house again.

The most bizarre thing though was Becky's bedroom. It was virtually unchanged from the last time she was in the house. Her closets, her drawers filled with her belongings, her bed with pillows and other ornaments covering it—none of it had been touched by her mother in all these years. Oh, she had dusted and vacuumed a bit, she told us, but that's all. Otherwise, it was like it had been preserved in a time capsule.

"Her room was always private. I never touched anything in it when she was alive, that was important to her to have that kind of privacy. And I've never violated it since her death either. This is still my Becky's room. Everything in it is just the way she left it."

I asked if Alex and I could look through the room. She hesitated at first. But I told her there could be something there that could jump-start our investigation. Especially since it was still the way Becky left it two decades earlier.

"Just make sure you put everything back the way you found it," she said.

"We will."

"Don't change anything in there."

"We promise to leave it the way it is."

Like a room in a museum, I thought to myself. Waiting for her daughter to come home again, even though that was never going to happen. Becky Benedict was dead and gone a long time ago. But I remembered my mother doing something similar after Caitlin died—in her bedroom and with her belongings. I guess it involved not accepting completely that someone we love is really gone. And if it helped Eleanor Benedict to deal with the loss of her daughter, then it wasn't any of my business.

"Let's see what we can find out in here," I said to Alex after Mrs. Benedict returned to the living room where she'd be surrounded again by pictures of her dead daughter.

SEVENTEEN

It was weird and definitely a bit off-putting to be going through the dead girl's belongings—which had seemingly been sitting there untouched—trying to look for something to unlock the doors to her past as a happy teenager growing up in this house. It brought back memories of going into my sister's room after her death. Seeing all Becky Benedict's things: clothes still left out; books with place marks to show how much she'd read; a to-do list she'd posted on a bulletin board attached to the wall. Like it was all waiting for her to come home again.

So weird.

I said that to Alex.

"Definitely weird," Alex agreed.

We each took half the room so we could look for anything significant, even though we weren't certain what that might be.

According to Eleanor Benedict, the room had never really been searched by police—either at the time of Becky's murder or more recently.

I sort of understood why they didn't care much about Becky's room twenty years ago. Daniel Gary Leighton had been arrested very quickly after the body was found, then confessed

—albeit falsely—to the murder. So the local police wouldn't have needed to look into the girl's life. The case was solved, the man that did it was in jail. Or so they thought at the time. I wondered who the police chief was back then. And if he was still alive and reachable. It was something I'd check out later.

What was a bit disturbing to me was that the police had not been back to check out the room—or any of Becky's belongings and possessions—since Leighton's admission that his confession was a fake. Not even after Alex and I arrived in town to re-investigate everything for the FBI. Wouldn't the local police want to retrace their steps from their initial investigation—even the steps that were omitted at the time—to try to track down the real killer?

I thought of a few possible reasons why Connor Nolan had not done this:

1) He had a small police force, and they were too busy dealing with present day crimes in Dorchester to prioritize a twenty-year-old murder with a trail that had long ago grown very, very cold.

2) Connor Nolan was embarrassed that the Dorchester police had done something—or maybe not done something—that messed up the earlier investigation and wanted to cover it up to defend his department.

3) Connor Nolan was simply not a very good cop.

The first thing Alex and I looked at was Becky's computer. She'd had a phone, but she presumably had it with her at the time of her death, and it had never been found. There was no such thing as an iPad or tablet in 2003, so I had hopes for the computer, especially if the police nor anyone else had never checked it.

It had not been turned on since then, I soon found out. It attempted to load updates when I started it, but that soon failed. The operating system from 2003 was so old that it wasn't compatible with anything out there in the computer world today. There might be some information about Becky's last days on there, but I couldn't access it. Maybe I could convince Mrs. Benedict to let me ship it back to Washington so our tech experts could take it apart and look for information on the hard drive or something.

"She liked *Lord of the Rings*, *Pirates of the Caribbean* and *Star Wars* movies," I said, looking at some of the posters that were on the walls of her bedroom.

"And *American Idol* and *Friends* on TV," Alex said.

"How do you know that?"

"*TV Guide*. I found one in her drawers. It had both shows marked like she wanted to make sure she watched them."

"Well, we know now she had good taste on *Friends*. Maybe not so much on *American Idol*."

"Which helps us how?"

"Not at all."

Her clothes looked pretty normal for a teenager. Lots of jeans and slacks. T-shirts and tops. Some sweaters for colder weather. There were dresses and skirts and blouses too, but I figured she wore the jeans and the T-shirts most of the time. That's what she was wearing when her body was found, too.

There was no identification or personal papers. Like her phone, she'd probably had that with her in her wallet when she was killed, and that had never been found. Only the ATM card she'd carried in it.

"Nothing exciting on her to-do list on the bulletin board," Alex said. "A dentist appointment. Cheerleading practice. A date for some big test at school that she had coming up. Stuff like that."

"Hey, what about this?" I said, holding up what looked like a greeting card. "I found it hidden underneath some clothes and other stuff in her dresser drawer."

It said, "Thank You For Being You." Below that, someone had drawn a big heart with the initials DM inside it.

"DM," I said.

"DM," Alex repeated.

"It could be a clue," I said.

"So let's see if we can find out anything else about DM and Becky in here, huh?"

We didn't, but we did hit the jackpot in another way. It was in another drawer of her dresser—hidden, like the greeting card, underneath some underwear and hosiery. Clearly she wanted to make sure her mother never found this stuff, even if she didn't ever come into Becky's 'private' room.

There was a pipe for smoking weed.

A small bag of marijuana.

A fake ID indicating Becky Benedict was old enough to buy beer in the state of Pennsylvania.

And—maybe most significant of all—a container of birth control pills it appeared she had been using.

"It looks like she wasn't Ms. Perfect at all," Alex said.

"Which makes her more like Jessica Staley," I pointed out.

"So if someone is targeting troubled teenagers..."

"We now know both Jessica Staley and Becky Benedict fit that mold."

"Do you think Becky's mother knew what her daughter was doing?" asked Alex.

"Let's go ask her."

EIGHTEEN

"Do the initials DM mean anything to you?" we asked Eleanor Benedict when we went back downstairs to see her in the living room.

"DM? I don't think so. Why?"

"They could be initials for the name of a boy."

"What boy?"

"Maybe a boy your daughter was seeing."

"My daughter wasn't seeing any boys."

"Are you sure about that?"

"Becky was only fifteen years old."

She said it defiantly, as if that should answer the question.

Which, of course, it did not.

"There's nothing wrong with a fifteen-year-old girl seeing boys," I said.

"The right kind of girl doesn't do that. Not a girl like Becky."

"I had a boyfriend when I was fifteen."

"So did I," said Alex.

"Well, Becky did not have a boyfriend. And I don't know

anything about a boy with the initials DM. Why are you asking me about all this?"

"We found a card hidden in a drawer in her room," Alex said. "I guess she wanted to make sure you didn't see it."

We showed her the card. She stared at it without saying a word at first, but eventually seemed to realize she couldn't pretend it wasn't there simply by ignoring it.

"We found other things in her bedroom too," Alex said.

"Did you know your daughter was taking birth control pills?" I asked.

"Becky? Why would she do that?"

The answer was pretty obvious, and I hoped I didn't have to upset Mrs. Benedict anymore by spelling it out for her.

Mrs. Benedict still didn't say anything, so Alex finally jumped in and blurted out, "It appears your daughter could have been having sexual relations with someone before she died."

"Oh my God!"

"Did she ever talk to you about this? Ask you questions about sex or birth control methods or..."

"No, of course not!"

"What about drugs?" I asked.

"What about them?"

"Did you know your daughter was using marijuana?"

We told her about the hashish pipe and the bag of weed we found hidden in her dresser drawer.

"Becky would never do that."

Just like she would never have a boyfriend or have sex, I thought to myself. At first, I figured Mrs. Benedict somehow really believed this. But then I recognized her reaction for what it was. I saw her defensiveness every time she'd said that none of what we were raising about Becky was true.

She knew.

She knew what her daughter had been doing.

She was in denial about Becky. A denial that had gone on for more than twenty years. She didn't want to do anything to ruin the image of her perfect daughter. Maybe because that was the only way to deal with her loss, to wear blinders to the truth. But Alex and I couldn't do that. We needed to confront the facts. And the facts showed that Becky Benedict had been no angel, the same way Jessica Staley was no angel either.

"I wish I'd never let you look through her things," she said to us now. "If I knew you were going to smear my daughter's reputation and her memory like this, I would not have allowed it."

"We're only looking for information to help us solve the case and find your daughter's killer," Alex said.

"Well, I don't want you talking about my Becky this way. I don't want you going through any more of her things. In fact, I don't want you in my house anymore. Please leave now. Leave me alone. Leave me alone until you find out who murdered my daughter. That's all I want from you."

"Then I guess you're not going to be happy with what I want to ask you next," I said.

"What is that?"

"We'd like to take Becky's computer with us."

She glared at me. "That computer belonged to Becky. Whatever is on there was no one's business but hers. It's an invasion of my daughter's privacy."

"Your daughter is dead," I said. It sounded brutal, I know, but I couldn't think of any other way to deliver the message. "She's been dead for twenty years. And her killer is still running around free and very possibly killing other young girls. There may be answers to Becky's murder, answers that could lead us to whoever killed her, on her computer. We can't access it at the moment, but our tech specialists may well be able to. It's worth a try. I'd like to do this with your cooperation, Mrs. Benedict. But if not, we'll get a subpoena and a search warrant to seize it from you. One way or another, we need to find out what was on Becky's computer concerning those last days of her life."

Eleanor Benedict eventually agreed to give us the computer. As she did so, I could see a look of resignation on her face. She knew it was all falling apart now; the fantasy she'd built up around her daughter's memory. She'd probably known the facts for a long time, of course, but she was finally confronting them at this moment.

I wondered if Becky's father had known all this about his daughter too before he died. Whether the stress of dealing with that or Eleanor Benedict's fantasy world played any role in causing his fatal heart attack.

"Are you sure the initials DM don't mean anything to you?" I asked one more time before we left.

"We just want as much information as possible about your daughter and her life and the people around her," Alex told her. "Anything you can tell us might help in finding justice for Becky even after all this time."

She hesitated this time before answering.

"Donald Maris," she said finally.

"That's DM?" I said.

"He's with the police department. He's an officer there, you might have met him. He works for Chief Nolan."

NINETEEN

Mrs. Benedict said she had a copy of Becky's high school yearbook somewhere in her house. She found it and let me look through the pages until I found Donald Maris. He was a good-looking guy, gorgeous brown hair, captain of the football team, a star wrestler too. Maris was a junior, while Becky was only a freshman that year, and it was easy to see how he would have been appealing as a boyfriend—if that's what he had been.

He had signed the yearbook under his picture, using the initials DM, and I saw another couple of references to him in the yearbook—talking about the football team—where he was referred to by those initials. So it was very likely the greeting card had been from Donald Maris.

I called the Dorchester police station and said I needed to talk to Maris. They said he was out on traffic watch right now and—once I identified myself—gave me his location. Alex stayed at the Benedict house to deal with the removal of Becky's computer and see if there was anything else interesting or significant in the bedroom. I went to find Donald Maris.

He was sitting in a patrol car, alone, at an intersection in downtown Dorchester. I wondered where his partner was. Or maybe they didn't need a partner in a place like Dorchester. Especially if he was only doing traffic duty.

"I figured you'd get around to talking with me," he said when I told him why I was there.

"Why didn't you come to me?"

"I already talked to Chief Nolan."

"About having a secret relationship with Becky Benedict before she died."

"Yeah, but it was no secret."

"Becky's mother said she didn't know about it. At least at first."

"She's pretty nuts when it comes to Becky. She's been bugging us at the station since the Leighton confession fell apart and it became obvious someone else killed Becky. Mrs. Benedict complained we weren't doing enough to solve the case. I guess that's why she wound up going to you people. Has the FBI done any better than us?"

I ignored the question and asked him about his relationship with Becky.

"That was a long time ago," he said.

It sure was. Maris looked like a different guy than he'd been in high school. Less hair, more weight—his police uniform was stretched tight on him, especially around his stomach. While Becky Benedict's beauty was frozen in time, Maris's good looks had been ravaged, even though he wasn't even forty years old.

"I've been married a long time now. We've got three children—two boys and a girl. I can't really remember a lot about Becky. That's what I told Chief Nolan, and it's all I can tell you. I was interviewed by the police when her murder happened, but they weren't too interested in me because they quickly nabbed Leighton for the killing. Like I said, it was all so long ago. Another lifetime."

"She was only fifteen when you were seeing her?"

"I guess."

"How old were you?"

"Seventeen. Going on eighteen."

"Did the age difference bother you?"

"No, why should it?"

"Well, for one thing, she was underage."

"Underage how?"

"For sex."

"Sex?"

"Or in this case it could be called statutory rape."

"That's crazy."

I wasn't sure why I was antagonizing him like this. Maybe I felt he had taken advantage of Becky as an older boy. Maybe it bothered me that he'd gone to Chief Nolan instead of me to discuss his relationship with her. Or maybe I was just trying to get him mad enough at me to reveal something he hadn't before.

"So there were never any sexual relations between the two of you?"

"No, we never got that far. Look, I was seventeen years old. We never did anything like that. We didn't have sex. We only fooled around a bit—necking, some petting, that kind of thing. That's all. And we weren't even doing that when she died. The relationship was over before then."

"What happened to end it?"

"I went away to a football camp that year. Becky... well, Becky found someone else. She told me that when I came back. I tried to see her again, but she was all hung up over this other guy."

"Do you know who he was?"

"Not a name. But I think he was older. A lot older. She talked about him like he was a man, not a kid."

"Do you know if she was having sexual relations with this older man?'

"I have no idea."

"We found birth control pills in her bedroom when we searched through her stuff earlier today."

"Well, she didn't use them with me."

"Because you never had sex?"

"That's right."

"Do you have any idea who might have killed her?"

"I told Connor—Chief Nolan—everything I know."

"What about telling me?"

"You don't talk to Chief Nolan?"

He smiled when he said it. Like he knew something about Nolan and me. Not that there was anything to know.

"Nah," Maris continued, "I have no clue who did it."

Just to keep him talking, I asked him one more time what he remembered about Becky Benedict from when they were dating. "What was Becky like?"

"Pretty. Fun. A bit wild sometimes. She liked to have a good time."

"Her mother described her to me as the perfect daughter—an angel of a girl who never did anything wrong or got into any kind of trouble."

"Well, that sounds like Becky's mother didn't know her very well," Donald Maris said.

Or didn't want to admit what she did know, I thought.

TWENTY

The Dorchester police chief twenty years ago had been a man named Stan Upshaw. He was still around, and I tracked him down to a house in the area. He was close to eighty, and the years had not been kind to him. He needed a walker to get around, and he looked extremely frail. I realized he must have been in his sixties—probably close to retirement age—during the Benedict case. I wondered if that had played a role in the way he handled the investigation. Would a young man like Nolan have done a better job?

"It was pretty much the last case of my law enforcement career," Upshaw said to me as we sat in his living room. "Definitely the biggest case. We'd never had a murder like that in Dorchester. I'd been police chief for a lot of years and on the force before that—and I'd never seen anything like that in our area during all that time."

There were plaques, awards and pictures from his police career all around the living room. Outside, in the back, I could see a beautiful garden of tulips, hyacinths and other plants that Upshaw told me he tended to diligently these days.

At my urging, he went through everything he'd done back

then—starting with the first call from Becky's mother about the girl not coming home from school, then the shocking discovery of her battered body, and finally the arrest of Daniel Gary Leighton.

"At first, it didn't seem like that big a deal," Upshaw said. "We figured she'd gone off to some party without telling her parents. Or maybe she ran away, kids do that. Or she'd been in an accident and was in a hospital. No one ever contemplated murder as a possibility when we first got the case. I know I sure didn't. Murder simply didn't happen in Dorchester. Not this kind of murder, anyway.

"But, as the days went by without any trace of her, we all became more desperate. Her mother. The search parties. And me. It became clear at some point that this was going to end badly. Then we found the body in that trash bin.

"It was a sight I'll never forget. The way that poor girl had been battered and beaten. She was so beautiful in life, but in death almost impossible to look at. All I could think about was catching the monster that did it. Putting him in jail for the rest of his damned life so he could never do it to anyone else. No matter how long it took, I was going to find him and make him pay.

"Then suddenly, almost without warning, it was over. Leighton used the girl's ATM card at a bank, we saw him on a security video, discovered he was already on record for previous violent crimes and he was picked up very soon after that. It was your people, the feds, that nabbed him. Then he was brought back to Dorchester to face the murder charge. And he confessed. He confessed to killing the Benedict girl. Plus a lot more."

Upshaw shook his head sadly. "It was over. It was done. We had the guy. And that was that. He went away to prison, and everyone moved on with their lives. But now... now I keep looking back on what I did and what I didn't do. Did I miss something at the time? Well, obviously I did, we put the wrong man in jail. Oh, he deserved to be there, but not for Becky Benedict. We know that now. That haunts me, Agent Cassidy. I let the real killer go free. That's something I can never forget. And you know what? I always had a feeling something was wrong about this case. There was stuff that didn't make sense. Things I could have pursued, but I didn't.

"Now I think about Becky a lot. I keep playing it all over and over in my head. I haven't been a cop in a long time, but I still have my memories from back then. Everything about that poor girl, about Leighton and about all the things I could have done—but never did—at the time to get at the real truth."

I was surprised by Upshaw's reaction. I'd expected him to be defensive about his role in the case, to tell me how he only did what everyone else did, believed Leighton's confession because it wrapped everything up so nicely. I wasn't even sure he'd talk to me much about it. But, instead, the exact opposite had occurred. He'd been brooding about it ever since the truth came out about Leighton, and now he welcomed the opportunity to talk about it with someone. Especially someone who might be able to finally find justice for Becky Benedict.

That's what he told me.

And I sympathized with him.

I'd come here planning to be critical of former Police Chief Stan Upshaw for doing a bad job investigating the case twenty years ago, but I didn't feel that way anymore. He'd done what any law enforcement official would have done. Even me, most likely. He'd followed the trail of evidence and the confession to what seemed like a logical conclusion. Even if it turned out not to be that way. Now he wanted to try to help right that wrong before it was too late for him.

I went through all the details of what I'd found out since his original investigation, and I asked what he thought might have been wrong about the case, about what didn't make sense to him back then.

"The mother bothered me. She kept pushing this idea of her daughter being such a wonderful, good girl; that there was nothing she'd ever done that could have led to her being abducted and then murdered. But the mother seemed to be living in a fantasy, not recognizing that her daughter was a normal teenage girl with flaws, who made mistakes like all kids did. She just kept talking about how the girl was perfect... well, it seemed too perfect to me to be true. But, again, we didn't have any reason to keep digging into those questions once Leighton had confessed."

I told him about the birth control pills I'd found in Becky's bedroom recently and about the card I'd found from Donald Maris, who had dated her at one point. "Did you question Maris back then?"

"Of course. But he was clean. He wasn't anywhere near here when she disappeared."

"Any other boyfriends that you found out about?"

Upshaw shook his head. "No, but we never pushed too much on her personal life after the Leighton arrest. But the questions about her personal life bothered me too, even back then. No idea who else she might have been with. But... well, I thought there was something weird going on in that house. With the father."

"The father who died right after all this?"

He nodded. "There was a strange dynamic going on between him and the mother. At first it seemed like she was blaming him for the girl being gone. I was on the job for a long time, and sometimes you got a feeling—an instinct or whatever —that something was wrong. Well, I had an instinct that something was wrong inside that house."

"Wrong how?"

"I wondered if maybe the father was... doing things to her."

"Sexual things?"

"Yeah, it just had that feel to it."

If what Upshaw was saying was accurate, Becky Benedict had definitely been unhappy in her home life. Just like Jessica Staley was when she ran away.

Was that the connection that got them both murdered twenty years apart?

TWENTY-ONE

I had questions for Dorchester Police Chief Connor Nolan. About his officer, Donald Maris, and Maris's connection to our victim, Becky Benedict. About what Nolan had done or not done so far in his investigation of Becky Benedict's death. About Upshaw's account of what his department did or didn't do during the initial investigation.

And, yes, I had questions for Connor Nolan too—whenever I figured out the best way to ask them—about his history with his dead wife. But that was for another time.

I called Alex and told her I was going to talk to Nolan at the station about all my questions. She asked me if I wanted her to be there too. I said no, I wanted to talk with him alone. She wasn't sure if that was a good idea, but she finally agreed.

"Don't make this personal, Nikki."

"Why would I make it personal?"

"Because of your... your interest in the guy."

"Hey, I'm a professional."

I meant that too. I wasn't fantasizing about a relationship with Connor Nolan right now. Talking again to Nolan was simply another part of my job as a professional FBI agent, nothing more than that. Or so I tried to convince myself anyway.

I parked my rental car in the lot of the police station, took a deep breath and then got out to see Nolan. But his answers didn't turn out to be what I thought they would once I got inside.

Because there'd been a big development.

"I was just going to call you," Nolan said when I got to his office. "We got an email from someone claiming to be the killer."

"The killer of Becky Benedict?"

"Her. The Staley woman in Ohio. And maybe a lot more."

"More?"

"Yeah, it's all in the message."

"Do you think it's for real?"

"You tell me."

I raised a questioning eyebrow.

"Because it's addressed to you." He handed me a printout of the email. It was a single page. Then he sat while I read through it.

Greetings Nikki Cassidy, FBI agent (and all my other law enforcement friends out there).

I watched you on TV in Dorchester the other day. You were talking to me, right? Even though you don't know who I am. Not yet.

You asked me to give myself up and stop what I'm doing. I'm afraid that's not going to happen, Nikki. I'm having too much fun. How about you?

Becky Benedict didn't have time for much fun in Dorchester before her untimely death, did she? Daniel Gary Leighton took the fall for that for a long time, but now you know the truth. Danny boy was a killer, but he was not the killer of Becky. That honor belongs to yours truly.

Then there's the case of Jessica Staley. Jessica wanted to run away from her parents in Michigan and see the world. That's what she told me—when she could still speak. But all Jessica got to see was Zanesville—posing there as Becky Benedict, no less!—and Huntsdale, huh? Not much of a world view before her time on the planet was over.

There's more too.

More victims out there.

Since Becky Benedict.

Before Jessica Staley.

And more to come too.

But I'll elaborate on that in a moment.

For the time being, the question is, Agent Cassidy: "Do you think you can ever stop me?"

Like you stopped the person—or the people—who killed your sister.

Or did you?

If I have one regret, it's that I didn't place a bouquet of roses on Becky Benedict's body like the beautiful bouquet of roses that were found with your sister. Too late to do anything about that now. But I didn't make the same mistake with Jessica Staley. She died with roses just like your sister did. And I even got dear Jessica to buy them—my last gift to her—herself. Wasn't that a nice touch?

I was bothered by the Zanesville reference and the mention of Jessica Staley buying the roses. A lot of the other things were known to the public from previous media coverage, but we'd kept the fact that Jessica signed into the Zanesville motel using Becky Benedict's name and her purchase of the roses on the convenience store security video private so far, in case we got another confession we had to check.

But whoever wrote this note knew about both details.

And that gave me the chills.

This was a cold-blooded killer, and he thought this was all a game.

A game he had dragged me into.

But the worst part of his message was at the end. It said:

That's all for now, Agent Cassidy. But you'll be hearing from me again soon. Very, very soon.

Becky Benedict.

Jessica Staley.

There have been more—many more—in the past.

And there will be more in the future.

Unless you can stop me.

TWENTY-TWO

"Where did you get this?" I asked Nolan, trying my best to keep my emotions under control and remain professional.

"It arrived about an hour ago. No one read it for another forty minutes or so. And then I saw it. I called you at the hotel and on your cell, and then you walked in."

"How did it arrive?"

"It was sent to the hotline set up for information about the Benedict murder. We've been running an appeal in the media for anyone who knows anything to come forward. Nothing we received really panned out. But now we've got this."

I read through it again. Looking for something—anything— that I might have missed before.

"It sure looks real," I said. "The Zanesville connection and the purchase of the roses at the Huntsdale store. Whoever wrote this connected both to Jessica Staley's murder. Which means he's the killer of the Staley girl, or at least knows the killer. Either way, this is no fake."

"What about killing Becky Benedict?"

"He could be making that part up. We can't be sure if he's

responsible for that too. It is hard to believe that they could be linked twenty years apart."

"He claims to have killed other women too."

"So did Daniel Gary Leighton. We have no proof of that."

"And what about the stuff regarding your sister?"

"I think he's just trying to goad me."

"But we won't know for sure until we find him."

I looked at the name and mailing address of the sender. It was a garble of letters from an unknown mail address, like the scam mail you might get from an "Iranian prince" who wants to give you a fortune or those that say you won the Irish Sweepstakes and you'll just need to send them all your bank information. I'd turn it over to our FBI techs to search for an internet trail, of course. But I was doubtful that it would take us anywhere other than a dead end.

Still, we needed to check every possibility. This note could hold important clues toward helping us track down the killer of Jessica Staley.

And maybe more deaths too.

Maybe even the long-ago murder of Becky Benedict.

But what about the connection with my sister? Why was that in the killer's note? How did that fit in? Was it there only because of all the media attention I'd gotten recently? Or was there something more to the killer bringing up the case of my dead sister again?

I'd had a vague feeling of uneasiness about my sister's case ever since I was in Huntsdale last time. I mean, I'd answered most of the questions about her murder, but not ALL of them. I'd figured, though, that what I didn't know—my remaining questions about Caitlin and the investigation by my father back then into her murder—weren't really important in the scheme of things.

Except now I wasn't so sure.

And I wondered if the Jessica Staley murder could give me

some of the answers I still needed about Caitlin, as far-fetched as that might seem.

"Let's assume—at least for the time being—that the same person did kill Jessica Staley and Becky Benedict," I said.

"Okay."

"That means if we can finally figure out who really killed Becky Benedict..."

"We might get the answers for Jessica's death and others too."

I told him about what I had found in Becky's bedroom. About my conversations with Upshaw and Maris. And more about the strange link that we'd found at the Zanesville, Ohio motel where Jessica Staley had used Becky's name to register.

"There's more I want to do," I said. "I want to speak to any teachers still at the high school who were there when Becky attended. There might be some. And I need to track down her friends from high school too; the other members of the cheer-leading squad she was on. And I want to go back to the last places we know Becky Benedict was at. The neighborhood where she was last seen walking home from school—and then the trash bin where her body was found."

"Why there?"

"It's where she was last alive."

"But it's been twenty years."

"I always like to visit the crime scene."

I called Alex from Nolan's office and told her about the email. Then I alerted Dave Blanton back in Washington and said I was forwarding it to him to get our techs to try to track down the sender, as impossible a task as that might be. I also asked him to get people to go back and look for other unsolved murder cases of teenage girls to see if there were any obvious links to Jessica or Becky's deaths. To see if the person who wrote the note might have been telling the truth when he claimed other victims.

"We should go back to Leighton again too," I said.

"Alex got nothing from him the first time," said Blanton.

"No, but that's before we got this message. Someone is claiming to be a serial killer the same way he did. Maybe the sender of the note got information from the media about Leighton's supposed murders—and made more cases up, just like he did. It could be linked somehow."

"Leighton's been in jail for years," Blanton pointed out.

"I'm just trying to cover all the bases, Chief."

At some point, Phil Girard came on the line with us. He was up in Elmsford, Jessica Staley's hometown, looking for more information about her. Blanton patched Girard into our phone conversation, and he gave us an update of what he'd found out.

"Everything we thought about the Staley girl is true, and more. Just before she left home, she got stopped by police on the street with a handbag full of pills and marijuana. She was already on probation from a previous police bust. There were two domestic violence complaints filed against Tim Staley by his wife. She later dropped the complaints, so no formal police or court action was ever taken. But there was clearly bad stuff going on in the Staleys' house. So if someone offered her a chance to get away from all this, she very likely was happy to take it."

"Any idea on who that person might be?"

"No. She told a few friends she was running away, like she did with her younger sister. But she didn't talk about leaving with anyone else. As far as they all knew, she left on her own."

We talked more about the details of how to proceed. Girard, for now, would stay in Elmsford to see if he could gather any more information about the Staley girl in the days and weeks before she left.

"What about Huntsdale?" Girard asked. "Who's going to handle things for us there?"

"Let me and Alex handle Huntsdale. It's my hometown."

"Along with Dorchester, where you are now?" Blanton asked.

"Yes."

"That's an awfully big job, Agent Cassidy."

"It's why you pay me the big bucks."

Blanton laughed. He didn't laugh much. Maybe I was getting to him, making a bit of a dent in his officious and business-like attitude.

"We'll need to work closely with local police and law enforcement on all of this," he said.

"I am."

"What about the chief in Huntsdale?"

"What about him?"

"You had trouble with him the last time you were there."

"Still do. I'm doing the best I can. He's a jerk, but I've dealt with jerky local law enforcement before."

"How about this Chief Nolan in Dorchester?"

"Better."

"You have a good working relationship with him?"

I looked over at Nolan sitting across the desk from me, waiting for me to get off the phone. "I'm working on it," I said.

TWENTY-THREE

I was woken up by a knock on my hotel room door. I looked at the clock next to my bed. 7:15 a.m. Must be Alex. She was always an earlier riser than me. I tumbled out of bed, walked over to the door and opened it.

But it wasn't Alex.

It was Chief Connor Nolan.

"Do FBI agents always sleep in this late?" He smiled. He was holding a cup of coffee in his hand. Two cups actually. He took a sip from one and handed the other to me. "It looks like you could use this," he said.

He was right about that. I took a big gulp of the coffee, and I let him into the room. I then realized how much of a mess I must look to him. I was wearing a ratty bathrobe I'd hurriedly pulled on when I thought it was only Alex at the door. My hair was a mess too. And God knows what my face looked like. If I was trying to impress the guy with my sex appeal, this was not a particularly good way for me to do it.

"What's going on?" I asked him. I sat down on the bed and drank some more of the coffee. That helped. Not a lot, but I was at least waking up now. All I had to do was get dressed and comb my hair to maybe look presentable.

"You told me you wanted to visit the spot where Becky Benedict's body was found—and the place where she disappeared, Nikki."

Nikki. He called me Nikki. He'd called me Agent Cassidy back in his office. This was a step forward. Maybe I didn't look quite as bad as I thought I did.

"That's right."

"So I'll take you there."

"Now?"

"I like to get an early start on the day."

"You're a morning person, huh?"

"I am."

"I'm not."

"I figured that out already."

A short time later, we were in his car driving through the streets of Dorchester. I was showered, dressed, caffeinated, and armed with a Glock 19M on my hip. Ready for another day as Nikki Cassidy, star FBI agent. I felt a lot more comfortable with Nolan seeing this version of me.

He said we'd first stop off in the neighborhood where Becky Benedict was last seen—and presumably from where she was abducted—then go to the area around the trash bin where her body had been found.

"What do you know about former chief Upshaw?" I asked as we drove.

"He was a good cop, from what I understand. Though not a lot of big cases happened while he was in office. Certainly no other big murders. The Benedict girl was a huge case for him. Lots of media attention at the time. Of course, there wasn't much for Upshaw to do. They stumbled onto Daniel Gary

Leighton using the girl's ATM card, then he confessed as soon as he was arrested a day later. So the case was over for Upshaw pretty quickly."

"Except he got it wrong."

"Lots of people were wrong about that. All the rest of the cases Leighton confessed to too. It wasn't only Upshaw."

"Do you want to get the Benedict case right this time, to make up for what happened when your department wasn't able to do that?"

"I want to solve this case because it's my job, Agent Cassidy. Just like you do."

I noticed he was calling me Agent Cassidy again. Maybe I'd offended him with my questioning. But there was still more I wanted to ask him and I figured this was as good a time as any to do it.

"How come you didn't tell me about Donald Maris?" I asked.

"Maris? What do you want to know about him?'

"He was dating Becky Benedict before she was murdered."

"That's not really relevant to the investigation."

"Wait a minute! One of the officers on your police force was having a romantic relationship with the girl, and you don't think that's relevant?"

Nolan sighed. "Did Donald Maris tell you the details of that relationship?"

"He said to ask you. That you knew."

"I do."

"And?"

"Donald Maris dated Becky Benedict briefly before she died. At the time she was abducted, he was in a dormitory on the University of Florida campus in Gainesville, attending a football camp. That was officially verified at the time. Gainesville is more than one thousand miles from Dorchester. So there's no way he could have been involved. Upshaw knew that. I know that. And now you know that too. Maris later joined the Dorchester police force. Upshaw hired him. He's been a solid and respected member of the force since then. Anything else you want to know about him?"

"No," I said, feeling a bit silly. "I think that about covers it." But I plunged ahead anyway with another question. I asked him about the computer and other stuff we found in Becky Benedict's bedroom. "Did anyone ever check that out before?"

"I don't know whether Upshaw did. Maybe not, since they had a suspect in custody so quickly and they were certain he did it. Me, I never realized the Benedict woman kept her daughter's computer and other stuff in the house so long after the murder had occurred. That's pretty damn unusual."

It was kind of what I assumed. Still, I kept pressing him on the issue. "You could have gone there and checked it out like we did."

"We probably would have. But you did it first. I guess you're just smarter and quicker and a better cop than me, huh?"

"I didn't mean to insult you."

"Go ahead. Anything else you want to know from me, Agent Cassidy?"

I was still Agent Cassidy. Not a good sign at all. But I had one more question I wanted to ask him. I knew I probably shouldn't do it, but I was curious. "What happened with you and your wife?" I said.

"She died."

"I mean about you being suspended afterward."

"I was reinstated."

"But—"

"I don't want to talk about my wife," he said.

We drove in silence until we got to the spot where he said Becky Benedict was last seen on the day she disappeared.

"I'm sorry," I said as we got out of the car. "It's really none of my business."

"You're right about that."

"I won't ask you anymore about her."

"Good."

"I just wondered what happened."

"It's private."

TWENTY-FOUR

The neighborhood where Becky Benedict had last been seen was a typical suburban block with a variety of houses and yards, which somehow, despite their different appearances, all seemed to have a quality of sameness about them.

It sure seemed safe though.

Looking around at the street where Nolan and I were standing, it seemed hard to believe a teenage girl had lost her life walking here.

Nolan pointed to one of the houses. "That's the house where someone saw Becky getting into a car. A green Ford."

"Can we talk to them again?"

"No, long gone."

"Moved away?"

"Dead. She was an older woman. Her name was Doris Johnson. Retired and a widow. She sat at her front window a lot of the day and watched what was going on outside. That's how she saw Becky Benedict and the car."

"But she didn't think anything was wrong?"

"Not until Becky went missing and we started canvassing the neighborhood."

"So there was no struggle or force used that she saw?"

Nolan shook his head. "She said Becky didn't seem scared or upset or acted like anything was wrong. The car pulled up alongside her, she had a brief conversation with whoever was behind the wheel and then she got in the car. She did it all voluntarily, the woman said."

"Just like the Staley girl going to the store to buy the bouquet of roses that would later be found with her body," I said. "That seemed to be voluntary too."

"Interesting. You figure the victims knew their killer? Trusted him until it was too late?"

"It seems likely. Or maybe he had some kind of hold over them that allowed him to get them to do what he wanted without using force."

"Drugs? Hypnotism?"

I shrugged. "And the woman at the window—the one who died—didn't give any more details about the car or its driver? No license plate or anything?"

"Only that it was a green Ford. According to the records, Upshaw questioned Doris Johnson pretty hard at the time—hoping she would remember more. But again, she didn't think anything was wrong until the news of Becky Benedict's abduction came out. Until then, she thought someone had just met Becky to pick her up after school."

I looked at the house where the woman had lived and at the window in front she must have been looking through that day.

That was more than twenty years ago. A long time to wait before coming back to look for more evidence. Leighton's phony confession had messed up this case—and a lot of others too—and left the trail very, very cold.

"And no one else in the neighborhood saw anything?" I asked.

"People were still at work at that time of the afternoon."

"Don't imagine it would do much good to go knocking on doors again, huh?"

"Most of the people who lived here then are gone. Either moved away or dead, like the Johnson woman. It's been a long time."

I walked over to the spot on the street where Doris Johnson had said she'd seen the green Ford pick Becky up. I stood there for a minute or two, trying to imagine what it was like for Becky Benedict on that day. Trying to imagine what had been going through her mind when the green car pulled up. Happiness. Fear. Or something in between. Well, whatever it was she seemed to have no hesitation about accepting a ride from whoever was inside. A ride that would turn out to be a fatal one for her.

"Do you want to check out the spot where her body was found?" Nolan asked.

"Let's go to her school first."

"Why?"

"I'd like to track her steps that day. Follow the same route that she did. That route—that trail—would have started when she left Dorchester High School."

The high school was only a few minutes' drive away. Probably a ten-minute walk or so for Becky that day. Nolan said that, based on accounts from people at the school, her last class ended at 2:50 p.m. She'd then attended cheerleader practice for an hour at the football field next door. After that, she left to walk home. Her encounter with the car happened around 4:30 p.m. according to the twenty-year-old account from Doris Johnson.

I walked from the high school to the cheerleader practice field like she must have done that last day. I looked in the direction of the neighborhood where we'd just been and she'd gotten into the car.

Something was bothering me.

"What direction from here is Becky's house?" I asked Nolan.

He pointed in the other direction from where we'd come.

"She was supposed to be going home, right?"

"That's what she told people when she left."

"Then why was she walking in the opposite direction?"

"I guess she wasn't really heading home."

"She was going to meet someone. Someone she didn't want to tell anyone about."

"Who?"

"The person who killed her."

We found nothing at the location where Becky's body had been dumped, not even the trash bin it had been in. That was long gone by now. There was another trash bin in a parking lot nearby, but it was a different one.

There was a building next door to the area. It was a corporate-looking place that looked like it housed a lot of offices.

"How many of these businesses do you figure were here when Becky's body was dumped outside?" I asked.

"Probably not many."

"But maybe some."

"There's never been any indication that the trash bin her body was found in had anything to do with any of the offices in this building. It was always assumed it was just picked at random by the killer."

"What if it wasn't random? Someone in that building might be connected to the murder. Or at least know something about the dumping of the body here. We need to find out if they do."

"C'mon, there must be twenty-five or thirty businesses in that building."

"Okay."

"You want us to interview them all to see if they were here

twenty years ago and, if so, whether they know something about Becky Benedict's murder?"

"Not us. You."

"Me?"

"Maybe not you yourself, but someone from your force could do it."

"That would take my people a long time and a lot of effort. You realize that, don't you? I don't have that kind of manpower available."

"What time does Donald Maris get off traffic duty?" I asked.

TWENTY-FIVE

I posted pictures—all the pictures we had—of Becky Benedict and Jessica Staley on a big whiteboard at the Dorchester police station. Along with a summary of the circumstances of each case and more details about both girls. It was the latest version of what I liked to call my "war room." An area I set aside when I'm working on a big case in order to go over the facts and the evidence with the other people I'm working with on the investigation.

Connor Nolan had let me use a conference room for this, and he was with me now for our first meeting. So was Alex and Donald Maris. Plus, I'd set up a Zoom conference call with Dave Blanton; Chief Frank Earnshaw and Edgar Daniels from Huntsdale; Ray Terlop, our FBI tech guy; and Phil Girard, who was still in Staley's hometown.

Looking at the pictures on the board, I tried to find some similarities between the two victims. There was nothing obvious. Becky Benedict had long blonde hair that hung down her back, and Jessica Staley was a brunette with a much shorter cut. The Benedict girl was taller and had a slender, sleek body, maybe from a lot of workouts at cheerleader practice. Jessica Staley was short with a bigger body, almost pudgy looking. Phil said people in Elmsford had told him she'd been dieting to get her weight down before she disappeared. And, of course, even though the victims were about the same age when they were murdered, those two killings happened twenty years apart. Different looks, different sizes, different times.

"So what's the connection?" I asked everyone as we looked at the pictures of the two dead girls. "Assuming for now that the note is true and the same person did kill both Becky Benedict and then Jessica Staley twenty years later, why do we think they went after these particular girls?"

"They were both troubled," Alex said.

I nodded. That was the same direction I was headed in my theory on this.

"Jessica Staley had run away from home," Alex continued. "We know now that Becky Benedict wasn't the 'good girl' her mother claimed she was. They both could have been looking for some way out of their unhappiness. And the killer... the killer must have somehow offered that to them."

"Which explains why they would have gone willingly with him," Blanton said.

"Like Becky Benedict getting into the car on her own," Nolan agreed.

"They wanted to be with the guy. They liked the guy. They weren't scared of the guy," I said.

"Until he killed them," Alex said. "Until it was too late."

We spent some time then trying to expand that idea a bit.

"Who might have knowledge of the troubles these girls were having in their lives?" I asked.

"Their parents," Earnshaw said.

"Maybe. Though Becky Benedict's mother seemed woefully unaware of what was going on with her daughter. Sometimes the parents are the last to know. So who else?"

"A psychiatrist or a psychologist," Daniels suggested.

"Or even a school counselor," Nolan said.

"Were any of the girls talking to anyone professionally about their problems?" I asked.

"Not that we've been able to determine," Alex said.

"Let's check it out."

"You really think that some shrink or school counselor preyed on these girls and killed them?" Earnshaw snorted. "That sounds like a pretty far-fetched possibility."

"Let's check it out," I said again.

I could tell Earnshaw didn't like me giving him orders like that. It wasn't really clear who was in charge of this investigation, us at the FBI or the local law enforcement operating at each crime scene. But somebody needed to run this and Blanton seemed to be okay with me running this meeting. I was happy to do that whether Earnshaw liked it or not.

Girard gave us a report from Elmsford. There was more about Jessica's troubles with her parents, school officials and the law there. And about the domestic violence inside the Staley house. But nothing new about how Jessica ran away or who she might have been with when she left Elmsford.

It was Ray Terlop, our computer tech guy, who provided the most intriguing aspect to the meeting.

"We got into the Benedict girl's computer," Terlop said. "Most of it was routine stuff. School work. Gossip about other students, especially girls on her cheerleading team. She had a big crush at some point on some kid named Donald Maris who went away somewhere for a football thing which left her pissed off at him."

I looked over at Maris. He didn't say anything. Obviously, Terlop didn't know he was right here with us. I could see a look of anguish on Maris's face. It had been a long time ago, but he probably still remembered that time when he and Becky Benedict were young and in love before it all went bad for her.

"But then, not long before she disappeared, her emails got more intense. She talked about some new guy she was interested in. She seemed quite taken with him. She said he was 'older and so much more mature' than the boys she was used to in high school. She didn't give much more of a description than that, except she did use a name for the guy. She called him 'Zachary.'"

"Zachary?" I said.

"Zachary."

"Is that a first name or a last name?"

"Not clear."

I turned to Nolan and said, "Let's go back and talk to everyone who was around when Becky disappeared. Including her mother. Find out if the name 'Zachary' means anything to any of them. Or if they ever heard Becky Benedict talking about someone with that name."

But there was something else we discussed too. Something that all of us were very aware of, but hadn't spoken out loud. I finally brought it up before the meeting ended.

"How about the elephant in the room here?" I said.

"What do you mean?" Blanton asked, even though I was pretty sure he knew exactly what I was talking about. But I guess he wanted it to come from me rather than him.

"Two girls murdered? Twenty-plus years apart? If this really was the same guy, what was he doing for those twenty years in between Becky Benedict and Jessica Staley? People don't stop killing like that, then suddenly start up again. So that means there probably—almost certainly—are more victims out there."

"We need to pinpoint who they might be," Alex agreed.

"Good luck with that," Girard grunted.

"Well, we need to try," I said. "The toll could be much higher than just Becky and Jessica. And, even more frightening, he could be targeting a new victim right now. He's pretty much come out and told us that he's not stopping killing these girls. We have to make sure we find him before that happens."

TWENTY-SIX

Nolan and Maris offered to give Alex and me a ride when the meeting was over.

"Anyone interested in a drink?" Alex asked as we pulled up to the front door of the lobby. There was a restaurant and a bar on the first floor of our hotel.

"I could sure use one," I said.

All of us agreed to stop off at the bar.

"That guy Blanton is your boss, huh?" Nolan said to Alex and me when we were all seated around a table next to the bar and ordering a round of drinks.

"Our new boss," Alex said. "We had another boss. Les Polk. He was pretty good. Better than this one. But now he's gone."

"Fired?"

"Kicked upstairs. He got promoted. So now we have Blanton leading us."

"What's the story with him?"

"He's a bit officious for my taste," I said. "He's very much a go by the book guy. He makes us call him 'Chief Blanton.' And he always refers to us as 'Agent Cassidy' and 'Agent Del Vecchio.' He never uses our first names."

"That is an officious boss."

"Yes, definitely."

"You don't seem like the type of person who would work well with someone who is 'officious.'" Nolan smiled at me.

Our drinks arrived. We all had beers. Except for Nolan. He was drinking Perrier water.

"No beer?" I asked him.

"Not tonight."

"Are you on the wagon or something?"

"I'm still on duty."

"So am I. But I'm still going to have a drink."

We talked some more about the meeting.

"What did you think of your contemporary in Huntsdale?" I asked Nolan. "Police Chief Frank Earnshaw."

"He didn't have much to say."

"That's because he has no ideas."

"You don't like him?"

"I can't stand the guy. And the feeling is mutual. I had to work with him on my last case. The murder of my sister a long time ago. It wasn't easy dealing with an asshole like that."

Nolan smiled. "Then I guess I must look pretty good to you in comparison."

I smiled at him. "You look very good to me, Chief Nolan."

Was I flirting with this guy?

Maybe I was.

But it was just a little bit of harmless flirting, right?

We all kept talking there for a while—about the case, about the meeting and sometimes about ourselves too. Finally, Alex stood up and said she was going to her room to call her son and husband. Maris left then too, saying he needed to pick up his daughter after a swimming class at the YWCA.

"That just leaves the two of us," Nolan said after they were gone. "Are you hungry? Want to grab some dinner while we're here?"

"I could eat."

"Let's check out the menu."

It wasn't the best selection of food I'd ever seen: barroom basics and comfort food like hamburgers and meat loaf and chicken dishes. I settled on a chicken pot pie, while Nolan went for a hamburger plate.

"Tell me about your father," I said. "The one on the Philadelphia police force that made you want to follow in his footsteps and go into law enforcement."

"What about him?"

"Was he a good cop?"

"I thought so. But then I loved him. You might question my judgement on the matter, I suppose. I mean, I'm not sure you even think I'm much of a good cop, based on our recent conversations."

I shook my head sadly. "I'm sorry about that. I sometimes come on a bit too strong. I didn't mean to imply you weren't doing your job well. I get very intense when I'm working on a big case like this."

"Don't worry about it."

"It's just that sometimes, well..."

"What?"

"It's hard being a woman in the FBI. Even in this day and age where things like an agent's sex is not supposed to matter. Unfortunately, it does.'

"You still get a lot of negative reaction because you're a woman?"

"Yes, and I think that's part of the problem with this guy Earnshaw. He doesn't like working with or, even worse, taking orders from a woman. He'd never admit that was the reason. But I'm pretty sure it plays a big part in his attitude. Bottom line is Frank Earnshaw's a sexist pig, along with being a lot of other not so great things."

"I understand that must be tough for you."

"What about you? Does it bother you that I'm a woman?"

"No, not at all." He laughed. "I'm very happy that you're a woman, Nikki."

There it was: a moment of flirting again between us. Innocent flirting. But still flirting, all right.

"Tell me about your father," he said now.

I gave him the whole story about him being forced to investigate his daughter's death when Caitlin was murdered; about how he had died afterward; and how I'd found out he'd also been murdered by my sister's killer. I also talked about how close we'd been. And how I still had a lot of questions I wished I could have asked him before he died.

"What kind of questions?"

"What he knew about my sister's death."

"But you solved that case."

"But why did the killer bring it up in his note? Why talk about my sister? Okay, maybe he was only doing it to get my attention because of all the publicity. But there's still some things about what happened to Caitlin that I don't understand. Some missing pieces to the puzzle. I think my father was hiding something he found out about Caitlin at the end, but I have no idea what that was. And I'll probably never be able to find out the answer."

The chicken pot pie wasn't great, but it was good enough. I've found in my experience that it's almost impossible to find a chicken pot pie that isn't good to eat. Nolan finished off his entire hamburger and a side order of French fries, so I guess his dinner was a success too. I didn't want the meal to end yet, so I suggested coffee and dessert. We lingered over that for a while.

"One of the things I left out in my apology before was asking you those questions about you and your wife," I said as we finished up. "You're right. That's private. None of my business."

"It's still very painful to me," he said.

"You still loved her?"

"Yes and no."

I gave him a questioning look.

"It was a complicated relationship," he said.

I nodded. I understood that. I'd been in a few of those kinds of relationships myself.

"Are you seeing anyone now?" I blurted out before I could stop myself from saying it.

"I am."

Damn.

"But nothing serious. Just casual dating. I'm still looking for the right woman after my wife, I guess."

Be still my heart!

Eventually someone brought us a check. Nolan started to grab for it, but I said I'd put it on my room bill for the FBI expense account. I mean we had discussed a lot of business, hadn't we?

I wondered if something might happen between us afterward. Would he walk me to the door of my hotel room? Maybe try to kiss me goodnight? Or say something to indicate this was more than simply a business dinner between us?

But there was nothing like that.

"Well, good night," he said after I'd paid the bill. "See you in the morning."

"In the morning," I said. Then I headed for the elevator and took it upstairs to my hotel room.

Alone.

TWENTY-SEVEN

"So what happened last night with you and the police chief after I left?" Alex asked me.

"Nothing."

"You didn't get it on with him?"

"Nothing at all happened, Alex."

"Your decision or his?"

"It was mutual."

"I'm surprised. I was pretty convinced something might be going on between you two."

"It was all very professional."

We were on our way to Dorchester High School where Becky Benedict had once been a student. I wanted to check out the lead we'd gotten about someone named Zachary being mentioned in Becky's last emails. Were there any students named Zachary back then? Or even teachers? It didn't seem likely the Zachary person would still be around anywhere in Dorchester, but we'd find out soon enough.

Alex was driving, and I was in the passenger seat of our rental car. I wanted to talk about the case, but Alex kept asking me about my love life. She might be happily married, but she still seemed to have an almost obsessive interest in my romantic ups and downs.

"I still don't understand why you walked away from that last guy you were set to marry," she said to me.

"Greg Ellroy."

"Right. He had a lot going for him. Big job as a lawyer. Politically connected. Good-looking. And he was crazy about you."

"I decided I didn't want to spend the rest of my life with Greg Ellroy."

"How about Connor Nolan?"

"Alex..."

"Could you see yourself spending the rest of your life with a guy like Nolan?"

I shook my head. "That's not going to happen."

"Why not?"

"Nolan's got a lot of baggage. Emotional baggage."

"Oh, you mean the business about his dead wife. Did you find out any more about that?"

Dorchester High School was in front of us now. Alex had pulled into the parking lot at a space near the front door of the building.

"We're here," I said to her.

The principal of Dorchester High School was a man named Bruce Sniderman. Sniderman was in his fifties and he said he'd been at the school a number of years. Not long enough to remember Becky Benedict though. That had been before his time.

He did show me a picture of Becky he said he'd found on one of the walls of the school. It was another shot of her from the cheerleader team. Becky belonged to the Junior Varsity squad because she had only been a freshman. She had a big smile—almost like she was laughing—in the picture. She looked really happy. There were four other girls in the picture with her. All of them were attractive, but Becky was the most attractive of all. And she looked the happiest. I wondered how long before her death this picture had been taken.

Looking at it again, I was struck again by how Becky Benedict was frozen in time now—eternally a teenage girl with youth and beauty and innocence about her. If she'd lived, she would be in her thirties by now. A grown woman. Probably married. Maybe a mother of her own teenage daughter. But instead it ended for her not long after this picture was taken.

"I don't think there's anyone still here who would have known the Benedict girl when she was a student," Sniderman said. "We have quite a bit of turnover. And twenty years is a long time."

"I understand that," I said. "But I was hoping you could check the school records for us. Maybe find the names of some of the teachers she had that year when she was a Dorchester freshman."

"If any of them are still around—and hopefully alive—we can track them down for interviews," Alex explained to Sniderman.

"We're especially interested to see if any of her teachers or anyone else here at the school back then was called Zachary," I said.

"Zachary?"

"Yes."

"Last name?"

"Probably."

"But could be a first name too, I guess," Alex said.

A bit later, we were going over a list of teachers from that time at the school. Specifically, teachers that had Becky Benedict in their classes. There was no one named Zachary on the list. But we made copies of all the names and contact information to try to interview them later.

"What about the school administrators?" I asked. "The principal at the time. Any assistant principals, deans or counselors or anything like that who would have been here?"

That list turned out to be a lot shorter. Only a handful of names. None of them was Zachary either.

I was disappointed, but not surprised. It had seemed like a long shot that someone named Zachary would simply turn up here.

So who in the hell was this Zachary she had seemed so interested in?

I went back over the list of teachers and went through all the names one more time; looking for a clue, any kind of clue. And that's when I saw it. Not Zachary as a last name. Or as a first name either. But some of the names had middle initials in them. And one of them was John Z. Crudele.

"Do you know what the Z stands for with this one?" I asked Sniderman.

"No idea. It might be in some personnel records from our old files."

"Please try to find them for us."

It took a while, but he eventually came back with the information.

"His full name was John Zachary Crudele," Sniderman said. "He was only a teacher here briefly. The year Becky Benedict was here. He resigned at the end of the school year. That's all I know."

It was enough.

A man named Zachary.

One of Becky's teachers and someone she might well have trusted.

Trusted enough to get into a green Ford with him.

TWENTY-EIGHT

It turned out there was another man named Zachary in Dorchester twenty years ago. His name was William Zachary and he'd lived in the town while Becky Benedict was still alive —according to the information Ray Terlop and our FBI people in Washington had turned up in their computer searches.

But he didn't go to high school with her. He was in college by the time she became a freshman, attending the Wharton Business School outside Philadelphia where he later got an MBA for a career in finance. He didn't go to Dorchester High School either, he went to a private military academy in central Pennsylvania before his college years.

Still, his name was Zachary.

He was older than Becky.

And, best of all, we knew where he was.

The computer people had tracked him to an address in Bucks County, Pennsylvania. He lived there and commuted into Philadelphia for a job with a big financial consulting firm. He was married and had a daughter.

Alex and I drove out to Yardley, the town where he lived, to knock on his door. We didn't call ahead first. It was a weekend—

a Saturday morning—and I figured he might be home. I wanted to catch him off guard, see what his reaction was when we showed up at his door with questions about Becky Benedict. That might indicate to us whether he might be a killer or if this was just a wild goose chase.

William Zachary's house was a big one. On River Road in Yardley, which means it was overlooking the Delaware River—and that was a pretty impressive sight. There was a Mercedes and an Audi parked in the driveway. It was two stories, with a three-car garage and a huge yard area filled with trees, plants and flowers. Somebody spent a lot of time making this place beautiful.

We walked up the driveway, onto the front porch and rang the doorbell.

A young girl answered the door. A teenager. She was dressed in cargo pants, sandals and a T-shirt which said "Save the Rain Forests." She was pretty with short blonde hair, but had a ring through her nose. That kind of ruined the whole look for me. I guess a ring through the nose must be trendy now. Me, I still like to wear my rings on my fingers.

"We'd like to talk to William Zachary," I said to her.

"Mom!" she yelled. "Someone here to see Dad."

"Who is it?" a woman's voice called out from inside the house.

"Who are you?" the girl asked us.

"We're with the FBI," we said, showing her our badges.

"Cops, Mom!"

A woman came to the door. She had short blonde hair and was pretty too. She almost looked like an older version of her daughter. No nose ring though, which was a good thing.

We introduced ourselves and said we were looking for information regarding a murder that took place in Dorchester years ago when her husband was growing up there. We said we hoped he might be able to help us track some things down. I tried to make it all seem as innocent and routine as possible, at least until I met her husband.

She seemed to accept this. She said her husband was out but would be home soon, and she invited us to come in and wait for him. We sat down in the living room with her, and the daughter disappeared after that. I thought about how she looked to be about the same age Becky Benedict had been when her father was in Dorchester. I had no idea what that meant, but the thought kept running through my mind.

Mrs. Zachary served us coffee and we talked for a while. She said her name was Laura and her daughter's name was Sandi. They'd lived in this house for the past eight years, and she and her husband loved the location very much. She said her husband was a senior vice president at a firm called Fields and Wiley that was located near Center City in Philadelphia.

She seemed fascinated that a couple of women like us were FBI agents, and asked us a lot of questions about the job, the case we were investigating, and even stuff like what kind of guns we carried. It was all very friendly, but I didn't like the fact we were wasting time here. I hoped her husband would come back soon.

"I'm sure Bill will be happy to tell you anything he remembers," she said to us when we asked her again how long the wait might be. "Although I can't imagine he'll know very much that could help. That was so long ago."

Finally, the door opened and William Zachary walked in. He was a good-looking guy with slicked down dark hair, wearing a suit and tie even though it was Saturday, and with a trim body that looked like he spent plenty of time working out at the gym. The kind of guy that might be appealing to a teenage girl if he focused his attention on her. Someone like Jessica Staley now. Or Becky Benedict when he was younger. But I was getting ahead of myself.

"Who are these lovely ladies?" he said with a charming smile when he saw us with his wife.

"Nikki Cassidy and Alex Del Vecchio," Mrs. Zachary said.

"A pleasure to meet you."

"They want to talk to you, Bill."

"Happy to talk with them." He smiled again. "About what?"

"We're with the FBI," I said, taking out my shield to show him.

That's when it all went bad. His smile disappeared and was replaced by an angry look. His face turned red with anger, and he clenched his fists, almost as if he was going to reach out and punch us.

"Get out of my house," he said.

"All we want to do is ask you some questions about a girl named Becky Benedict who you might have known a long time ago in Dorchester and—"

"I said get out! Now!"

"I don't understand," Alex said. "You see, we're investigating Becky Benedict's murder and we thought maybe—"

"You want to talk to me get a warrant. You want to search this house, get a search warrant. You want anything to do with me, talk to my lawyer. In the meantime, get out of my house."

I looked over at Mrs. Zachary. She seemed as confused as we were as we got up and left.

"That was interesting," I said to Alex once we were out of the house.

"Not sure what it means."

"But interesting."

So now we had one Zachary we couldn't find. And another Zachary we had found but didn't know what to make of.

What next?

TWENTY-NINE

"Do you ever think about wanting to be more than the police chief in a small town like Dorchester?" I asked Connor Nolan.

"Huh?"

We were in his car riding back to the station after an interview with someone who had known Becky Benedict as a teenage girl. We didn't find out much from the interview, but it gave me a chance to spend time with Nolan. And find out more about him. I still had a lot of questions.

"I mean, you're a big fish in a little pond here, as the saying goes. You could be a smaller fish but in a bigger—and a lot more interesting—pond somewhere else."

"Where else could I go?"

"Big city force, like Philadelphia, maybe. Your father made a career there, right? You might too. Or else go to some kind of top-level private security firm, they're always looking for people from law enforcement backgrounds. Or the state police. Maybe even look into federal job openings."

"Like the FBI?"

"Why not?"

"Then I could be a big-time crime fighter like you, I guess."

"I'm only saying...'

"I know what you're saying. That this is a crappy little job, compared to yours."

This conversation was not exactly turning out the way that I had hoped.

"Well, maybe I don't feel that way, I like my job," Nolan said. "I'm proud of my job and what I do here. There's nothing wrong with being a small-town police chief. Hell, your father was one, wasn't he? Did you tell him to get a better job? Did you ever ask him why he stayed on doing his job in Huntsdale?"

"Once I did."

"What happened?"

"He said pretty much the same thing you did to me now."

"But you, you're different, Cassidy." I noticed he was back to calling me Cassidy again. I realized he did that whenever he got upset or mad at me. "You went for the big time. The FBI. No messing around, top of the line for you right from the start."

"All I'm suggesting is maybe you think about your options. You're still a young guy, you could have a big future ahead of you. You might be happier in a job with the bureau or somewhere bigger than Dorchester."

"Except you don't even think I'm that good of a cop. You told me so the other day."

"I said I was sorry for that."

"I'm still not convinced that you don't think you're better at your job than I am. Maybe you are. But don't tell me how to do my job, okay?"

"Okay," I said.

We drove in silence for a while.

"So how do you feel the case is going?" Nolan finally asked.

I knew I should keep my mouth shut, but I said there were still some things bothering me about what the Dorchester Police Department had done. Or, more specifically, what they had not done.

"You're back to criticizing my job performance again."

"I'm not trying to be critical of you or the department. I'm simply trying to understand things better."

"Hey, we're just small-town cops. We simply muddle along on a case as best we can. It takes a real crime fighter like you to help us solve a big murder case."

I ignored the sarcasm as best I could.

"So what else don't you understand, Cassidy?"

"Well, I still don't know why you didn't tell me earlier about Maris. He dated Becky Benedict, she broke it off with him, she started seeing—and presumably sleeping with—another man. Even if Donald Maris does have an alibi for the actual murder, that gives him motive for wanting her dead."

"Like I told you before, Don's a good man. I know him, you don't. It wasn't relevant for you to know about his background with the Benedict girl. I'm sorry if that still bothers you. But you're wasting time thinking about Donald Maris as being some kind of a player in all this."

"What about Eleanor Benedict? She told me she tried repeatedly to get you to re-investigate her daughter's murder after the Leighton confession turned out to be false. But she said she never got any real results from the Dorchester police. That's why she finally came to me. She couldn't get the answers she wanted from you."

"We were working on the case. We just couldn't tell her anything substantial she wanted to hear. So she got frustrated and went to you."

"Then there's that building near the trash bin where her body was found. Once Leighton's confession turned out to be bogus, you should have been back immediately interviewing everyone—even though it was twenty years later—to see if anyone was still there who might have known something about what happened that day."

"We did wind up going back to do that—and found out nothing."

"But you only did it after I said you should."

"It turned out to be a waste of time."

"Still needed to be done."

"Why?"

"It's called proper police investigation."

Nolan looked over at me with an expression on his face that seemed to be a combination of anger and bemusement. "Did anyone ever tell you that you're overly critical and sometimes just need to keep your mouth shut?"

"A few people."

"You should listen to them." He smiled.

He was probably right about that. I'd blown up my engagement with Greg not long ago after I began looking for things wrong with him and—soon enough—I found some. Enough for me to decide not to marry him. I'd done the same with Billy Weller, even though our relationship had never gotten beyond the flirtatious stage. And now I was doing it with Connor Nolan. I had no personal relationship of any kind with him, of course. But, if I ever had any hopes of having a relationship with him, I needed to learn from the past and stop tearing apart every guy in my life looking for faults.

"I'm sorry," I said.

"Again?"

"This time I mean it."

"Good to hear."

"I get really intense when I'm on a case like this. I want to make sure we don't miss any possible clues or leads."

"I suppose there were things we could have done better."

"We all have things we could have done better," I said.

THIRTY

"What about DNA from Becky Benedict's killer?" I asked Nolan and Alex. We were back at the Dorchester police station, still looking for some kind of break in the case.

"There is no DNA evidence," Nolan said.

"Nothing at all turned up from the body or the trash bin area where she was found dead?"

"Nope."

"Are we sure about that?"

"What do you mean?"

"Maybe there is a DNA trail there, and we simply haven't found it yet."

"I went through the police reports from back then and all the old documents on the case we have. I asked Upshaw, the old police chief, about possible DNA evidence too. But there was nothing found. Absolutely nothing. C'mon, I know you don't always have a high opinion of the Dorchester police force, but don't you think we would have checked out something like that back at the time of the murder? I mean there was DNA evidence back in 2003 too."

"Yes, but the technology to find it—and for tracking DNA—wasn't nearly as sophisticated as it is now."

He stared at me in surprise. Alex seemed surprised too.

"You think we might be able to find some DNA now from this old case?" Nolan asked me.

"Maybe. Do you still have the evidence from the case? Clothes Becky was wearing, blood samples from the body, anything else tangible we could actually examine?"

"I guess. I mean that's evidence from a murder investigation. We'd still have it all on file... somewhere in our system."

"Let's find it and take a new look."

I knew Alex had figured out where I was going with this by now, but I explained it to Connor Nolan. I'd taken some extra courses on crime detection in Washington, and one of them was on the history and progression of DNA testing.

DNA was unheard of for many years in crime fighting. Fingerprints were the way law enforcement tracked criminals, not DNA. But that all began to change in the 1980s when it was discovered that every person had a unique DNA identity. Within a few years, DNA began to be used—at least in a rudimentary way—to track killers and other criminals.

Today, of course, anyone can send away for a DNA kit for a small amount of money on Ancestry or some other genealogy website. But back in 2003 when Becky Benedict was murdered, the usage of DNA was not so easy or common. For one thing, many criminals' DNA had not yet been collected in any federal data bank, so it was much more difficult to match with an unidentified suspect. Also, the process to compare DNA samples took much longer than it does now. And the biggest problem was being able to detect DNA at a crime scene, which was much more difficult to pinpoint and accomplish than it is today.

But in recent years great strides had been made in technology for detecting DNA in even a small amount of blood or semen or other evidence from a crime scene. A bloodstain, for example, used to have to be a least the size of a quarter in 2003 to recognize a DNA sample in it, but today, investigators can detect DNA in a much smaller amount of blood or even from tiny skin cells left behind by the criminal.

"What do you think?" I asked.

Nolan jumped at the idea, and soon reached out for blood samples and other evidence in the case to send to our laboratory in Washington for more analysis.

Later, we got our answer from Washington.

My idea had worked.

Well, sort of...

"We've been able to extract a DNA sample—a DNA signature—from a tiny amount of blood that was found on the girl's body," said Chief Blanton over a Zoom call.

"That's great news!" I said.

"There's also some not so great news."

"We don't know who it belongs to?"

"Right."

"No match for the DNA from anyone in our files?"

"We came up empty on that."

"So we have the DNA of the killer, but we don't know who that DNA belongs to."

"It's definitely not Daniel Gary Leighton's DNA, if that matters at this point."

"Not really. We already know Leighton didn't kill Benedict."

"I guess all it proves is that Leighton was telling the truth when he said his confession was a lie."

"But at least we do have the real killer's DNA, Chief. We've identified that."

"Yes. If we catch someone, we can match the DNA we have

to the suspect's. That way we can prove we have the right person."

"Well, that's something. That's progress."

"Now all you have to do is catch that killer, Agent Cassidy."

THIRTY-ONE

There were four cheerleaders who had been with Becky Benedict at that last practice she attended at Dorchester High before her disappearance. Their names were: Carole Kaiser, Susan Young, Kasey Podesta and Linda Sanderson. I figured I had the best chance of finding out about Becky's last hours from one of them. I also knew it was likely going to be hard tracking them down after twenty years.

The first name turned out to be the easiest to get answers on. Carole Kaiser was dead. Killed in a car crash a few years after Becky's murder when she was a senior in high school. She and some friends were joyriding and drag racing after a night of heavy drinking. The car went out of control and into a tree. The other kids survived, but Carole Kaiser died instantly from the impact.

At first, I wondered if there was any significance in the fact that two members of the junior varsity cheerleading team had died before they got out of high school. But it really didn't seem like one had anything to do with the other. Tragic events like that happen for no reason most of the time.

Susan Young had moved away from Dorchester. Far, far

away. She lived in Japan with her husband—who was a corporate executive with a company there—and her family. I probably could track her in Japan if I really wanted. But it would take a lot of effort, probably for little to no reward. So that left Kasey Podesta and Linda Sanderson.

Kasey Podesta lived outside of San Francisco. I was able to get her on the phone and she was happy to talk to me about Becky Benedict, and what she remembered. But she didn't remember very much.

"I was never really into the cheerleader thing," she said to me on the phone. "I really only did it because I thought it would help me meet boys. It did, but I never took the cheerleader stuff too seriously. Never was that friendly with the other girls on the squad. I had my own friends back then."

I brought up the death of Carole Kaiser in the joy-riding accident.

"Carole was pretty wild, as I recall." She sighed. "She was getting into trouble back then even when we were just freshmen. Hey, we were all wild in our way, I suppose. But Carole always seemed headed for some kind of a tragic end like that. But I'm sorry how things turned out. Not much else to say after twenty years, is there?"

"What about Becky Benedict? Was she wild?"

"Nah, not really. More messed up than anything."

"Messed up how?'

"Becky wasn't what she seemed. She was supposed to be this A-student, perky happy cheerleader, the ultimate Ms. Perfect who had it all. But she didn't act like she had it all. She seemed troubled, unhappy... you know what I mean?"

"Do you think that could have had anything to do with her being murdered?"

"Hey, I never saw that coming."

"Do you remember what happened at her last cheerleader practice? Did she say anything at all that you can remember?"

"I told all this to the police twenty years ago."

"What did you tell them?"

"I told them that I didn't remember anything unusual at all. It was just a routine cheerleader practice. And then we found out Becky had been murdered. I don't know anything more about it. I didn't understand how it could have happened back then twenty years ago, and I still don't understand."

Linda Sanderson was different. She was living in Florida, and I got her on the phone at her home in Boca Raton—outside Miami. She said she had only gone to Dorchester High for that one year. Her father had gotten a job in Florida and she transferred to a high school there not long after Becky's murder.

"To be honest, I was glad to get out of Dorchester. My parents were glad to get me out too. It was such a mess there after Becky died. Everyone was worried that other girls might be killed too. Girls were afraid to go to school, to walk down the street or even to leave the house, even after they said they caught the guy who did it. It was a crazy scary time."

But—even though she had left Dorchester soon after Becky's abduction and murder—she had some interesting things to tell me once we started talking.

"I knew Becky better than any of the other girls on the squad. We hung out together sometimes, even double dated once or twice."

"With a guy named Donald Maris?"

"Yeah, that sounds familiar. We were really young though, of course. Becky had to sneak around a lot when it came to boys, I remember that. Her parents thought she was this innocent, naïve teenager. Well, Becky was no innocent, naïve teenager. Take my word for it."

"Do you remember her being with anyone named Zachary?"

"Zachary who?"

"I'm not sure."

"It doesn't sound familiar."

"But you did remember Donald Maris."

"Only because you mentioned his name."

"Did she talk about the boys in her life—the romances in it —during that last day at cheerleader practice with you at all?"

"God, yes. I mean she was always talking about boys back then. I guess we all were. Anyway, back then, at that last practice, she kept talking about a guy she was really smitten with."

"Any idea who he was?"

"No. She wouldn't tell me his name."

"Do you think he was another boy in your class?"

"I'm pretty sure he wasn't a student there."

"Why not?"

"The way she talked about him made him sound older than we were."

"A lot older?"

"Maybe. Could have been."

"Did you get the impression that she was in a sexual relationship with him?"

"Well, I knew she was having sex with someone."

I told her about the birth control pills I'd found hidden in her bedroom.

"I guess they didn't work," Linda Sanderson said.

"What do you mean?"

"Because Becky told me she'd gotten pregnant."

THIRTY-TWO

"Is there any possibility Becky Benedict was pregnant when she was murdered?" I asked Connor Nolan.

"I never heard anything like that."

"Did Upshaw?"

"No, not that I'm aware of."

I told him about my phone conversation with Linda Sanderson, the girl on the cheerleading squad with Becky.

"Did Sanderson tell anyone this at the time?"

"She doesn't remember."

"How can she not remember something like that?"

I'd asked Linda Sanderson the same question. Her only answer was that she'd been in a state of shock at the time. A girl at the school she knew—a girl she'd just spent time with at cheerleader practice—had disappeared, then been found brutally murdered. She couldn't remember who she'd told what to or if she'd even told them anything.

Also, she said her parents had whisked her away to Florida as soon as the horrible news about Becky Benedict's murder broke, fearing for their daughter's safety. She was receiving grief counseling too, which encouraged her to try and not think about what had happened to the member of her cheerleading squad.

As a result of this, she didn't dwell a lot on any of her final conversations with Becky. And, because she was in Florida, the police in Dorchester never specifically questioned her about anything she might have discussed with the victim. She had put all that behind her when she and her family moved. It wasn't until now, twenty years later, that someone like me had started asking her questions about Becky Benedict.

"The autopsy report never said anything about Becky Benedict being pregnant, did it?" I asked Nolan.

"Of course not."

I thought about it for a minute.

There was another possibility. "What if she had an abortion?" I asked Nolan.

"An abortion," he repeated.

"Would that show up in an autopsy?"

"I don't know... I'm not sure.'

"Can I see the autopsy report?"

The autopsy report turned out to be a surprisingly detailed one. Much more detailed than I would have expected from a small-town medical examiner. But this was a rare murder case for Dorchester—and the murder of a popular young cheerleader—so I guess the authorities back then, led by Chief Upshaw, wanted to make sure they did everything by the book and covered every base of the investigation.

I read through a lot of it, even what I knew were parts of the generic autopsy report procedure and pretty meaningless to this specific case. But I wanted to make sure I didn't miss anything. Finally, I got to the summary of the cause of death of Becky Benedict and a description of what was discovered about the victim.

No surprises there either. It said she was fifteen years old, five feet six inches tall and weighed one hundred and eighteen pounds at the time of her death. She had no obvious health issues. Heart, lungs, and other organs seemed normal prior to her death.

The estimated time of death was between midnight and 6 a.m. on May 12, 2003. That was four days after she disappeared, and several hours before her body was discovered inside the trash dumpster.

The cause of death was a stab wound to the heart that punctured the girl's aorta and, according to the report, would have caused her to lose enough blood to die within a matter of minutes, or even seconds. However, there were also more stab wounds on the body. Some of them were believed to have occurred before death, others apparently happened postmortem, as if the killer was in such a rage that he kept slashing her even after he must have known she was dead.

There were also numerous bruises and lacerations where she had been struck repeatedly by some kind of a blunt object, like a hammer or a piece of metal or wood. But no such object was ever found during a search of the area. And the knife or whatever object had been used to stab her to death was never recovered either.

There was nothing about a baby or a pregnancy. I didn't think there would be. Otherwise someone would have known about it back then, which no one seemed to. So what was the real story? Was Becky Benedict pregnant? There was no indication of that in the autopsy report or from anything else I'd read or heard. Until Linda Sanderson said Becky had told her about getting pregnant.

I checked and found out that a medical examiner could detect if there was evidence of any recent surgical—especially gynecological—procedure performed on the victim prior to death. In other words, an abortion. Did Becky Benedict get pregnant at some point, then have an abortion to get rid of the baby? If she did, there was no evidence of this in the autopsy report.

"So she wasn't pregnant," Alex said when I told her what I'd been doing. "And, as far as we know, she hadn't been pregnant in the past."

"As far as we know."

"So why did she tell Linda Sanderson she was?"

"Maybe she thought it was true."

"Or fantasized it."

"Yeah, I thought of that possibility too," I said. "Okay, Becky Benedict was not pregnant. But she told her friend Linda Sanderson that she was. So maybe Becky told some other people the same thing."

"Someone like this Zachary guy who was one of her teachers."

"Or the Zachary who supposedly was away at military school back then who threw us out of his house when we started asking him questions about Becky Benedict in front of his wife and family."

"Or maybe she told someone else she was having sex with back then—when she was supposed to be the perfect teenage girl at Dorchester High—that she was pregnant with their baby."

I nodded. "And maybe that person—whoever he is—decided he couldn't let her tell anyone else about having a baby."

THIRTY-THREE

Alex left the Dorchester station house before me that night and took the rental car we were using. So I started to call an Uber from outside the station. Connor came out while I was doing it and asked me if I needed a ride. I said sure.

He drove me back to my hotel. He asked me if I wanted to have a drink at the bar. Just one, I said, it was pretty late. I ordered a vodka tonic, but all he asked for was a glass of Perrier like the last time we were there. I was curious, so I asked him about it.

"You don't drink?"

"I drink."

"Okay."

"I'm just not drinking now."

"How long has 'now' been?"

"Six months, two weeks and four days."

I got the message.

Or at least what I figured was the message.

"You're an alcoholic?"

"No, I am not an alcoholic."

"But you said…"

"Not drinking does not mean someone is an alcoholic. In fact, not drinking can be the exact opposite of being an alcoholic. Me, I choose not to drink. Right now. That doesn't make me an alcoholic."

I nodded. "Do you mind if I drink?"

"Not at all."

I took a sip of the vodka. "You're an unusual man, Connor Nolan."

"Unusual how?"

"Unusual in that you are different from pretty much every other law enforcement official I have ever met."

"Is that good or bad for me?"

"I'll let you know when I figure it out," I said, flashing him a big smile.

Afterward, he walked me to the elevator that would take me up to my room. We stood there, waiting. It seemed to take an eternity coming down to the hotel lobby for us.

I was aware of the awkwardness of the moment. At least it felt awkward to me. Should I ask him to take the elevator with me and accompany me all the way to my door? Should I invite him into the room when we got there? Should I rip the clothes off him, throw him down on my bed and let him have his way with me?

I got the feeling he was as uncomfortable as me in this situation, but maybe that was only me overreacting on my part.

"Well, see you in the morning," he said when the elevator finally arrived.

"In the morning."

"Bright and early in the morning. We've got a lot of work to do."

"Big day," I agreed, then got into the elevator.

Alone.

Up in my room, I didn't go to sleep right away. I suppose I had too much on my mind. I turned on one of the cable news channels on TV for a while, but its commentator was just spewing out stuff about politics instead of talking about news. I switched to a rerun of *Friends*. Joey and Chandler were having some kind of argument about being roommates, and somehow Rachel was involved. But I was having trouble keeping my mind on that too, so I finally turned down the sound. My mind was still on Connor Nolan.

I knew there were a lot of very good reasons I should not get involved in a personal relationship with this guy. For one thing, it was inappropriate. He was the lead police officer investigating a murder, and I was the FBI agent on the case. I wasn't exactly sure what the police or FBI manuals said about this kind of thing, but I was pretty sure that sleeping with each other would be frowned on, professionally speaking.

Then there was the other problem of his ex-wife dying and him being suspended during that investigation. I still wasn't sure what happened there or what he did or didn't do. Nope, I did not need to open myself up to that kind of a messy personal relationship. I was better off doing what I had done downstairs —just walk away from Connor Nolan and don't look back. That was the smart thing to do, the right thing.

So why didn't I feel right about it?

I was still too wound up to go to sleep, so I ordered an apple pie à la mode from room service—that ought to cheer me up— and something to drink with it.

I turned the sound back up on the TV while I was waiting for it to be delivered. There was an episode of *Criminal Minds* on now. I liked watching shows like that because they made solving crimes look so easy. In every episode, they caught the bad guy within an hour. I wished crimefighting was that easy in real life.

There was a knock on the door.

Must be my room service order.

I got up off my bed and went to answer it.

"Wow, that was quick!" I said as I opened the door.

But it wasn't room service at all.

Connor Nolan was standing there.

"What's going on?" I asked him. Damn, that sounded stupid.

"I think we have some unfinished business," he said.

"What kind of unfinished business?" That sounded even stupider, but I couldn't think of anything else to say.

It didn't really matter though.

He moved closer to me, put his arms around me and kissed me.

We kissed each other for a long time, almost as if we wanted to make up for all the time we'd wasted getting to this point. Until we were interrupted by room service, but I sent them away with a wave of my hand. I think they could see I was busy.

Then I pulled him into the room and eventually over to the bed.

He took off my clothes slowly—deliciously slowly—while I did the same thing to him.

And then we made love.

I hadn't had sex with a man since I broke off my engagement to Greg Ellroy. I'd wanted to have sex with Billy Weller, the cop I'd worked with in Huntsdale, but he died before that could happen. So I was ready for this. I was more than ready to make love with Connor Nolan.

There was no awkwardness now, just two people who were where they wanted to be. We did it slowly, passionately and intensely, all at the same time if that makes any sense.

We made love like that for a long time.

And then, when it was over, I held onto him tightly, desperately wanting to cling to every moment of being together with him after all my waiting and expectations and fantasies.

Yes, I knew there were still a lot of reasons for me not to have a sexual relationship with Connor Nolan.

Reasons to keep it professional between us.

But I sure couldn't think of any of them at the moment.

THIRTY-FOUR

In the morning, Alex showed up before I was ready for her. I was awake, but barely. I'd just come out of the shower and put on a robe to answer the door and let her in. My clothes were still strewn on the floor from the night before.

"Running late, huh?" Alex said, looking at me and around the room.

"A little."

"Everything okay with you?"

"I'm terrific." I picked up the skirt I'd been wearing the night before from the floor and then a few other articles of clothing.

"What happened here?"

"Great night."

"Great how?"

"I slept with Connor Nolan."

"Wow!"

"Yes, wow indeed!"

I hadn't been sure if I should tell Alex about it. Or at least when was the best time to do it. But now I'd simply blurted it out to her, so the deed was done. It was probably the right thing to do. I mean Alex is my friend. More importantly, she's my partner. We don't keep secrets from each other. Especially a secret as juicy as this one.

I gave her all the details about Connor Nolan's late-night visit to my room and a play by play—well, a sanitized play by play—of what happened.

"Does anyone know?"

"You know."

"Besides me."

"You think I should alert TMZ to get the news out there to everyone?"

She made a face. "I'm talking about Blanton."

"I'm not in the habit of sharing my sexual escapades with my boss."

"Even if the guy you're sleeping with is the lead local investigator of our case here?"

"That does make it a bit tricky."

"Blanton's not going to be happy if he finds this out."

"It does kind of violate the official FBI rules and guidelines for personal behavior on the job. So I think I'll keep it to myself —and to you—for now."

I started getting dressed while Alex peppered me with more questions about me and Connor.

"What happened next?" she wanted to know.

"What do you think happened?"

"You know what I mean."

"Was this a one-night stand or something more?" I said.

"Yes, is this the beginning of a serious relationship between the two of you?"

"I don't know."

Connor and I hadn't talked about that much last night. We just kind of enjoyed being in the moment as we made love. A while later, he'd gotten dressed and left. I thought about asking him to stay the night, but realized at the same time that was probably not a good idea. Imagine the look on Alex's face if she'd walked in and seen him in my bed. So we said our good-byes and went to bed separately. Me here, and him at home. I explained all that to Alex.

"Should be an interesting morning," she said when I was done.

"You think anyone at the station will figure out I had sex with him?"

"It could be very obvious, depending on how you two handle it."

"I'm not going to make a public announcement or anything."

"People still can pick up on sexual vibes in a situation like this."

"I'll do my best to control my sexual vibes."

"Hopefully, he will too."

As it turned out, Connor acted totally professionally once we got to the police station. All business, no lustful glances at me, no words of love or affectionate whispers in my ear. The truth is I was a bit disappointed by this. But, like Alex said, I knew it was better if we kept professional in front of everyone else.

We all met in his office where he brought us up to date on everything he and his people had found out. Connor, me, Alex, Donald Maris and a few other people from the Dorchester police force were there.

"The substitute teacher whose middle name was Zachary only worked here for six months. It was at the time of the Becky Benedict murder. But he moved on after that, and no one ever really gave him a second look. No reason to at the time. He'd worked at a bunch of other substitute teaching jobs at places around the country before that. Until he stopped here for those six months at Dorchester High."

"Is it even possible to get a substitute teacher job that easily?" I asked.

"He had a teaching certificate. From some small school in the south, but it was valid. Schools are pretty desperate for teachers sometimes, especially substitute teachers. It didn't take much to get into the classroom on a temporary basis."

"Any criminal record?"

"Nothing showed up."

"Okay then, the big question: where is he now?"

"No one has any idea. He disappeared after leaving Dorchester that year when Becky Benedict was murdered. Like I said, no one thought much about it at the time. We can't even be sure if she had any classes with him since he was a substitute, not a regularly assigned teacher. John Z.— for Zachary— Crudele was just gone. We don't know where he went or what he did after that."

"Maybe he committed more murders," Alex said with a sigh.

"Or he's dead now," someone else said.

"We'll keep looking," Nolan said.

"And I'll alert the FBI to initiate a national search for any record of this guy in recent years," I said.

There was also more information about William Zachary, the financier who'd thrown Alex and me out of his house when we went to see him. It turned out that Zachary was the target of a federal probe into fraudulent money moves by the company where he was a senior vice president. He'd refused to talk to investigators or show his books or cooperate in any way.

"It's possible he thought that was what we were there for when we introduced ourselves as FBI agents," Alex said. "That might have been why he got so upset. Thinking we were there to question him about his financial dealings."

"Except we did mention Becky Benedict's name to him."

"That's right. But he seemed to explode before that, as soon as he found out we were from the FBI. We can't be sure he even heard us mention the Benedict murder. His reaction could have been all about the financial scandal he was involved in, not murder."

"Or he could have committed financial fraud AND murdered Becky Benedict twenty years ago."

We made plans to continue pursuing information about both Zacharys until we could either confirm or eliminate them as potential suspects in Becky Benedict's murder.

And then suddenly everything changed.

My phone buzzed. I planned to ignore it until the meeting was over, but I looked down at the screen and saw who the call was from.

Dave Blanton in Washington.

"I'm in a meeting right now, Chief," I said. "With the Dorchester police. Can we talk afterward?"

"Forget the meeting. Forget Dorchester for now. We're pulling you out of there."

"But the police here have some leads we want to pursue."

"You've got to get back to Huntsdale right away."

"Why? What's in Huntsdale?"

"There's been another murder."

"Another teenage girl?"

"Yes. And a note. A note to you. A note that says you're going to be the killer's next victim."

THIRTY-FIVE

The victim's name was Carolyn Garms. She was sixteen years old and a sophomore at Huntsdale High School.

The day before, her class—an American history class—had gone on a field trip to a museum in the area that featured artifacts of Native American tribes who had lived here during the nineteenth century before many of the towns in Ohio were built and populated. The group of about thirty students and their teacher was transported by school bus to the museum that morning and then returned to the school in the early afternoon.

Carolyn Garms was on the school bus when it arrived at the museum. She was there when the class toured the museum. And she was seen on the bus that took the students back to the school. Except, when everyone returned to their classroom afterward, Garms was missing.

A few hours later, her body was found in a parking lot not far from the school.

She had been beaten and stabbed to death.

Just like Jessica Staley.

And Becky Benedict so many years before.

"No bouquet of roses?" I asked Chief Frank Earnshaw when Alex and I got to the station.

"No roses."

"Interesting."

Earnshaw had a piece of paper on his desk. He handed it to us to read. It was the note from the person claiming to be the killer. Earnshaw said it had been left at the Huntsdale police station not long after the body of Carolyn Garms was discovered. It looked very similar to the note found with Jessica Staley.

Alex and I read the note.

It was everything I had feared it would be.

And more.

Dear FBI Agent Nikki Cassidy,

Did you like the present I left you?

 I'm sorry it had to be so rushed. No assortment of roses this time. No note on the body proclaiming it to be my work—this is my belated effort at that. Nothing ingenious enough to match the crime fighting ability of a top investigator like you, Nikki.

 But Carolyn Garms did wind up dead.

 Like Jessica Staley.

 And Becky Benedict a long time ago.

 And now...

 What happens now?

 Well, I'll come back to that later.

 I imagine you are wondering a lot about me right now. Using all your famed FBI expertise and equipment to try and create some kind of a profile on me. What would make someone do the things I do? Did my mother neglect me as a child? Did a teenage girl break my heart when I was that age and that is why I am seeking revenge against young females now? Did I wet my bed as a kid? Did I not get enough love? Do I have some kind of horrific brain disorder?

The truth is—and it is the truth, Nikki—that none of those things are true.

I'm the only one who knows the reason I do what I do.

Maybe you'll find out too before the end of all this, or maybe you won't.

I have done my work quietly for many years. Often letting others take credit for my achievements, like pretend serial killer Daniel Gary Leighton did with all those murders he "confessed" to having committed.

But now I embrace my identity. I want you to know who I really am. I want them—all those young girls out there—to know me. I want the world to know who I am.

And they will, with your help, Nikki Cassidy.

Yes, Carolyn Garms isn't the end of this game.

Any more than Becky Benedict was the beginning.

We have been doing this for a long time.

And so I will continue to do what I do—take these young girls places, give them pleasure, open their minds for them in a way no one has ever done before in their shallow, drab lives.

I make them happy.

Yes, they really are happy.

They are happy right up until the end.

You see, I save them.

I save them all.

I save them from growing up to live in this evil world.

I make sure they stay forever young.

I know that you are after me, Nikki Cassidy. I've seen you on television and in newspapers and on the internet talking about me. And I am aware of all your accomplishments in the past. Including the solving of your own sister Caitlin's case. Poor Caitlin. She never got a chance to be happy before she *died like Jessica Staley or Becky Benedict or my others. Or did she?*

I'm sure you have many questions for me. Things you want to ask if you ever catch up with me.

Well, I have answers for you when that happens.

In fact, I believe we will meet very soon, Nikki.

You and me.

The serial killer and the FBI agent who's solved every big case she's gone after until now.

But—and I say this because I respect you as a worthy adversary—let me give you a warning before you pursue that route.

Be careful.

Be very, very careful.

Yes, you're coming after me, I'm aware of that.

But I'm coming after you.

My last kill.

See you soon, Nikki Cassidy.

"Are we sure this is real?" Alex asked.

"It's real," Earnshaw said.

"How can you be sure? There's nothing in here that isn't out in the media. Could be another phony like Leighton was."

"There was a picture attached to the note," Earnshaw said. "Take a look." He showed us another piece of paper he'd pulled out. It was a picture of Carolyn Garms lying dead in the parking lot near the school. It had to have been taken before anyone found her body.

"Okay." I sighed. "The note is real. It was sent by the killer. And he is one sick son of a bitch."

THIRTY-SIX

"Tell us about Carolyn Garms," Alex said to Earnshaw. "What do you know?"

"What is there to know? She was a sixteen-year-old high school student. That's all."

"Any record of trouble?" I asked, thinking about what we'd found out on Jessica Staley and Becky Benedict.

"What kind of trouble?"

"With the law. At school. With her parents. Drinking. Drugs. Playing hooky from school. Anything like that turn up in her background yet?"

He shook his head. "The kid's record was clear. Just an average teenager, according to her parents and friends. Why would someone pick her to grab off that bus? No idea. But it doesn't seem like it had anything to do with anything she was involved in."

"Is it clear when she was abducted?" Alex asked.

"It had to be on the school grounds after the bus got back," Edgar Daniels said. It was the first time he'd spoken although he'd been sitting in on the conversation from the beginning.

"We have witnesses that saw and talked with her on the bus

ride back from the museum. There was no indication anything was wrong. She sounded normal and unconcerned, people said. Then, when everyone returned to the classroom, someone noticed she wasn't there. They searched the school for her first, then went back and checked the bus and finally widened the search past the school grounds until they found her body nearby. It was fully clothed. No indication of a sexual attack."

"Who knew the class was going on a field trip to the museum?" I asked.

"Uh, I guess a lot of people at the school. Their teacher. The principal. Other kids at the school, whoever the students in her class talked to about their field trip with. I mean it wasn't a secret or anything."

"No, but it also wasn't public knowledge. For someone to be in position to grab the girl, that person presumably knew in advance about the bus trip. We're going to need to talk to as many of those people as we can. Their teacher. The principal. Anyone else. We'll need your department's help."

Daniels nodded enthusiastically, but Earnshaw simply shrugged. I could tell he thought this was all a waste of time. Maybe it would turn out that way, but it was basic investigative procedure. It needed to be done. I didn't want to get in another argument with the guy though. Earnshaw was a jerk, but we needed to work with him even more now with this new murder.

"What about her parents?" Alex asked.

"They're still in a state of shock," Daniels said. "They have two other girls, seventeen and eleven. They want to make sure those girls are safe from this killer. We tried to talk to them last night, but we couldn't get much. I have someone with them now. We're going to keep talking. Hopefully, they can tell us something more—something significant—about their daughter today. Do you want to talk to them, too?"

"No," Alex said, "we'll let you handle that for now. Nikki

and I will focus on the school. The teacher. The principal. The kids who went on that field trip with her."

"Sounds like a plan," Daniels said.

Earnshaw didn't say anything.

I figured that meant our meeting was over.

"There's something bothering me," I said to Alex after we'd left Earnshaw's office.

"You mean Earnshaw? Different from Dorchester, huh? I don't think you're going to be having sex with this police chief anytime soon."

"Carolyn Garms doesn't seem to fit the pattern of Benedict and Staley. The troubled girl looking for someone to run away with."

"We can't be sure of that.'

"No, but we are sure this one happened quickly. One minute she was on that school bus, then she was dead. Staley and Benedict both spent time with the killer before they died. We know for a fact that Staley checked into the Zanesville motel and bought that bouquet of roses without seeming to be under any duress. And Benedict got into that car voluntarily, days before she was finally murdered. This one is different."

"So what does it all mean?"

"The killer is in a hurry this time."

"In a hurry for what reason?"

"To show off another killing. To show us how smart he is. And maybe, just to... well, draw me back here to Huntsdale."

"The worst part is he seems to be targeting you now," Alex said.

I nodded. She was right. But I was interested in some of the other things the killer had to say too.

"He indicates Becky Benedict wasn't the first victim. What

does that mean? She died twenty years ago. Was he killing young girls even before that?"

Alex just shrugged.

"And what about the line where he said 'we' instead of 'I'? 'We have been doing this for a long time.' Does that mean there's more than one killer?"

Alex didn't have an answer for that either.

"The weirdest thing was what he said about my sister. Like he knew something more about her. But how? Why? I assume he was just trying to get to me with that. Like he left the bouquet of roses with Jessica Staley because he wanted to make it look like when my sister's body was found. But it doesn't mean anything. It can't mean anything. Because if it does... well, I have no idea what that might be."

"I think you're missing the main point of this, Nikki. He's coming after you. You're his target now. His last kill, he says at the end of the note. Doesn't that worry you at all? There's a serial killer out there who wants to get you."

It did worry me. More than I wanted to admit to Alex or Earnshaw or anyone else. I realized it that night when I walked back to the hotel. It wasn't a long walk, but I realized I was uneasy. Especially after I had left the lighted area around the station house and began walking on the deserted nighttime streets of Huntsdale.

I'd tried my best to act unconcerned about the threat against me in the note from the killer. And the truth was I didn't scare easily. I'd been in plenty of dangerous spots before. I was armed, and I was a trained FBI agent. I knew how to take care of myself. Still, I'd never been in a situation like this. When I was a target. The killer had made that very clear in his note: I was going to be his ultimate victim. Which meant he could be here around me, following me and watching me, right now. Waiting for his chance to make his move against me.

I started walking faster. It suddenly seemed important to get to the safety of my hotel as soon as possible. I looked around behind me to see if anyone was there. But the streets were empty.

Until I stopped at an intersection a few blocks from the hotel. A car pulled up alongside me. I froze at first. Then I whirled around and faced the car, my hand on my gun and ready to pull it out if I had to.

"Hey, honey, you're looking good," a voice said from inside the car.

"Mighty fine," another voice said.

"Do you want to come party with us?" a third voice shouted out at me.

I looked at the occupants of the car. Three young men. They'd obviously been drinking, I could see a beer can in the hand of one of them. This wasn't anyone out to kill me. Just some of Huntsdale's male youth out for a night on the town.

"Don't take this the wrong way, but you're all assholes," I said. "Get lost."

They laughed, the light changed and they drove off.

I kept walking briskly until I made it to the hotel. I took the elevator directly up to my room, checked just to make sure there was no one in there waiting for me and then locked the door behind me.

I felt safe now.

I also felt a little foolish.

But I slept with my gun on the table next to my bed that night, just in case.

THIRTY-SEVEN

The teacher of the class, Alan Gilmore, appeared to be in as much a state of shock over Carolyn Garms' murder as Earnshaw said the girl's parents were.

"I don't understand... I just don't understand," he kept repeating when we met with him in his classroom at the school. "I mean we were all on the bus, at the museum for a few hours, took the trip back here and then... then she was gone. I can't understand how something like this could ever happen."

Gilmore was a remarkably unremarkable man. Somewhere in his forties, thin, balding, dressed in drab clothes, no real charisma of any kind when he talked. The kind of bland, boring teacher that I remembered having too many of when I was a student at Huntsdale High years ago. Not exactly an inspiring instructor. If my theory was right that the killer was someone who charmed his young female victims before he killed them, this guy sure had to be ruled out as a suspect.

The classroom was empty except for Gilmore, me and Alex. School hadn't been officially called off, but most of the students —the ones who showed up after Carolyn Garms' death—were undergoing grief counseling sessions to deal with the trauma from her murder. Gilmore looked like he could use some of that kind of counseling too, but he was here talking to us right now.

We asked him to recount the day of the field trip as best he could.

"Oh God, I don't know... it was a field trip. That's all. We'd planned it for a few weeks, talked about in class, put it on our calendars—there was nothing at all unexpected about it. What happened that day? Nothing. Until the end. The students were really excited about going out of the classroom for the trip. There was a lot of shouting and singing on the bus ride there. Everyone seemed to enjoy the tour of the museum. And we were all talking about the stuff we'd seen there on the bus ride back. Then we came back inside the school, and that's when someone noticed Carolyn wasn't with us anymore."

He was on the verge of tears. "I've been going over and over in my mind if there was some sign of trouble or a problem that I missed. But I can't think of anything. I saw her on the bus, acting just like everyone else. So whatever happened must have been after we disembarked from the bus. But I didn't notice anything wrong then either. Why would I? Why would I have any fear or concern that something like this might happen right here on the school grounds? I really don't understand any of it."

Now he started crying.

It could have been a performance, of course. Covering up guilt on his part—either guilt from killing the girl or guilt over somehow allowing it to happen. But I didn't think anyone, particularly Alan Gilmore, was capable of an acting performance like that.

No, he was devastated by the tragic death of his student.

Vernon Ackerman, the principal of the high school, reacted a lot differently. He was much more defensive about the Garms girl's murder. Oh, he professed his sadness and grief over her death, but it was not as overwhelmingly or sincere sounding as we'd gotten from Alan Gilmore. He spent much of the time explaining why the school had done nothing wrong that allowed something like this to happen. CYA, I thought to myself. The guy is covering his own ass. Making sure this doesn't hurt him or his career. Understandable for a career educator, I guess. But still pretty despicable in my book. Hey, we were just the FBI though, not the moral police.

Ackerman was a lot better looking, a lot more personable and a lot smarter than Gilmore. I got the impression he spent a lot of time dealing with parent groups, teacher unions and maybe raising money for school facilities instead of dealing with the day-to-day education of the students.

"Every potential safety issue and security regulation was followed," Ackerman insisted to us. "There was never a moment that she wasn't under supervision from the teacher from the time the students left the school until they returned. We are not responsible for this. We are not at fault. We took every possible precaution to ensure the safety of each and every student on that trip."

"And yet one of them got murdered,' I said.

He glared at me.

"Can you tell us some more about Carolyn Garms?" Alex asked, trying to keep the interview on track—like she had other times in the past when I let my emotions show too much. "Were there any kind of issues with her, any obvious problems?"

"No, nothing. I've checked with her teachers. She was a decent student, B and C. Not outstanding, but nothing bad either. Involved in a few extracurricular activities. Carolyn Garms was simply an average student here. Nothing about her that could have suggested she might be the target of someone to do something like this."

I didn't like Ackerman. Not that that really meant anything, of course. But I also felt we were wasting our time with him. He wasn't going to tell us anything that might help the investigation, he only wanted to make sure the school—and, even more importantly, himself—suffered as little damage as possible to their public image from the murder.

"We'd like to talk to some of the other students that were on the trip with her to the museum," I said. "Can you arrange that for us?"

"I suppose so. As soon as they're finished with the grief counseling."

"And maybe some of Carolyn's friends outside the class too?" Alex suggested.

"I'm not sure who they might be."

"Could you check for us?"

"I'll ask around," Ackerman said.

We wound up talking to a large number of students. Some were forthcoming, some were not. But none of them really told us anything that changed what we knew. All we'd been able to find out after several hours at the school was that Carolyn Garms was an average teenage girl that no one could understand why someone would want to kill.

"Something is missing here," I said to Alex as we were driving away from the high school. "There's no reason Carolyn Garms was targeted. Not like with Jessica and Becky who could have been picked because of all the problems they were having. They would have been more vulnerable. But not Garms. Why her?"

"Maybe it was random."

"God, I hope not."

"Yes, that makes finding out who did this even tougher. So what next?"

"Something will happen," I said optimistically.

THIRTY-EIGHT

"This is unlike any serial killer I've ever seen or heard of before," I said to Phil Girard.

Girard had flown into Columbus Airport that morning. Blanton wanted "more FBI boots on the ground," as he put it, in Huntsdale because of the second murder. Girard was the agent joining us. Alex and I had picked him up at the airport and were driving him back to Huntsdale now.

"How so?" he asked.

"He seems to woo the girls before he kills them. As far as we can tell, they go voluntarily with him, at least the two of them that we know about for sure. Becky Benedict and Jessica Staley did. There's no coercion or force or threats that we've been able to find. Everything seems wonderful with him until... well, until he kills them."

"Except for the last girl. Carolyn Garms," said Alex.

"That didn't fit the pattern," I agreed.

"We think he killed her in a hurry to send us a friggin' message," Alex said.

"But you figure there were others—between Becky Benedict and Jessica Staley during the past twenty years—that this guy convinced to follow him. To trust him. To believe in him. And then, after a period of time in this relationship—or whatever it was with the girls—he killed them," said Phil.

"That's our working premise," I said.

"And all of the girls are in the same age group?"

"Pretty much. Early teens, fourteen to sixteen or so."

"That makes sense."

"You have a theory?"

"He's Charles Manson."

"What?"

"Charles Manson. The guy who got young girls to kill Sharon Tate and a lot of other people in Hollywood back in the sixties."

"Charles Manson is dead," I pointed out.

"But your guy here is following Manson's pattern."

I was never quite sure how much I could count on Phil Girard. I knew from past experience with him that the guy was an FBI veteran just hanging on until his retirement. He spent most of his day doing crossword puzzles, playing online word games and reading conspiracy books on everything from the JFK assassination to UFOs to true crime stories.

But, back in the day, he'd worked as an FBI profiler, putting together scenarios and descriptions of killers the bureau was chasing. He was pretty good at it. So he was back here in Huntsdale with us in the hopes he could come up with some ideas to help. I figured it couldn't hurt to hear what he had to say. Besides, I still owed Girard a favor for helping to save my life the last time he'd come here to Huntsdale to help with a case—my sister's murder.

The problem was keeping his mind on the job.

"As I recall, there weren't a lot of great places to eat the last time I was in Huntsdale," Girard said now. "Have you two found any better restaurants since then?"

"There's a pretty good Italian place not far from our hotel,"

Alex said. "Lots of pasta choices. And they have a lasagna special to die for. I'd recommend the veal too."

"Sounds promising."

"Let's talk about your Charles Manson comment," I said.

Girard explained that he'd read a lot of details about Charles Manson since Manson's death a few years ago—and he said he saw some similarities between him and the killer we were looking for.

"One of the things people never understood about Charles Manson was how he convinced all those cute young girls to follow him and do everything he wanted them to do—including killing people," Girard said. "I mean Manson was a funny-looking little man with no apparent sex appeal or anything like that. But the first thing he did was to target particular kinds of girls. The pattern was always the same. A young, confused teenage girl with an unhappy home life. All of the girls he recruited were like that. Teenage runaways. Abandoned by their families. Looking for someone—anyone—to love them. Charles Manson did that. He loved these girls, all of them. He made them feel good about themselves.

"One of the girls he recruited put it this way: 'When I first met Charlie, he gave me a big hug and said: I'm so happy to see you. I felt, ah, someplace where I finally belong, someplace somebody finally wants me.'

"Once he'd found a girl like that, he gave them his full attention and made them feel like they were special to him. These young girls were searching for that kind of love. And Charlie was the only person who gave it to them. He also used sex to control them. For many of them, it was their first sexual experience. So it drew them closer and more dependent on him. Until they were so devoted they would do anything he wanted.

"You see, they also had to give up everything they had to him. All of their possessions, any money or anything else they had. They had no identity anymore except to belong to Charles

Manson. Which made them feel safe and secure and comfortable for the first time in their lives. He was like a Pied Piper to them. And so they followed him everywhere, even to murder. Your guy sounds similar. What do you think, Cassidy? Make sense?"

I thought about everything he'd said.

It did make sense.

For a burnout case, Phil Girard still could come up with some good ideas. Just like he had last time he was in Huntsdale with me.

"And Manson used this obsession to get these girls—who were young innocent things when he met them—to do the unthinkable. To maim and torture and murder people like Sharon Tate and all the other victims of the Manson family back during their bloodbath that took place in the late sixties," I said.

"Exactly."

"Except our guy doesn't use his women to kill other people."

"Okay, that part is different," said Phil.

"He convinces them to come with him, to stay with him and do everything he wants. That part is like Manson. But the ending is different when they die. Maybe they figure that part out at some point, but by then it's too late. He holds them in his power right up until the end—and maybe even at that point—until he takes their lives."

"And he does it horribly cruelly and violently, not with any of the kindness or affection you say he showed these girls earlier," Alex said.

"That part is different from Manson," Girard agreed.

"But why?" I asked.

"Why does he kill them?"

"Yes."

"Who knows? Maybe he gets tired of them. He wants

another girl, another conquest. Or he simply enjoys the act of murder. Lots of possible reasons. No way to know for sure. Hey, maybe he'll tell you all about it when you catch him."

We had arrived in Huntsdale now. We were sitting in the hotel parking lot outside the front door. We got Phil's suitcases out of the back and then made our way inside to check him into his room. I was glad Phil was here. I thought he could help Alex and me. I told him that.

"Yeah, yeah, but let's get to the important stuff now," he said, waving off my effort to praise him.

"What important stuff?"

"Take me to that Italian restaurant you were talking about."

"That's what is important to you?"

"Hey, I want to check out that lasagna."

THIRTY-NINE

I knew it was time for me to do something really unpleasant that I'd been avoiding ever since I came back to my hometown to deal with these new murders. This would be even more unpleasant than meeting up again with Police Chief Frank Earnshaw.

I was going to see my mother.

My relationship with my mother had always been complicated, even when I was growing up. But it fell apart completely after Caitlin's murder. She blamed me for not watching Caitlin better at a town carnival that day and allowing her to be abducted, then later killed. It was a traumatic thing for an eighteen-year-old girl to deal with. My father helped me get through it for a while, but then he died. Instead of turning to me—her only living family member—for support and love, my mother wanted nothing to do with me. I guess I was a reminder to her of everything she had lost in my sister and my father.

I had desperately needed my mother to help me get through this terrible time, but she'd made everything worse for me. We'd reconciled a bit when I came back to track down my sister's real killer, but I hadn't really been in much contact with her since then. I sure wasn't looking forward to seeing her now, but someone would likely tell her I was here. Of course, she could reach out to me. But I decided to bite the bullet and go talk to her.

She was living in an apartment complex in Chillicothe—a few towns away. She'd sold the family home a number of years ago. I drove to her place, passing some of the landmarks from my youth on the way: the old house where we'd lived; the high school I attended; a burger place where I'd hung out with my friends before my sister died and everything went bad. All of these memories came rushing back to me as I went to see my mother. And then I'd have to deal with all the memories that would bring back for me.

She seemed surprised to see me when she opened the front door. I guess no one had told her I was back in town. But she knew about Becky Benedict.

"I saw you on TV," she said. "Talking about that girl in Dorchester."

"There's been another murder too. Two murders. Back in Huntsdale." I told her about Jessica Staley and Carolyn Garms.

"I heard about the Staley girl. But she wasn't from Huntsdale. The body was just left here, right?"

"Yes, but there could be more of a connection to Huntsdale than just the body turning up here."

"What kind of connection?"

"To Caitlin."

She glared at me. Just like she had in the past when I'd brought up my sister's name. Caitlin was a loving memory for my mother, a memory that she could embrace and maybe find some solace in. She was a bit like Eleanor Benedict, I suppose. But I kept interrupting that memory every time I asked questions about Caitlin. Still, it had to be done.

"There was a bouquet of roses next to the Staley girl's body," I said. "Like the roses we found with Caitlin."

"That doesn't mean anything," she said quickly.

I wasn't sure if she was trying to convince me, or herself.

"Everybody knows about that with Caitlin. And you did all those media appearances recently. The killer was probably just reacting to that. Trying to get your attention for some sick reason."

"That's one possibility."

"What else could it be?"

"The same person could have been involved in Caitlin's murder."

"That's crazy. You solved her murder. You found out it was that horrible Tommy Thompson who killed her and then murdered your father because he was getting too close to the truth. But Thompson is dead now. That's all over."

I hoped she was right. But there was something still bothering me about my sister's case.

"There were some questions about Dad's investigation into Caitlin's murder," I said. "I read his police report. There were pages missing in it. No one ever found out what was on those missing pages. Or what happened to them. I keep hoping that he might have said something to you about why he might have removed those pages from his report. There were some other unanswered questions about what he did—and didn't do—before his death. If you can remember anything at all..."

"I'll tell you what I remember!" She was yelling at me now. "I remember your father working day and night on the case. First to try to find Caitlin. Then, once she was found dead, to catch the person who did it. He put his heart and soul and every part of his being into that investigation. So don't you dare question anything about what your father did for Caitlin. Don't denigrate his memory like this, for God's sake. I hope you find out who killed these other girls, but it has nothing to do with your sister. So just leave it all alone with this nonsense about these new killings being somehow about her."

"I'm not going to leave it alone. I'm sorry if this opens up old wounds for you. But I'm going to do whatever I have to do to find out the truth. About Jessica Staley and Becky Benedict. And Caitlin too, if there is more to her case."

My mother shook her head sadly. "You never did listen to me, Nikki. You always did whatever you wanted. No matter what the consequences turned out to be. Like..."

She didn't finish that thought, but she didn't have to.

Like the time I didn't listen to her and took my sister to the carnival.

And Caitlin wound up dead.

"She's your mother," Alex said after I finished complaining to her about our latest confrontation. "Most families aren't perfect. Hey, we all have mother problems."

"You too?"

"Did I ever tell you that my mother didn't want me to marry Bob? She didn't think he was 'good enough for me.' She loves him now, but I went through some rough times over it."

"Except you did go ahead and marry Bob."

"Yes, we got married very soon after that."

"Because of your mother?"

"Uh, no. Because I found out I was pregnant with Jonathan."

"I never knew that."

"Like I said, not everyone's life is perfect, Nikki. Sometimes you just have to accept people the way they are."

FORTY

The Garden Island Motel in Zanesville, Ohio—where Jessica Staley had stopped on her fateful journey from her home in Elmsford, Michigan until she was found dead in Huntsdale— was a small twelve-unit structure with a blinking sign out front that said: "Single Rooms Available—Cut Rate Prices."

I decided to check it out in person to find out what I could about Jessica Staley's last days on this planet. And to try and figure out how—and why—she had signed into the place as Becky Benedict. I wasn't sure what I hoped to find there, but I did have one idea. DNA. Whoever killed her might have left his DNA in that room, if he was there with her, as I suspected. We now had obtained DNA from the Becky Benedict crime site two decades ago. If DNA from the motel room somehow matched up with it, then that would be final confirmation for us that the same person murdered both Staley and Benedict. Even if we didn't know who that person was yet.

The office in front of the Garden Island Motel had a broken window, the entire place was covered with peeling paint and somebody had sprayed graffiti on the doors of several of the rooms. It was in a bad location too, some three miles from the main highway. All in all, the Garden Island Motel was not an ideal place to stay at. Unless you were a young girl on the run like Jessica Staley had been when she was there.

I'd wondered how a fourteen-year-old girl like Jessica Staley had managed to check into a motel on her own without any questions. Or presumably without even anyone checking her ID, since she signed in as Becky Benedict. How did the people at the motel allow that to happen?

Well, it was a lot clearer now that I saw the Garden Island Motel up close.

And especially after I met the man behind the desk in the front office.

His name was Lester Eldridge, and he said he was the manager and owner of the place. I was there with some police officers from the Zanesville force I'd coordinated this visit with and a DNA team to examine the room where Jessica Staley had spent the night.

Eldridge wasn't happy to see any of us. He first tried to refuse us access to the place, until we served him with search warrant paperwork I'd gotten from a judge before arriving. Then he complained about how the police had closed off the room where Jessica had stayed as part of a crime scene.

"That's costing me money not being allowed to rent that room because of you people," he said. "Am I going to get some kind of compensation from you for doing this? I'm trying to run a business here."

I looked out the window at the parking lot. There were two cars outside besides ours, one of them I assumed belonged to Eldridge. Most of the units seemed to be empty. I pointed that out to him. He grumbled something about how the reason there were no customers now was because they'd been scared off by all the police presence.

Eldridge himself was a squat, overweight, balding man wearing a dirty white T-shirt that looked like it hadn't been washed in weeks, and sucking on a cigar that was so wet and sloppy it probably had been in his mouth even longer.

I showed him a picture of Jessica Staley. "Recognize her?"

"Yes, I think so."

"She checked in to your motel not long ago."

"If you say so."

"I say so."

"Okay, I guess she did."

"Let's see the registration."

He fumbled around in a big old book—no computer listing for this place—and found the page for the night Staley showed up here.

Not surprisingly, there was only one guest listed. Becky Benedict was the name in the book that she had signed in as, like Phil Girard had been told earlier.

"Her real name was Jessica Staley, not Becky Benedict," I said to Eldridge.

"Whatever." He shrugged.

"Did you check her in?"

"I imagine so, I'm the only one here most of the time."

"She was only fourteen years old."

"I wasn't aware of her age."

"So this girl is underage, she's using an assumed name and she's all alone, as far as you know. But you have no trouble checking her in as a guest. Is that your normal procedure here, Mr. Eldridge?"

"Hey, she paid me thirty-eight dollars for the room. In cash. Her money was just as good as anyone else's, as far as I was concerned." Eldridge said he didn't know anything else about the girl. He didn't see what happened to her after she went to the room. He never saw anyone else join the girl in the room. And he never saw her leave in the morning.

Finally, he took us to the room where she had stayed. It was Room 11.

All of us—me, the Zanesville cops and the DNA people—went inside.

The room was exactly what you'd expect in a place like the Garden Island Motel. Small, dingy, battered old furniture and a musty smell that made me wonder if the place had even been cleaned recently. I thought about how Jessica Staley had grown up in what Girard told us was a nice big house in a beautiful suburban town in Michigan, and I wondered what pushed her into winding up in a dump like this. Was she really that unhappy at home? And was her departure completely voluntary?

It seemed so, given the way she'd been alone when she checked in here and when she'd bought the roses at the convenience store in Huntsdale. But it still didn't make sense to me.

There'd been someone else staying in the room after Jessica, then it had been shut down, by police request. So the only DNA in the room should be Jessica's plus the subsequent tenant. Maybe something from a cleaning person too, although I'm not sure the Garden Island Motel really cleaned much in between guests. And, because of that, there could be DNA from another guest before Jessica Staley.

But all of them weren't important. I knew what we were looking for.

DNA that matched the DNA found at the Becky Benedict murder scene some twenty years ago.

The DNA people did a complete sweep of the place, then sent everything back for comparison in their lab. While this was going on, I checked the rest of the room in case there was any evidence or trace of anything from Jessica Staley. But there was nothing. She had spent the night here—presumably with a man who was with her, accompanying her before murdering her—and then left with him to meet her fate in Huntsdale.

"What do you think?" Alex asked me afterward when I called to tell her we'd finished up at the motel.

"I think the guy with her—the killer—knew exactly what kind of place this was. No one was going to ask too many questions about a fourteen-year-old girl by herself and using a name that wasn't hers. This guy is smart. He's shrewd. He knows all the angles and checks everything out to make sure it's the way he wants it to be."

"Then why do you think he might be sloppy enough to leave his DNA behind?"

"Because I believe—and we'll find out as soon as we get the results back—that he left his DNA in this room deliberately. Just like the way he had the girl sign in as Becky Benedict. Maybe he figured out that we'd eventually match it up with DNA from Becky's scene. This guy wants us to know he's responsible for both murders. And probably a lot more too."

"But why? Why would he do that?"

"He's the only one who has the answer to that, Alex."

FORTY-ONE

Whenever I come back to my hometown, I visit some of the places I remember from growing up in Huntsdale until I went away to college at the age of eighteen. I did that not long ago when I was here investigating Caitlin's murder. And I knew that, sooner or later, I would be following my normal routine, reliving the memories of my hometown.

The good memories.

And the bad ones.

Not that I had spent that much time in Huntsdale after my sister was murdered. I went away to college and only returned on school breaks when I had to. After I started working, I hardly ever came back. There wasn't much in Huntsdale for me anymore. My father was dead, my sister was dead, and my mother was... well, we didn't have much of a relationship. And, whenever I was in Huntsdale back then, all I could think about was getting away again. I was nervous, uptight, sad and even panicky—to the point where a few times I thought I was suffering an anxiety attack—being around my memories. All I wanted to do was get the hell out of town and go back to Washington and my life and my job.

But here I was again.

Back in Huntsdale.

With all the memories.

So I took another trip down memory lane.

I'd already visited the high school to question the principal and teachers and students about Carolyn Garms. It was always a weird experience going back there. The high school was in the same location as when I'd attended, but it was pretty much all a new building, with an additional wing that had been constructed since I left. The football field had been moved to a different spot alongside the school, as had the spectator grandstand. I'd been a cheerleader at Huntsdale High— just like Becky Benedict had been in Dorchester—but the football field looked strange and unfamiliar to me now.

Different building, different football field, different teachers and students and administrators. It was definitely not the Huntsdale High School I remembered.

One place in town that did look the same was the movie theater. There was only one. I'd been back there the last time I was in Huntsdale when a teenage girl disappeared from the theater. I was surprised then to see it had not been torn down or turned into a multiplex. There was something very quaint, very historic about it.

I stood on the street outside now and remembered going there on dates or with my girlfriends. I had a sudden flashback of sitting in the theater watching one of the Bourne movies and developing a crush on Matt Damon that I thought would never go away. Actually, it still hasn't.

My favorite diner was still there too. I'd eaten there again the last time I was in town, delighted to find out that the triple-decker tuna fish sandwich special I used to love so much was still on the menu.

But most of the rest of the stores, shops and restaurants had changed from my childhood days. The ice-cream stand, the music store, the clothes shops from then had been replaced by CVS, Starbucks and other chain outlets.

But these weren't the only places I returned to when I was in Huntsdale. There were other locations too. Places that were more painful for me.

One of them was the site of the carnival where Caitlin disappeared fifteen years ago. The place where my sister was suddenly gone in an instant on a long-ago summer day. She was watching me getting on the Tilt-a-Whirl with my friends, and then minutes later when I got off, she was gone.

Gone forever.

There was no Tilt-a-Whirl there anymore, no carnival—only a strip mall of stores that had been built years earlier. Not much to see. But it was still the crime scene for me. The crime scene of my sister's abduction.

Her body was found murdered several days after she disappeared in a spot called Grant Woods. It was an area with miles of woods and trails just outside of town. The place where Caitlin's body had been found, with a bouquet of roses on top of her. Just like the roses with Jessica Staley. Another teenage girl's body had been found in Grant Woods the last time I was here. How could such a beautiful spot—a beautiful town like Huntsdale—be the home for this kind of evil?

Finally, I wound up at the most vivid memory I had of Huntsdale. The house where I grew up.

It was a white, two-story house with a big porch in front within walking distance of town, where my father had worked as the police chief. He and I used to sit on that front porch, and he'd tell me police and crime stories that held me spellbound. Then he'd make up imaginary crime puzzles, and he'd get me to try to solve them. I got pretty good at it, although my father was invariably one step ahead of me. There was always one important clue that I could never quite figure out from him. But I loved those moments on the front porch. I guess that's why I got into law enforcement as a career. Because of my father.

The last time I'd been in Huntsdale I'd come back to this house with the now dead Billy Weller. I'd stood on my old front porch with him, and he encouraged me to knock on the door and ask if I could see the inside of the house once more too. I didn't do that. Should I try now? I was still thinking about it, standing on the porch, when the front door of the house suddenly opened.

"Can I help you?" a woman said.

She was middle-aged, about the same age as my mother was back when we lived here, and for just a second or two I could see my mother standing there again as she did when my father and sister were alive.

The woman said her name was Maureen Wilcox.

"I'm sorry," I said, "I was just looking at your house." I took out my FBI credentials and showed them to her to make sure she felt comfortable talking with me.

"Is there some problem?"

"No, my name is Nikki Cassidy, and I—"

"I know you now. I saw you on TV."

Of course, she did.

"But what are you doing at my house?"

"I used to live here."

She hadn't known that, she said. The house had been sold to someone else by my mother when she moved out. And Maureen Wilcox wasn't aware of who the previous owner, my mother, had been.

I talked a bit with her about growing up in this house.

"Would you like to come inside and see it again?" she asked me at one point.

It was the same thing Billy Weller had suggested I do.

People do it all the time, he said to me that day. Knock on

the door of a house where they grew up and ask to look around inside to relive some of the memories of their childhood.

That's what this Wilcox woman was inviting me to do.

It would be very easy to take her up on the offer. But what would I find inside?

My sister Caitlin was not living there anymore. My father wasn't. Even my mother was long gone. It would be a different house and a different look and different furniture and, most importantly of all, different people.

"No, thanks," I said to her. "I've got to get back to work." Then I left the porch, went down the front steps and never looked back as I left the house where I once lived as a young girl a lifetime ago.

Sometimes it's best to just leave memories alone.

Let them be what they were supposed to be.

Memories.

Only memories.

FORTY-TWO

"I used to be like you, Cassidy," Phil Girard said to me.

"Really?"

"Hey, I was like you and Alex both."

"How is that, Phil?"

"Gung-ho. Dedicated to the job. Willing to put my life on the line for the sake of the bureau. Seeking justice for all, all for justice and that kind of crap. All the stuff you two believe in. That used to be me, honest, it was."

"But not now?"

"I'm not that guy anymore."

"Yeah, we've noticed."

I'd learned a while ago that you couldn't insult Phil Girard with comments like that. He made them about himself all the time. It was no secret to anyone that he was pretty much mailing it in on the job these days, and he had been for a long time. Counting the days until he retired while he focused on things like padding his expense account at fancy restaurants and immersing himself in various conspiracy theories like UFOs and the JFK assassination and even—although I wasn't sure he wasn't kidding us when he said it—expressing doubts about whether Neil Armstrong ever really landed on the moon.

But I'd also discovered that Phil Girard could be useful.

Most importantly, he had saved my life in a shoot-out the last time I'd been in Huntsdale.

There were plenty of other times too when he used his years of experience with law enforcement and the FBI to help me in investigating cases I was involved in. Girard knew stuff. He understood things about cases that I sometimes hadn't thought about very much.

Like what he'd told Alex and me before about Charles Manson.

"I'm not saying that this guy is anything like Manson," Girard said now as I pressed him on the idea. "He doesn't necessarily have to have long hair, a beard, a crazy look in his eyes or get people hooked on LSD or other mind-altering drugs, like Manson did. I'm talking about something a lot more subtle. Manson had this fascinating ability to win his followers' trust and get them to follow his orders, no matter how crazy they were. No one could ever understand how this strange little guy had accomplished the whole Manson family thing. But he was somehow able to get all of these young, impressionable girls to do what he wanted. I think whoever we're looking for here is doing the same thing."

Girard and I were having dinner at a restaurant in Huntsdale. Well, not simply a restaurant. The most expensive restaurant in the area. It was a steak place, and Girard assured me he could put the whole bill on his expense account. "Dinner with investigative source," he said with a laugh when I asked him how he'd claim this was a valid business expense to Blanton and the higher-ups in Washington.

Alex was back at the hotel again talking with her family. It was just Phil and me. I was hoping that might get him to open up a little more and talk about his ideas on the investigation.

"Who would you think might gain that kind of control over someone like Becky Benedict or Jessica Staley?" I asked him.

"Maybe someone with a lot of authority," Girard said. "Authority that made them feel safe. Like they could trust the person."

"Like a schoolteacher?"

"Maybe."

"Or a school counselor."

"Exactly."

"Who else?"

"Someone older."

"Uh-huh."

"Someone who had a lot of money."

I thought about that guy William Zachary back in Dorchester. He was older. And he had a lot of money, based on his job and his house and his cars. Of course, he was in Dorchester. But Dorchester wasn't that far from Huntsdale if someone like Zachary wanted to travel to kill young women.

"Anything else?" I asked.

"What about someone in a uniform?"

"You mean a military person?"

"Or a police officer."

"A cop?"

"These girls might well have felt safe with a cop, right?"

I knew four cops involved in these cases. Chief Frank Earnshaw. Edgar Daniels. Donald Maris. And Chief Connor Nolan. Did I really think that any of them could be serial killers? Not really. But then I would have never imagined Tommy Thompson, a longtime district attorney, had murdered my sister and other girls until I uncovered the truth.

"What do you think, Phil?" I asked now.

"I think that this steak I'm eating is overpriced. It's a little chewy and too well done. Maybe I should have gone for the prime rib or the lamb chops. Are you sure this is the best steak place in town?"

"I'm talking about our murder investigations."

"Oh, that."

"Do you have any more ideas about Jessica Staley or Becky Benedict or Carolyn Garms?"

"You'll figure it out." He laughed. "You and Alex. The two of you are real FBI hotshots, right? What do I know, I'm just a guy dreaming about my pension and the fishing boat I'm going to buy soon in Florida."

"C'mon, man..."

"Hey, something will happen. There'll be a break in the case. There always is. You just have to wait for it. Sooner or later, something will happen."

We were in the car driving back to the hotel when something did happen.

Phil's phone buzzed. He answered it, listened to whoever was on the other end and then turned to me with a big smile on his face. "It was the DNA results from Zanesville. They were a match. The same DNA at the motel as the DNA found twenty years ago at the Becky Benedict crime scene."

"Oh, my God, it really is the same killer."

"Two decades apart."

"Jeez, it's the answer we've been looking for."

"And now that leaves us with one big question."

"How many other girls has he killed in between Becky Benedict and Jessica Staley over those twenty years?"

FORTY-THREE

Alex, Phil and I called up Dave Blanton on a Zoom call. We talked with him about the DNA match between Staley and Benedict. But we also brought up the other obvious conclusion from this.

"We need to seriously consider at this point the likelihood that there are more victims of this killer than just Becky Benedict and Jessica Staley," I said to Blanton. "And, of course, Carolyn Garms too. And we need to figure out who these victims might be."

"I agree," he replied.

"Great."

"But how do we do that?"

"I have a plan."

"What is it?"

"I want to take a look at all the unsolved murders of teenage girls over the past twenty years. The time period between Becky Benedict and Jessica Staley. And we see if we can find other victims who appear to fit the same pattern. We should get our FBI research people on this right away, Chief."

"Are you talking about every teenage girl murder case?"

"Not every case. We can narrow it down." I told him the theory about the girls going willingly—even eagerly possibly—with their killers because they were unhappy and had troubles in their lives.

Blanton still wasn't sure how practical that would be. "That's a helluva lot of cases to check out. Almost impossible to do. Is this your theory, Agent Cassidy—the stuff about the killer targeting unhappy, troubled teenage girls?"

"It's not my theory, it's Phil's," I said. "But I agree with it."

"Phil?" Blanton asked.

"Yes, boss."

"This is your idea?"

"That's right." Phil talked more then to Blanton about his Charles Manson-type profile of the killer. About a Svengali-like figure who somehow convinced troubled girls to follow him. Which they did, even though it eventually led to their deaths. "That's what happened with Becky Benedict and Jessica Staley," he said.

And then Girard told Blanton how he believed it was very possible that more young girls had met the same fate. "A guy like this doesn't kill a girl twenty years ago, then do nothing until now. He's been out there. He's been active. He's been taking other girls and murdering them. We just never knew about it. We were never able to put it together until we made the DNA match between the Benedict and Staley cases."

"But we ran that DNA through our computer. Every case in it, every suspect ever arrested. No match. Why would he never leave DNA anywhere else, then suddenly do it in the motel room now with the Staley girl?"

"If we assume the Benedict murder was his first one, and that's the presumption I'm operating under, then he left DNA there because he was inexperienced in committing murder twenty years ago. He didn't know how to clean up a crime scene. But after that he figured out how to do it better.

How to do it clean. So there was no DNA trail until Jessica Staley."

"Then how did the DNA show up with her?"

"He did it deliberately."

"You mean he wanted us to find it?"

"Right. It was a message."

"Like the messages he's been sending to Cassidy," Alex said.

"He wants us to know he's the same guy, for some reason," Phil said to Blanton. "That's the only conclusion that makes sense."

"And he knows we can't match up the DNA unless he's in our criminal justice system. Is that what you're saying, Agent Girard? That we can't identify the guy from our systems?"

"Not until we catch him."

Blanton seemed to be warming to the idea. Which pissed me off a bit. I mean, he didn't take it seriously when it came from me, not until Girard talked about it. Maybe he felt more comfortable working with a veteran male FBI agent than a younger female one. Who said sexism was dead? It sure seemed to be alive and well at FBI headquarters, Nikki.

But I put my resentment about this aside for the moment. The important thing was to get the records of all these past cases for us to go through. And Blanton agreed at the end to set that in motion.

I updated him on everything else we'd found out in Huntsdale and Dorchester since Alex and I had been assigned to the cases. I tried to keep it as professional as possible. No specific criticism about Chief Frank Earnshaw or anything in Huntsdale. And no overly gushing praise of Police Chief Connor Nolan from Dorchester.

But Blanton knew about my personal history with Earnshaw—just as I'd had similar issues in the past with local police force officials who I felt weren't cooperating with us as much as they could.

"Then you're getting along better with Huntsdale's police chief than you did the last time you were there?"

"Uh, sure."

"Agent Cassidy?"

"Okay, Earnshaw is still an asshole."

"But you haven't told him that, have you?"

"I've been on my best behavior. Honest."

"What about the guy from Dorchester? Alex had good things to say about him last time we discussed this."

"He's so much better to deal with."

"Good."

"I've been on my best behavior with him too."

"You were nice to Nolan, the Dorchester chief?"

"Very nice."

"So keep on being nice to him."

I saw Alex smirking next to me when he said that. Blanton couldn't see her, thank goodness.

"I'll do my very best to keep on working closely with Chief Nolan," I said.

FORTY-FOUR

I'd gone back to a lot of the places I remembered from my days growing up in Huntsdale. I'd been to my old high school, my old house, the diner where I used to hang out with my friends, and, of course, I'd been to the police station where my father was once the police chief, and I'd followed him around in awe, like a female Opie Taylor from the old *Andy Griffith* TV show. But the one place I hadn't yet returned to was the Huntsdale Cemetery. Where my sister and father were buried.

It was late in the day, and the cemetery was almost empty when I got there. I saw one family at a gravesite way in the distance and a white car sitting at another location nearer to me, probably just arriving or leaving. Other than that, I was all alone. No one except me and the ghosts.

Caitlin and my father were buried side by side next to a pond, surrounded by trees and grass, with ducks swimming in the water. I'd visited the site last time, after solving my sister's murder. I guess I wanted to 'tell them'—my father and my sister —what I had done. But maybe I also had some unanswered questions about Caitlin's case.

I still did.

I thought again about playing those games with my father on the front porch. How he'd give me a set of clues, and then I had to solve the crime. Sometimes I would, but a lot of times he was too smart for me. "Just give me one more clue, Dad," I'd plead with him.

Damn. I wished I could play the game with him again. Tell him everything I knew so far, then he'd somehow make sense out of all of it. Like he used to do when I was a little girl dreaming about one day growing up to solve crimes the same way he did.

"Am I still missing something, Dad?" I asked aloud at his grave. "Where do I go next on these new murders? What do I do now? Just give me one more clue, Dad."

But there was only silence. Nothing but the sounds of the ducks on the water and the wind blowing through the trees.

It's difficult to get answers from someone when it's a one-way conversation.

It was starting to get dark. The family at the gravesite in the distance was leaving. The white car was still there, but I figured they'd be gone soon too. I got in my car, mouthed a silent goodbye to my father and sister and then started driving back to the hotel.

As I was leaving the cemetery, I noticed the white car pulling out behind me.

I guess it was time for everyone to leave.

I didn't feel like going right back up to my room and being there alone until I fell asleep. It wasn't that late yet anyway. I decided to have a drink before I went upstairs. There was a bar across the street from the hotel that I hadn't checked out. The parking lot was filled with cars. I figured that meant it must be a popular place.

A woman drinking alone in a bar is always a target for men.

But I was ready for that. I knew how to handle myself. And carrying an FBI badge and a gun also helped. Sure enough, I'd only been there about five minutes when a guy on the prowl slipped onto the barstool next to me and tried to start up a conversation. I told him I wasn't interested. He ignored me, and I told him again—a bit more forcefully this time. But he still didn't get the message.

"I am simply not interested," I finally said, hoping the blunt, direct approach would work.

"Oh, you'll come around if you have another drink or two."

He was about thirty with bushy black hair and he was wearing a flashy sports shirt and what looked like designer jeans. He had an earring in one ear and a tattoo on his arm with a heart that said Ladies Man. Jeez. I guess maybe he wasn't used to getting rejected by women in bars like this. Hey, if it was another time and another place, maybe I might have been interested. But not tonight.

"Go away," I said.

"Why should I?"

"Because you're harassing me."

He smiled. He wasn't going to give up easily. "What's wrong with a little harassment, honey?"

"It's against the law."

"What are you gonna do... call a cop?"

"I am a cop." I pulled back the jacket I was wearing and showed him my FBI badge on my belt and the Glock 19M I had on my hip.

That did it. He disappeared quickly. He must have spread the word about me too. No men bothered me after that. I drank two vodkas, which is normally my limit. But then I decided to go for a third before leaving. What the hell, it was only a short walk to my hotel.

I was feeling a bit of buzz from the alcohol when I stepped out the front door and into the night air. I took a deep breath, then looked around the parking lot to make sure there was no traffic before I started walking.

That was when I saw it.

A white car was parked not far from the door where I stood.

Of course, there were a lot of white cars on the street. But this one looked like the one I'd seen earlier at the cemetery. What was it doing here? Was it a coincidence? Or was it following me for some reason?

I tried to convince myself I was overreacting again. Like the time I almost pulled out my gun when the car filled with drunk guys pulled up alongside me and scared the hell out of me. That turned out to be nothing. This was probably the same kind of thing.

You're really being paranoid, Nikki, I told myself. Then I continued walking across the parking lot.

I was in the middle of it when I suddenly heard the roar of an engine as whoever was behind the wheel of the white car started it up.

Before I could react, it was speeding toward me.

Even with my not so quick reflexes after the drinks I'd consumed, I knew I had to get out of the way in a hurry.

I almost pulled it off. But not quite.

I jumped to get out of the way, but the car clipped me as it roared past. I saw the tail lights in the distance, tried to make out the number on the back license plate—but it was all a blur.

Then the force of the car's blow hurtled me into another car. I smashed my head into that car's windshield and suddenly everything went black.

FORTY-FIVE

"You were lucky," the doctor said to me.

"How was I lucky?"

"If that car had struck you a foot or so—maybe even a few inches—more head-on, you could have been seriously injured or even dead right now."

"If I was really lucky, the damn car would have missed me completely."

I was sitting on an examination table at Huntsdale Hospital. I hadn't been in the hospital as a patient since I was in the fourth grade, and I broke my wrist on the school playground. My father drove me there in a squad car then, this time I went by ambulance. I protested, saying I didn't need to go to the hospital. But the EMT people on the scene insisted, and so here I was.

Fortunately, even though I had been hurt when the car hit me, the injuries turned out to be pretty minor. I'd blacked out very briefly—only a matter of seconds, they told me later—when the force of the collision had hurled me toward the nearby car. My head hit the windshield, then I bounced off the hood face down on the pavement, opening up a small gash on my forehead. I had a few other lacerations and bruises, and I had felt some soreness in various parts of my body when I sat up for the first time on the examination table a few minutes earlier.

The doctor was finished working on me now.

"Can I get out of here?" I asked.

"You really should spend the night."

"I'm not spending tonight in the hospital, Doctor."

"You suffered a nasty blow to the head."

"I'm fine."

"Someone should monitor you tonight to make sure you don't suffer any complications or additional problems."

"I'll self-monitor."

"You can't self-monitor when you're asleep."

"Okay, I'll stay awake all night. Where's my stuff?"

He sighed. "I'll have a nurse get everything ready for you."

Edgar Daniels had been there earlier to fill out a police report on the incident.

"Did you happen to get a license plate number?" he asked.

"Uh, no. I would have told you that if I did."

"Too bad, that would have made it easier."

"I was a little busy at the time trying to get out of the way of a car speeding toward me, Edgar."

He smiled. "What do you remember about the car?"

"It was white."

"Anything else?"

"I'd seen it before."

"Where?"

I told him about seeing a white car—presumably the same car—when I'd visited my father and sister's graves earlier that evening. And how I'd noticed the car leaving at the same time I did. It was obviously following me, although I didn't realize that until later, I explained to him.

"Make of the car?"

"I think it was either a Honda or a Toyota. Something like that."

"And the driver?"

"No idea."

"You never saw who was behind the wheel, even when the car was bearing down so closely on you?"

"No, it all happened very quickly."

Daniels had been off-duty when he heard what happened to me, so he'd showed up at the hospital in casual clothes, which consisted of khaki pants, sandals and a T-shirt which said "Born to Run" on the front. I remembered Daniels telling me what a big Bruce Springsteen fan he was.

"Is that your favorite Springsteen song?" I asked, just to talk about something else for a few minutes besides cars trying to run me down.

"'Born to Run'? Great song, great rock anthem. But not my all-time favorite, even though a lot of people like you think it must be."

"What's your favorite Springsteen song?"

"'Rosalita (Come Out Tonight).'"

"How come 'Rosalita' over 'Born to Run'?"

"I don't know. I guess maybe because I heard Bruce do a twenty-four-minute version of 'Rosalita' at one of his concerts that just blew me away. I never get tired of listening to that song. Are you a Springsteen fan?"

"I like him, but I don't love him the way you do."

"Go listen to 'Rosalita,' and you will." He smiled.

Daniels said he would send out a bulletin asking all officers to be on the lookout for a white Honda or Toyota that might have damage to its front from the collision with me. But he didn't hold out a lot of hope.

"There're a lot of white Hondas and Toyotas around here," he said.

Before I left the hospital, the curtain to the alcove where I was waiting opened again and Alex came in. She'd been there earlier. The first person on the scene and then at the hospital when she found out what had happened. Now she was going to drive me back to our hotel.

"Are you going to live?" she asked.

"For a little while longer anyway."

"What does the doctor say?"

"He wants me to spend the night here so they can observe me."

"Good luck with that."

"Yes, I was ready to shoot my way out of here, if necessary." I started putting on my clothes. Then I told Alex we needed to get out of there in a hurry before the doctor treating me changed his mind about letting me go.

"Let's get you back to the hotel as soon as possible," Alex said once we were out of the hospital. "You've had a tough night."

"I want to go back to the bar first."

"The place where the car hit you?"

"Yes."

"Why?"

"I want to look around there again."

And so there we were standing again at the spot where a short time earlier someone in a white car had tried to run me down for some reason.

I retraced my steps. Leaving the bar. Walking across the parking lot. And then seeing the car come speeding toward me. I wasn't sure what I accomplished by going through all this again, but it seemed important for me to do.

"You could have been killed, Nikki," Alex said when I'd finished the run-through and told her again how it had all gone down.

"I don't think so."

"Huh?"

"Whoever did this wasn't trying to kill me."

"Then why in the hell try to run you down with a car?"

"If he was trying to kill me, he would have hit me straight on. But he didn't. The car swerved at the last minute, I remember that now. That's why it only struck me a glancing blow, not a direct one."

"Then why..."

"He didn't want to kill me. He didn't even want to hurt me badly. He wanted to scare me. And he wanted to send me another message. A message that he was out there. Waiting for me. Just like he said in the note he sent. He's right here with us in Huntsdale, Alex. He's playing a game with us. Mostly with me. And I have to keep playing his game."

"This isn't a game, Nikki."

"It is for him."

"Well, you don't have to play the game."

"I do if I hope to catch him. It's the only way."

FORTY-SIX

Blanton was sure right about there being a lot of unsolved teenage girl murder cases over the past twenty years. There were hundreds of them.

And that didn't even include other cases that were ostensibly solved—like the cases on Daniel Gary Leighton's list of "confessions"—where the wrong man might have been convicted or admitted to a crime he didn't really commit for some bizarre reason while the real killer remained free.

We started by narrowing down the age bracket. We concentrated only on cases where the victim was a teenage girl between twelve and sixteen years old. That was the age bracket for Becky Benedict, Jessica Staley and Carolyn Garms. That seemed to be the age bracket that a sexual predator like this would most likely focus on. For what it was worth, my sister was also twelve when she was murdered.

Of course, he might be attracted to someone seventeen or eighteen, or even eleven or younger in the other direction. But twelve to sixteen seemed to be the best area for us to look for more possible victims.

We also cut down the field by doing some racial and

economic profiling. That kind of thing might not sound politically correct, but the reality was that killers tended to have a type. All the victims we knew about so far—Benedict, Staley and Garms—had come from nice middle-class homes—not rich, but certainly very comfortable. And all three of them were white. Not black or Hispanic or Asian or any other ethnicity. So for this case, our killer's type of girl was white, pretty, and from a middle-class social background. We simply could not ignore that in our search for other victims.

We also looked for girls who seemed to come from troubled homes, like Staley and now Benedict, according to what we had found out. Girls in trouble with the law, in trouble with school officials or from homes where domestic violence may have been occurring. Teenage girls unhappy with their lives and looking for a way out.

But the thing that really streamlined the process—and limited the number of cases we were looking at—came when we eliminated all but the teenage girls who had disappeared for a period of time before they were found dead.

And, to focus even more on what we were looking for, we then went only with cases in which the victim seemed to go voluntarily with their captor.

These girls were the perfect prey for a Svengali like figure—like Charles Manson, as Phil Girard put it—to offer them an escape, convince them to join him and then—for reasons known only to himself—murder these young women.

By the time we'd narrowed everything down, we were looking at six cases that seemed to fit all the criteria. There were no other obvious links between them. They had all occurred at different times over the two decades since the Benedict murder, and in different locations, none of them even in the same state. But, and this seemed important, the method of murder was always the same. No guns in any of the cases. All the victims had been beaten and stabbed to death. And all the deaths were particularly brutal. Just like they had been with Becky Benedict, Jessica Staley and Carolyn Garms.

"We need to do a deep dive into all six of these murders," I said to Alex and Girard once I got the list from Blanton.

"What are we looking for?" Alex said.

"I'm not sure."

"That makes it tough."

"We'll know something is important when we see it."

"Okay."

"Something specific that connects any of these cases with our cases here."

"Like if one of them was going out with someone named Zachary?"

"That would be nice."

"How about DNA from any of these cases?" Girard asked.

I shook my head. "We already have the DNA from the Benedict murder at the beginning, and what we found in that motel room where Staley was in Zanesville. But none of that matched anything else when we ran the DNA through all the FBI crime data. There's no DNA from any of these cases."

"That's right," Alex said. "In fact, if someone did find DNA with any of these possible additional victims, we'd have to eliminate them from our possible connections. Because their DNA would not be a match to Benedict or Staley. So DNA is no help to us here."

"What do we tell local police when they ask us why we're checking back on these murders?" Girard asked.

"Tell them we're just working on some old cases to see if we can turn up any leads," I said.

"You think they'll buy that?"

"I guess we'll find out soon enough."

"And the media?" asked Alex.

"We should try to keep the media out of this as long as possible."

"Good luck with that."

"Yeah, someone is going to find out what we're doing sooner or later, Nikki," Girard said.

"Well, let's hope it's later. After we catch the killer."

I looked again at the six cases, and at pictures of the girls who had been killed. They all looked like normal teenage girls to me. Not like they would in the later pictures, the ones from the crime scenes where they were beaten and battered and covered in blood.

Why? Why would someone do that?

How could someone snatch away these young lives like that?

These girls had been cheated out of their chances for a life ahead of them, like Caitlin had been, by a person who murdered just for the thrill of it.

I couldn't do anything about that now. But I still had a chance to find justice for all of them.

And to make sure there weren't more victims.

Like Becky Benedict.

Jessica Staley.

Carolyn Garms.

Like all six of these new cases.

And yes, like my sister too.

FORTY-SEVEN

There was a surprise waiting for me when I showed up at the Huntsdale station house the next morning. A good surprise. Someone was talking to Chief Earnshaw in his office. When I got closer, I saw who it was. None other than my favorite police chief, Connor Nolan.

What was he doing here?

"The link from the DNA being found at both crime scenes changes everything now," Nolan said to me when I talked with him and Earnshaw.

"Chief Nolan and I are going to coordinate our investigations going forward," Earnshaw said. "We know now—or at least we believe strongly based on the evidence in Zanesville— that the same person committed both murders. And likely more too, because of the notes he sent claiming responsibility for Garms and others."

"We think working together—and merging the resources and manpower of our police forces—makes the most sense," Nolan said.

He was right about that.

Of course, I was glad he was here for other reasons too.

And it would definitely make my job easier if I didn't have to worry about shuttling between Huntsdale and Dorchester for a while.

"How long?" I asked.

"Excuse me?"

"How long do you expect to be here in Huntsdale?"

"We'll see how things go. There's nothing more important than these cases right now. My people back in Dorchester—like Donald Maris, you know him—can handle the routine crime stuff until I get back. This is a once in a lifetime law enforcement opportunity. A chance to finally get justice for Becky Benedict and solve—plus maybe prevent—a series of new murders by the same person. I want to be a part of that."

Edgar Daniels came in then. Earnshaw introduced him to Nolan and said he had been working with us on the cases too.

"All the resources of the Huntsdale Police Department are available to help us on this, Chief Nolan."

"Great, let's get to work!" Nolan said.

We all walked to the "war room" I'd set up at the Huntsdale station. Me, Alex, Phil, Earnshaw, Daniels and Nolan. Earnshaw and I told Nolan in great detail everything we knew so far, concluding with more specific details about the DNA we found in Zanesville, which matched that from the trash bin burial site of Becky Benedict all those years earlier.

"The Staley girl was at the Zanesville motel," I said. "I'm sure she was there with her killer. But we don't have any actual proof of that. No one saw anyone with her while she was there. At least no one we found or talked to. The owner/manager of the place was the only person we could find there. I think he runs it pretty much all by himself, and he claims he only saw the girl when she registered. We also have no idea why Staley stayed there, why she was apparently willingly traveling with the man who would later kill her and, maybe most significantly of all, why she signed in at the Garden Island Motel as Becky Benedict."

At some point, Earnshaw and Daniels left to take care of some other business. Eventually, Alex and Phil were gone too. Leaving me alone with Connor Nolan, surrounded by all the pictures and documents and notes about the murders.

"Did Earnshaw suggest the joint task force?" I asked him. "Or did the idea of you in Huntsdale come from you?"

"It was my idea. But he agreed right away. It's a good idea. The best way to handle all of this."

"Any other motivation for you wanting to be in Huntsdale?"

"Actually, the answer to that is yes."

"What's the reason?"

"I was worried about you."

"Worried how?"

"There's a crazy killer out there who has you in his sights. He seems fixated on you for some reason. No one knows who he is. But we know this puts you in danger. A lot of danger. The last one to die, he said that would be you, Nikki. Do you know how terrifying a thought that is? Tell me about the car that tried to run you down? Earnshaw just told me about that."

I gave him the details of what happened in the parking lot of the bar and our search for the car that hit me.

"My God, Nikki."

"I'm fine."

"You're in danger here."

"But now you're here to protect me, huh?"

"I'll do my best."

I shook my head. "I'm fine, and I don't need you to protect me just because I'm a woman. My ex-fiancé used to do that too, he wound up smothering me. Yes, it scares me. But I'm a trained FBI agent. I guess I should be grateful for your concern, but it seems a bit sexist to me. Would you be so worried if I was a man?"

"Probably not."

"Okay." I smiled. "Glad we resolved that. Any other reason you decided to leave Dorchester and come here?"

"Such as?"

"Well, we did have sex in Dorchester, Connor. Or did you forget?"

"Oh, I'd never forget something like that."

"Is that one of the reasons you're here?"

"To have sex with you?"

"Yes."

Alex and Phil were walking back to the war room. We could hear their footsteps in the hall outside. Connor moved closer to me so they couldn't hear what we were saying once they walked in.

"We have to be professional about this," he whispered.

"Professional?"

"That's right. We can't let our personal feelings get in the way of us doing our job as law enforcement officers."

"Of course not."

"So we have to remain professional, okay?"

"Totally professional, Connor."

"Or at least make it look professional." He smiled.

FORTY-EIGHT

Connor and I made love again that night.

No big surprise there. I was pretty sure it was going to happen, and I guess he was too. No late-night knocks on my door this time or frantic disrobing and jumping into bed. This was more comfortable and leisurely and... well, even nicer than the first time.

All four of us—me, Connor, Alex and Phil—had eaten dinner together at the Italian place that Alex and I had taken Phil to the night he got here. We all had quite a bit to drink, trying to relax I suppose after all the stress we'd been under. Except for Connor. He was still drinking nothing but Perrier water. I wondered what that was really all about. But I'd already asked him about not drinking back in Dorchester, and he'd been kind of evasive in his answer. So I didn't push it. Maybe he was an alcoholic on the wagon. Maybe he was simply trying to stay alert and healthy. Or maybe he simply liked Perrier water.

When we got back to the hotel, Alex and Phil headed for their respective rooms. Connor stayed with me while I took the elevator to the floor where my room was.

Alex knew what was happening between Connor and me, I could tell from the look on her face. I wasn't sure whether Phil had picked up on it. Probably didn't care much one way or the other. He had a *New York Times* crossword puzzle under his arm, and he said he was going to start working on it as soon as he left us.

I wondered at one point if Connor Nolan had really come to Huntsdale for this purpose of being with me, not only because of the DNA match with the Becky Benedict case. He could have still worked on that with us from back in Dorchester. Didn't have to show up in person. But I was glad that he was here. And I was glad to realize he probably wouldn't have made the trip if it was only Alex and Phil here to meet him.

The lovemaking was slower and more intimate than last time. There's always a bit of nervousness and some urgency the first time you have sex with someone. No one is quite sure how it's going to work out. Now it was better. We were more familiar with each other, and more familiar with each other's bodies. More like a real relationship instead of a couple of people who simply jumped into bed together in a moment of passion.

Afterward, we lay in each other's arms, talking about a lot of stuff. Some of it about the case, some other things too. Like when we looked over at a nightstand by the bed and saw that we'd piled our guns, badges and handcuffs on it when we disrobed.

"Definitely looks like two law enforcement types that were having sex here, huh?" Connor said.

"Or else a couple of really kinky people who like to play with handcuffs and guns in bed."

"Did you ever?"

"Did I ever what?"

"Play any games like that to spice up your sex life?"

"Well, I did meet a guy once who wanted me to handcuff him spread-eagled to the bed and have my way with him."

"Did you do it?"

"I have the right to remain silent. If I decide to forgo that right, I have the right for a lawyer to be present before I answer that question."

He laughed. "My wife used to like to play some fantasy games when we were married. Like I'd stop her for a driving violation, and then she'd made love with me as a police officer. Believe it or not, that's how we met. I stopped her after she went through a stop sign. Later, we started dating. So it was fun to play it out as a fantasy thing after she was my wife."

His wife.

His damn wife again. She was dead, but she still seemed to be there on his mind a lot.

"Do you want to talk about this more at any point?" I asked.

"What?"

"Your wife."

"No."

"You brought her up, not me."

"That was a mistake. I shouldn't have mentioned her. Let's change the subject of conversation, okay?"

We talked about the case for a while. I told him more about Phil's theory on the killer's profile—a Svengali-like figure who convinced troubled teen girls like Becky Benedict and Jessica Staley to leave home and to follow him.

"Of course, that doesn't fit the mode of the last killing. The Garms girl. It sounds like she just got grabbed from the school bus after the field trip, then immediately murdered. Nothing Svengali about that. An old-fashioned abduction and murder. The question is why now? Why start doing it all over again all these years later after he killed Becky Benedict?"

"There could be more, right?"

"We're looking into that now. The people back in Washington have been checking a lot of cases around the country. Looking for similarities. It would make sense if there are more victims like this. We've already found about a half dozen murders that seem to fit the pattern."

"I'm talking about more killers than one. What do you think about that idea?"

"It's a possibility."

"Murders twenty years apart. Different locations. Different states even. Maybe there is more than one killer. Maybe they know what the other one is doing and has done in the past. Maybe they're even working together. A serial killing team of people—not just one crazy, screwed up guy."

I thought about The Nowhere Men. The website that Tommy Thompson—the man who murdered my sister—had operated with other sick men that preyed on young girls. Murdered them, made snuff films of their deaths and then sold these horrifying videos on the sexual black market. Thompson was dead now. And we'd closed down the site. But were there more of them—more Nowhere Men like Thompson—still running around free out there?

"That's a very scary thought," I said.

"Don't worry, you'll figure it all out."

"We'll figure it out."

"You and me together." He smiled.

He kissed me again then. I kissed him back. One thing quickly led to another after that. And very quickly we were back to the lovemaking.

It was nice.

Really nice.

So nice that I almost forgot about the murder—or murderers —who were still free stalking young girls.

And it was so damn nice I almost forget about my questions about Connor Nolan's wife too.

Almost.

FORTY-NINE

"We just got a complaint about you," Dave Blanton said to me on the phone.

"What kind of complaint?"

"Unprofessional behavior."

"Who was I unprofessional with?"

"Chief Frank Earnshaw."

"Oh."

"Were you unprofessional with him?"

"Probably."

"Nikki..."

"What does he say?"

"That you're verbally abusive, uncooperative and treat him like he's some kind of an idiot instead of giving him the respect he deserves as the town's chief law enforcement officer."

"He is some kind of an idiot."

"I'm trying to keep this whole thing under control, Nikki. Can't you try to help me do that?"

I sighed. I'd been having problems with Earnshaw ever since I came back to Huntsdale to investigate my sister's death.

But this was worse than that. Going over my head to Washington to try to complain about me was a new low.

"So Earnshaw filed an official complaint with the bureau against me?"

"Uh, huh."

"And?"

"It made its way through the system to me today. Imagine my surprise when I heard about it. I thought you were getting along with him better. That's what you told me anyway."

"It was the other police chief I was getting along with. Connor Nolan, the one from Dorchester."

As soon as the words came out of my mouth, I knew it was probably not a good idea to say that to Blanton. But fortunately, he didn't pick up on anything.

"What is Earnshaw asking you to do?" I asked him.

"He wants me to fire you or, at the very least, pull you out of there and let Alex and Phil handle the case from here on in."

"Are you going to do that?"

"No. I do not take my orders from local police chiefs. I deploy my people the way I feel will be the most effective on a case. And that, right now, means keeping you on the job. So you're staying in Huntsdale."

"What do I do about Earnshaw in the meantime?"

"Be nice to him."

"That's not going to be easy."

"Do your best."

I walked into Earnshaw's office a few minutes later, shut the door and sat down in front of his desk. "I understand you've been complaining about me to my boss," I said.

"Damned straight I did."

"It didn't work."

"Huh?"

"He's not pulling me off the case."

Earnshaw didn't say anything to that, he just glared at me across the desk.

"Look," I said, "I'd like to try and let bygones be bygones. Start over fresh. Establish a solid, professional working relationship between you and me, Chief Earnshaw."

Be nice, Blanton had said. So I was trying my best to be nice.

"What do you think?" I asked him.

"What do I think? I think you're an embarrassment to the FBI. I think you're a joke. I think you should stop trying to do a man's job and go be a mother or a housewife or something where a woman belongs. I don't like women in the FBI. I don't like women on my police force. I don't like women in law enforcement at all. And I especially don't like you. This is my town, not yours. So just stay out of my way, you bitch!"

I guess Earnshaw was expecting me to blow my top at him again. But I didn't do that. Instead, I just smiled at him when he'd finished his diatribe against me and women in general.

"I guess we're past the point of letting bygones be bygones," I said.

"Get the hell out of my office."

I did. I left and headed back to the war room.

There was just no being nice to this guy.

FIFTY

"They found the car that hit you," Alex said to me when I got to the station house the next day.

"Where?"

"A parking garage about a mile away from the bar. One of the attendants noticed it had gone unclaimed by anyone from the garage, and he recognized it from the FBI bulletin looking for a white Honda or Toyota with damage to the front."

"Anything inside that tells us who was driving?" I asked, even though I was pretty sure there wouldn't be.

"That's all I know at the moment. Some of Huntsdale's finest are checking the vehicle out now."

"Let's go join them."

The parking lot was next to a strip mall of about a dozen stores outside downtown Huntsdale. It was twelve stories high, and the car was on the top floor. It was the only one up that high, and I wondered if that was deliberate by whoever left it so no one would have noticed it for a while.

I was right about the model. The car was a 2020 white

Toyota Camry. The entry ticket on the dashboard said it had checked in at 9:15 on the night I was hit, a short time after the incident at the bar. The driver must have gone directly here to get rid of the car before anyone spotted him in it. Did he have this parking space picked out in advance before he made a run at me? Or was it a spur of the moment decision to leave it here?

I looked at the car more closely and saw that the left front headlight was broken and there was a significant ding on the fender next to it where he had hit me. It made me realize how close I could have come to being seriously injured—or even killed—if the car had hit me head-on instead.

Somebody had already opened the trunk. It was empty except for a spare tire and a jack. Daniels was there, watching it all.

"License plate check?" I asked him, looking at the plates. They were from Indiana, not Ohio.

"Stolen. The plates were reported taken off a vehicle in Indianapolis a while ago. The car was stolen too."

"Big surprise," I said.

"Yeah, the car was snatched out of some guy's driveway in Macksburg a couple of towns away from here a few hours before it hit you. The real owner's registration and insurance cards were found in the glove compartment. We contacted him, and he told us how he'd reported the theft to the local police after it went missing. He's very happy we found it."

"I'll bet. And, of course, he has no idea who stole the car."

"Not a clue."

I turned to the garage attendant who had been listening to all this. "Is there any surveillance video?" I asked him.

"Nothing."

"No video camera?"

"The one on that floor is broken."

"How long has it been broken?"

"We found out it wasn't working when we checked it now," he said, pointing to a camera above us.

"Of course."

"You figure the driver of this car broke it deliberately so no one could identify him?" one of the Huntsdale cops asked.

"Either him or her."

"Are you saying this could be a woman?"

"I'm an equal opportunity crime fighter."

"I figure the driver was a man."

"Yeah, me too," I said.

We did get a break though. The car had a GPS device. Not a phone or anything that was removable, this was part of the car's audio system—the way they used to install GPS a few years ago —so it couldn't be removed by the driver before fleeing.

"We should be able to tell from this exactly where this car has been," I said.

One of the Huntsdale cops pulled up the list of destinations from the GPS. Most of them—the older ones—were clearly from the owner of the car as they were in the Macksburg area. Including his home address.

There were three destinations listed after that. One was the address of the bar where the driver had been waiting for me in the parking lot. That made sense. The address before that was the cemetery. That one made sense too. But the final address was a surprise.

"It's in Huntsdale," Alex said when she checked it out. "A familiar address too."

I looked at it again.

She was right, I recognized it too.

It was the address for the Huntsdale police station.

"I guess the driver and the car could have been there trying to pick up your trail, since that was a likely place to find you," Alex said.

"That's one possibility." I looked over at the Huntsdale cops, then back at Alex. "Can we step away for a second?" I said to her.

We walked over to a corner of the garage away from the Huntsdale police officers and others standing around the car.

"Okay, what is the other possible reason the police station shows up on this Toyota's GPS?" Alex asked, although I was pretty sure she already knew what my answer to that was going to be.

"The guy behind the wheel of the car that tried to run me down worked at the goddammed Huntsdale police station."

"Jeez, now you're really getting paranoid, Nikki."

"I might be paranoid," I said, "but that doesn't mean there's not someone here in Huntsdale out to get me."

FIFTY-ONE

"Is it true that you have linked the murders of two teenage girls more than twenty years apart?" a reporter yelled out to me.

"Why did no one ever detect a connection between Becky Benedict and Jessica Staley until now?" another wanted to know.

"How does the murder of Carolyn Garms fit into all this?"

"Agent Cassidy, is there any connection between all of this and the murder of your sister here in Huntsdale?"

The questions came fast and furious at a press conference we held, and most of them were directed at me. Chief Earnshaw, Alex, Phil, Chief Nolan, Mayor Harris and several other political leaders and members of the Huntsdale police force were there. But I was the center of attention, which is what happens when you become a high-profile media figure, like I had somehow become.

We'd tried to keep this all under wraps from the media for as long as we could. But there was only so long we could do it. And we were at that point now. We needed to go public with even the sensationalist and scary parts of the investigation. Yes, it made my job even tougher in some ways. But maybe it could help us to get some tips to catch the killer. And maybe, just maybe, this publicity could be a warning to other girls out there in time to save their own lives.

I went through everything we knew so far about the murders—and also what we did not know.

"The FBI—working in conjunction with local police departments in Huntsdale and also in the town of Dorchester, Pennsylvania—has recently confirmed that a DNA sample found at the murder of Becky Benedict twenty years ago in Dorchester matches DNA found in a motel where fourteen-year-old Jessica Staley stayed in Zanesville, Ohio, several days before her murdered body turned up here in Huntsdale.

"The obvious conclusion from this is that both girls were murdered by the same person—twenty years apart and in different locations hundreds of miles away from each other.

"A third teenage girl, Carolyn Garms, was murdered here recently, and we are still attempting to see if there was any substantive link—DNA or otherwise—between this and the other murders.

"I can also tell you that someone has been sending messages to law enforcement—specifically directed at me—claiming responsibility for all three of the murders. This person has also claimed to have killed other teenage girls in the past. We have no independent confirmation of these claims, but we are pursuing all the evidence in an attempt to determine the truth of these messages.

"In addition, based on this new information, we have begun at the bureau an examination of other unsolved murders of teenage girls around the country that might fit the same pattern as Becky Benedict and Jessica Staley. So far we have discovered six cases that possibly—I emphasize the word possibly—could fit the criteria of being committed by the same person or persons.

And we are continuing to look at more cases as we expand our investigation to see if there are more beyond these six unsolved murders."

There was an audible gasp from the people in the media.

"A serial killer?" someone said.

"You think someone has killed a number of teenage girls over a period of years?"

"You said 'person or persons.' Do you believe there is more than one killer at work out there, Agent Cassidy?"

I answered the questions as best I could. A few times I deflected specific questions over to Chief Frank Earnshaw or Chief Connor Nolan to answer when it concerned their towns and their police forces.

Earnshaw, Nolan and Alex talked a bit about how Benedict and Staley had both seemed to leave willingly with their captors more than twenty years apart—and urged parents to look for any suspicious signs of activity like that in their daughters that might lead someone to target them in the same way.

Still, most of the media questions kept coming back to me.

"Agent Cassidy, there have only been a handful of murders in Huntsdale over the years, none of them involving teenage girls, until your sister's death," one reporter said. "Now, since you've been back here in recent months, three more girls have been found murdered and another abducted and nearly killed. Can you tell us why this is happening?"

"I cannot."

"Do these murders have anything to do with your sister's murder?" someone else asked.

"My sister was murdered by former Huntsdale District Attorney Tommy Thompson for sick reasons known only to himself. Thompson also murdered my father, the police chief back then. Since Thompson is dead now too, he took a lot of his secrets to the grave with him.

"He was part of an online group of male predators of young girls. They called themselves The Nowhere Men, and made snuff videos of the girls they killed—like my sister—for sale on the Dark Web. It is possible that some of these people from The Nowhere Men are still out there. We have been—and are continuing—to actively look for them. So far, there has been no evidence of a connection between The Nowhere Men and these other murders. That's all I can tell you at the moment. We will continue to keep you informed as more details of the investigation become clearer."

I knew that wasn't going to satisfy anyone, but it was the best I could do.

It was almost time to end this. I'd survived the press conference, and I'd managed to deal with the worst of the questions the reporters could ask.

Or so I thought.

But then one of the reporters suddenly looked down at his phone, and saw something new on the screen. "We just got a bulletin from TMZ about something else breaking on this case," the reporter said to me. "It's a picture. A picture of you, Agent Cassidy. You and Dorchester Police Chief Connor Nolan. It's very interesting. Do you want to check it out, and explain to us what's going on in this picture?"

I clicked on my phone and went to the TMZ site. I saw it right away at the top of the site with a big headline. Everyone else at the press conference had seen it too by this point. I looked at the site in stunned shock. I wasn't sure what I was expecting to find on TMZ, but it sure as hell wasn't this.

There was a picture of Connor and me at the elevator in my hotel. I was either on my way from or on my way to my room, I wasn't exactly sure when the picture had been taken.

Not that it really mattered.

What mattered was what Connor Nolan and I were doing.

We were kissing.

The headline above the picture said: MURDER CASE REALLY HEATS UP FOR SEXY STAR FEMALE FBI AGENT.

FIFTY-TWO

"How in the hell did this happen?" I asked Alex.

"You tell me."

"Okay, I kissed Connor Nolan. And someone took a picture of me doing it. That's all I know. End of story."

"Not quite the whole story."

"What do you mean?"

"You slept with him too."

"I sure hope no one got pictures of us in bed."

"How many times have you slept with him?"

"Uh, twice."

"Twice," Alex repeated, shaking her head.

"So far."

"Jeez."

"What's your point?"

"The point is you're in some trouble here, Nikki."

She was right about that. We'd gone back to her room because I was afraid the media might come looking for me in mine. Same if we went to a bar or back to the Huntsdale station house. I'd slipped back to the hotel as soon as the press conference was over. That's where Alex had met up with me. I'd only had a brief text exchange with Connor, telling him we'd have to talk more later. That ought to be some interesting conversation.

But the conversation I was really dreading was the one I had to have with Dave Blanton. I kept checking my phone because I expected to hear from him at any moment. Of course, he might not have heard about the press conference yet, so I could call him to break the news. But I decided it was better to wait and let him explode at me later, rather than igniting the explosion myself. Either way, it was going to be bad. For a guy who was so obsessed with agents following the rules and guidelines strictly by the book, I figured me having sex with a local police chief on the case I was assigned to was not going to go over well.

"Are there specific rules about doing this kind of thing?" I asked Alex.

"I have no idea."

"That could be my defense."

"That no one told you not to screw a local law enforcement official while you're working a case? That's your defense?"

I suddenly remembered an episode of *Seinfeld* I'd always loved. In the show, George Costanza is confronted by his boss who says he just found out George had sex with a cleaning woman on his desk. "Was that wrong?" George asks. "If I had any idea that kind of thing was frowned on..." I also remembered though that George got fired by his boss. I hoped that didn't happen with me.

"What do you think is going to happen with Blanton?" I asked Alex.

"There're a lot of possibilities."

"He'll yell at me, right?"

"Definitely."

"Suspend me?"

"Possibly."

"Pull me off the case? Reprimand me? Maybe even fire me?"

Before she could answer, my phone buzzed. I looked down at the screen. It was from FBI Headquarters in Washington. Dave Blanton. Time for me to face the music.

He was more controlled than I expected. At least at first.

"Tell me what happened."

"I met up at the hotel bar with a local police chief. The guy from Dorchester. Connor Nolan. I meet up in bars with a lot of people."

"You don't kiss them all, do you?"

"No. But Connor Nolan kissed me. And then I kissed him back. These things happen sometimes."

"Any idea how TMZ just happened to get a picture of it?"

"They've been interested in me since this case began. Remember the piece about the "star agent" in Dorchester when I first went there? I guess they see me as good copy. A high-profile media subject, or whatever, that they can use to boost online traffic or whatever they do."

"Great, I have a celebrity agent on the case."

"I'm not really a celebrity."

"You said you were a high-profile media subject."

"Okay, but I'm not exactly like Kim Kardashian or anything."

I knew there was a big question he still wanted to ask. And he did that now.

"What else do I need to know?"

"Well, there's been some interesting developments in the case—"

"About you and this police chief."

"Oh, that."

"Did you have sex with him?"

"I did."

"That night the picture was taken?"

"Not sure."

"But you did have sex with him?"

"Yes."

"Was that the only time you had sex with him?"

"No, we had another sexual event too."

There was a long silence on the phone.

"I think we have to pull you out of there and bring you back to Washington," Blanton said.

"You can't do that."

"What choice do I have?"

"I'm the only one who can crack this case, Chief."

"You don't trust Agents Del Vecchio and Girard to do a good job there without you?"

"Of course, I do. But the killer has targeted me for some reason. He's sending messages to me. He's talking to me, not to the others. It's all been directed at me. He's made this personal. I think he wants to make me his ultimate target. His last kill. That's what he said in one of the messages. We can use that, Chief. We can use that to give us the best chance to catch him. But only if I'm here to keep on drawing his attention."

"You want to stay there as bait for this guy."

"It makes the most sense." I believed that. I only hoped it made sense to Blanton too.

"What about the cop?"

"I'll stay away from him."

"Tell him to go back to Dorchester."

"Understood, Chief."

"Whatever you do, you can't work with him anymore. He has to deal with Alex or Phil."

"He went for it?" Alex asked after I hung up with Blanton.

"Yes, for now anyway."

"So you're really going to let yourself be a target in the hopes this crazy guy tries to kill you for real this time?"

"That's how I convinced Blanton to let me stay here."

"Lucky you," Alex said.

FIFTY-THREE

I couldn't rely on Connor Nolan anymore for help because of our personal entanglements. And I sure couldn't rely on Chief Earnshaw or the Huntsdale Police Department with my growing doubts about them.

If there was one person in Huntsdale I thought I could trust besides the members of my team, it was Mayor Stacy Harris. I'm not exactly sure why I trusted her. I'd only met her a couple of times in my life, and I really didn't know too much about her. But she was a woman, which helped when it came to looking for someone to trust who I was pretty sure wasn't a murderer of teenage girls. She was relatively new to Huntsdale, which meant she'd had less of an opportunity to become involved in any wrongdoing or corruption here. She was black, the first African-American mayor in Huntsdale history, which seemed like a positive thing too. She'd helped me out when I first went to her with my suspicions about Tommy Thompson. And she'd been the one who called me back to Huntsdale by alerting me about Jessica Staley's body being found. All in all, that seemed to qualify her as a candidate for earning my trust.

We met up and I told her about the information on the GPS

device in the stolen car that had hit me—and some of the concerns I had about the Huntsdale Police Department.

"We had a similar conversation not long ago about Huntsdale law enforcement when you came to me during the investigation of your sister's death," she pointed out.

"I was right about Tommy Thompson, the D.A."

"Yes, you were. And now you have questions about the police department. I hope you're wrong. The D.A.'s office and the police department... I don't even want to think about that."

"I hope it's not true too, Mayor."

She sighed deeply. She really didn't want to have this conversation with me, but she knew she had to. "Look," she said, "I know you've had your problems with Chief Earnshaw. But I find it difficult to believe he would—"

"This isn't necessarily about Chief Earnshaw."

"But you said the police."

"It could be anyone at the station." I mentioned Phil Girard's theory that the killer could be someone in uniform. Someone like a police officer. Someone a young girl might trust. Someone she could feel safe with until it all turned bad.

"Do you really think that the killer is someone in our police department?" she asked when I was finished.

"I'm saying I have questions about the Huntsdale force."

"Questions you want me to ask?"

"Yes. It would be easier for you to ask these questions than me."

"Who do I ask?"

"Start with Chief Earnshaw."

"But—"

"Earnshaw won't talk with me about something like this. But you're the mayor. He has to talk to you."

"And you think he'll tell me the truth about anything he knows."

"I hope so. Hey, Earnshaw's an ass. But he's probably not

the bad guy we're looking for. Someone else there might be. So if we have to talk to Earnshaw to get some answers, we do that. And you're the one to do it, Mayor Harris."

After I left Mayor Harris's office, I felt better. A little better anyway. And I also remembered someone else in town I trusted. Michael (Big Mickey) Franze, the Medical Examiner, and a good friend of my father's.

"Who would have thought we'd have had all these murders in this quiet little town?" he asked when I talked with him in the ME's office. "I thought I'd seen everything the last time you were here. But now you're back again. And more teenage girls are dead." He said his office had done the autopsies on both Jessica Staley and Carolyn Garms. "I guess that's what you came to see me about, huh, Nikki?"

"I've already read the autopsy reports."

"No questions?"

"I think the autopsies pretty much speak for themselves. You always do a good autopsy report, Mickey."

He smiled. He'd been so close to my family when I was growing up. That's why I was here now.

I told him my suspicions about the police force. I said I didn't have anything specific except for the GPS tracking on the white Toyota, which listed the Huntsdale police station as one of the places the car had been. But I said I wasn't sure I could trust Earnshaw or anyone else in the department completely at this point.

"Once, I would have said you are being totally paranoid about the Huntsdale police," Franze said. "But after Tommy Thompson?" He shook his head sadly. "I mean, who could have ever imagined the district attorney was a serial killer? I guess that anything is possible, Nikki."

"Can you check around for me? Discreetly, of course. Let me know if you find out anything at all?"

"I'll see what I can do."

I had one more thing I wanted to ask Franze.

About another murder case he was involved in.

A long time ago.

The death of my sister Caitlin.

The last time I'd been in Huntsdale I'd talked with him while I was investigating my sister's murder, and I figured out in the end how Tommy Thompson had done it. Franze had been friendly and cooperative, even if he had not been able to help me much. At least, not about questions I still had about what my father knew—or didn't know—about Caitlin's death. There were pages missing—about a half dozen—from my father's final police report on Caitlin's death and his investigation at the time, and I thought then that Franze might be able to shed some light on this, but he couldn't.

Still, I figured it was worth asking him again.

"What does your sister's murder have to do with this?"

"I don't know."

"Then why are you bringing it up again?"

"I'm still bothered by the missing pages in my father's report I asked you about last time I was here."

He shook his head. "I told you then, Nikki, I don't know what happened to those pages. Or why they're missing. The only person who presumably knew that was your father. He never mentioned anything about it to me."

"I understand. I just wanted to ask you again."

"But what could that possibly have to do with these new murders?"

"I have no idea," I said.

The last person I went to talk to that day was the toughest conversation I needed to have.

It was with Connor Nolan.

I knew it wasn't going to be easy. But it had to be done.

"You need to go back to Dorchester," I told him.

"I'm not going back to Dorchester yet."

"My boss said I needed to convince you to do that."

"I don't work for your boss."

"Well, you can't be part of our investigation here anymore."

"I can help, Nikki. I have helped you. And I want to keep on helping you."

"Don't you understand the position I'm in, Connor? My career is on the line. Maybe you don't care about your career, but I care about mine. We can't be working together anymore. It would turn into a friggin' sideshow. All about us having sex, not about the case. My boss isn't going to let that happen. I'm not going to let that happen."

Connor didn't say anything at first, just looked at me sadly. "Would it make any difference if I told you I loved you?" he said finally.

I stared at him. "Are you in love with me?"

"Are you in love with me, Nikki?"

"I don't know, Connor. We really don't know each other well enough yet for me to answer something like that."

"Which is why we should keep on seeing each other."

"I can't do that."

"Is your career that important to you?"

"It's not only my career. It's the cases of these young girls. I need to solve them. And I need to be in the FBI to do that. My boss won't let me stay on the job here if you're with me. So there's no decision to be made. I have to focus on catching the killer. That's my priority right now."

"And when that's over?"

"We'll see..."

FIFTY-FOUR

My immediate priority—as I told Mayor Harris—was to check out everyone at the Huntsdale police station, and make sure I didn't find anything, or anyone, suspicious. Maybe I *was* being paranoid, but I wanted to be sure. So I asked Phil and Alex to do some checking too—just like I'd asked Harris and Franze—into the people we were working with on the Huntsdale police force.

And Alex came up with something.

"Eighteen months ago, a police officer—now on the Huntsdale police force—was arrested on suspicion of child abuse," Alex told Phil and me. "Guess who that police officer was?"

"Frank Earnshaw?" I asked. I didn't figure that was the right answer, but I could always hope it turned out like that.

"Edgar Daniels."

Edgar Daniels? The genial, long-haired older guy that we'd been working with? That seemed hard to believe. You never know about some people though. And I had wondered what happened in Columbus that wound up with Daniels leaving for a job in a much smaller town and smaller police force.

"The girl was a runaway. At least that's what she claimed

when they found her. She went to high school in the Columbus area. Was reported missing by her parents a few weeks earlier. Everyone was looking for her. Then the Columbus police found her with... well, one of their own. A neighbor saw a girl in the window at Daniels' house, called police and they found her inside. Daniels was arrested on charges of kidnapping, child abuse and sexual abuse. But the girl insisted she was there voluntarily. And that she and Daniels had never had sexual relations of any kind."

"There was no evidence of sexual activities with the other girls either," I pointed out.

"Yeah, I know."

"So what happened?"

"Eventually all the legal charges were dropped because the girl wouldn't bring any charges against Daniels. Like I said, she claimed she was there voluntarily. Said she'd been on the street once before, Daniels had helped her then—so she looked him up when she ran away again. There was no kidnap and no sex or child abuse of any kind to charge the guy with."

"But that's what must have cost him his job on the Columbus police force, right?"

"Duh, it sure did. I mean he'd violated all sorts of rules and regulations. And then not telling anyone when the whole city was out looking for the girl. They might not have been able to charge him with anything legally in court, but they weren't going to keep him on the force. He got canned immediately, no doubt about it from the records I read."

"Interesting," Phil said.

"Damn interesting," I agreed. "But how in the hell did he wind up on the Huntsdale police force with a background like that?"

"That's where it gets even more interesting. Your buddy Chief Earnshaw made it happen. Gave him the job as soon as he applied. Even with all that on his record."

"Any idea why?"

"They were friends."

"Earnshaw and Daniels?"

"Uh, huh."

"How did that come about?"

"From the Columbus force. Earnshaw worked there too. He told me once before this latest stuff started that he and Daniels were partners on the street in Columbus at one point. So when Earnshaw needed someone for Huntsdale after Billy Weller died, it made sense that he picked his old buddy. Despite what he knew had happened in Columbus."

"Awfully nice of him."

"Well, Daniels was his partner."

"I'm your partner. Would you do that for me if I had a record of wrongdoing?"

"Depends what you did wrong?"

"Well, there's only one way to find out why Earnshaw did what he did."

"Ask him?"

"You got it. This should be fun," I said.

On the way to Earnshaw's office, we passed by Daniels sitting at his desk. Looking pretty much the same way I'd seen him before. Long hair, a few too many pounds around the middle, a middle-aged guy working at a small-town police station in the twilight of his law enforcement career.

But what if there was more about Edgar Daniels that we didn't know? What if he had a fascination with young girls like the one he brought into his house in Columbus?

Yes, she said she'd gone there voluntarily with him. But Becky Benedict and Jessica Staley and girls like that seemingly went with their abductors the same way for some unexplained reason.

What if Edgar Daniels was the man we were looking for?

The man in authority that got young girls to feel safe with him.

The police officer that befriends them in their time of need.

We didn't go through all our suspicions with Chief Frank Earnshaw when we met with him though. We simply told him how we'd been checking on the backgrounds of numerous people here in Huntsdale, including members of his force. That's when we found out about Edgar Daniels' controversial departure from the Columbus force after the discovery of the young girl in his house. And then how he came to join the Huntsdale police force after that.

"Edgar Daniels is here because I brought him here," Earnshaw said when we were done. "I wanted him on my force. Edgar is a good man. I know that better than anyone. I was his partner. You get to know your partner as a police officer on the street. I got to know Edgar really well. I wished I could have brought him here when I first got the job as chief, but there were no openings. Then, when Billy Weller got killed, I went back to Edgar and offered him Billy Weller's job. He accepted, and he's been here ever since. He's done a fine job too. That's all there is to tell you."

"You weren't bothered by the incident with the girl?" Alex asked.

"He was cleared of the charges."

"But he still lost his job in Columbus because of it."

"And now he's investigating the murders of young girls here," Phil said.

I didn't say anything, because I knew I would piss off Earnshaw even more if I did. Better to let Alex and Phil handle most of this with him.

"That was then, this is now," Earnshaw said. "There's no

connection to what happened with him in Columbus." He shook his head. "Look, here's the truth about that girl in Columbus. Edgar found out—we all found out later—that her stepfather was forcing her to have sex with her at home. That's why she ran away the first time. She thought he might stop after that, but he didn't. So she went back to the man, to the police officer, who had helped her before. Edgar Daniels. And he helped her again. He kept her safe from her stepfather. Even at the expense of his career. He knew what he was doing was wrong, but he cared about saving the girl. That's why he did what he did. To help that girl. That's all there was to it."

"It still was a pretty stupid thing to do," I told Earnshaw.

"Edgar knows that now."

"So you gave him a second chance?"

"Everyone deserves a second chance, Cassidy."

FIFTY-FIVE

A murder investigation can turn out to be funny sometimes. Well, not funny, I suppose. It is murder we're talking about here. I guess I mean a murder investigation can turn out to be strange. Or unusual. Maybe even shocking.

You see, the thing is with a murder investigation that you follow the evidence.

You follow the evidence wherever it takes you.

And sometimes that can be surprising places.

It's not always a straight-forward trip either. You can follow the evidence in a case and find nothing that will help you in the investigation. But then, after going in a different direction and finding a different kind of evidence, you double back on the first track and find out more that is new and significant. One bit of evidence can lead to more evidence in an area or a place you never expected.

A murder investigation—and the evidence you find in it—is never static. It is always changing.

I learned that lesson a long time ago when I was starting out my career as an FBI agent—and I'd seen the phenomenon play out many times in my investigations since then.

Just like it did now with this one.

We had someone now, we had a specific person in Edgar Daniels who we were trying to find out more about. And so we needed to go back to some of the places we'd checked out before. Only this time we had more specific questions. Questions about Daniels and how he might be connected with Jessica Staley, Carolyn Garms or Becky Benedict, or any of the other young girls who had gone missing and later turned up dead.

Alex and I managed to get a picture of Daniels from the station—without telling anyone there what we wanted it for—and began showing it around to some of the places we had visited. Eventually, we made it all the way back to Zanesville—the town not far away where Jessica Staley had registered under the name of Becky Benedict at the Garden Island Motel right before her body was found in Huntsdale.

Lester Eldridge, the owner/manager we'd met before, was on duty again in the front office. Maybe he was the only one who was ever on duty. He was wearing another shirt with a food stain on the front. Then I realized it probably was not another shirt. It was the same shirt. He'd never changed it. Classy guy.

Eldridge wasn't happy to see Alex and me again, he made that clear. But he didn't really have much choice except to talk with us. We told him we could either talk informally there or we'd take him back somewhere else for more official questioning. He agreed to talk to us there.

I took out a picture of Edgar Daniels and showed it to him. "Have you ever seen this man before?" I asked.

"Who is he?"

"Doesn't matter," said Alex. "Just tell us if he looks familiar or not to you."

He looked at the picture of Daniels for a long time. I

thought at first he might be screwing with us, trying to waste our time because he was pissed at having to talk to us. But then he looked back at me and Alex, and he nodded.

"Yes, I remember him."

"How?" I asked.

"He was here at the motel."

"As a guest?"

"No. At least he never registered or anything. But I saw him outside one of the rooms. Standing by the door. He was smoking a cigarette. Then he opened the door and went back inside. I didn't think it was important. Is it?"

"Do you know who was staying in the room where he was standing outside the door?"

"Sure. It was the girl. The one you asked me about before."

"Jessica Staley?"

He shrugged. "She called herself Becky Benedict then. But, yeah, that's the one."

We had Edgar Daniels with Jessica Staley now, just before she died. That was pretty huge. Enough to go ask Daniels what in the hell he was doing that night at the motel with a girl who later turned up dead.

But, even before we did that, we got some more possible evidence tying Daniels to the murders from Phil Girard.

"I showed the picture of Edgar Daniels around to people from the school who'd been on that field trip when Carolyn Garms went missing," Girard told us when we got back to the station. "A few of them said he looked familiar from that day. They couldn't make a positive ID, but they said a man who looked like him was hanging around the school parking lot when they got back from the field trip."

"He wasn't wearing his uniform?" Alex asked.

"No, but the description sounded like him. Long hair,

general physical build and—like I said—they seemed to recognize him as the man in the picture I showed them of Daniels. He looked like Edgar Daniels."

"Damn," Alex muttered.

"There's more," Girard said. "I made some more quiet checks at the station. About Ed Daniels' work schedule. On the day the Garms girl disappeared, he was supposed to be on duty. But he called in sick. Showed up for work again the next day."

"What about the night Jessica Staley's body was found?" I asked.

"I checked that too. He worked the morning shift that whole week."

"So he could have spent the night in Zanesville with the Staley girl," Alex said.

I nodded. "And then dumped her body another night in the parking lot of that convenience store where she was found. He knew there was no video outside in the lot. He knew because he was a police officer."

"We have to question Edgar Daniels," Alex said.

"He's not here," Girard told us. "I've already called him at home. I left a message on his phone saying we needed to speak to him right away. But he hasn't returned my call yet."

"That's suspicious," Alex said.

It got even more suspicious when we checked with the sergeant on duty and found out Daniels was supposed to have reported for work an hour earlier, but there hadn't been any sign of him.

And they didn't get any answer when they tried to call him either.

"We were just going to send someone out to his place to check on him," the sergeant told us.

"Let us do it," I said.

"Really?"

"We'll let you know what we find out."

A few minutes later, all three of us were in a car headed to Edgar Daniels' house.

"What do you think, Nikki?" Alex asked.

"I think that maybe he suspects we're on to him. That's why he didn't take our call or come to work. He doesn't want to talk to us."

"So where is he?" Girard asked.

"Maybe on the run," I said. "Let's get there and find out. If he's gone... well, then I think we have our answer. Edgar Daniels is the guy we're looking for."

FIFTY-SIX

Edgar Daniels lived in a small house on the outskirts of town. The place didn't look very expensive, and the neighborhood it was in didn't either. If there was a poor part of Huntsdale, this was definitely it. I guess being a police officer in Huntsdale didn't pay enough for the finer things in life. I thought again about how this guy had once been on a big city force like Columbus, and how far he had fallen in his career since then.

"Did you tell Earnshaw we were coming out here to confront Daniels?" Phil Girard asked me.

"No."

"That could get hairy if something bad goes down between us and him."

"I'm not sure I trust Earnshaw or anyone else on the Huntsdale force right now," I said.

"Phil's right," Alex said. "This could get ugly. What if we have to shoot Daniels or something? Earnshaw's not going to be happy with us shooting his deputy. What do we do then?"

"We shoot Earnshaw too, I guess," I said.

"You're kidding, right?"

"Yes, Alex, I'm kidding."

"At least Earnshaw knows that we're suspicious of Daniels," Phil said.

"Do you think he alerted Daniels to that?" Alex asked. "Does Daniels know?"

"Given the fact that Daniels didn't show up for work this morning, I think that's a real strong possibility," I said.

Alex shook her head. "I still have trouble accepting the idea that Edgar Daniels is the serial killer of all those young girls," she said.

"Why?" Phil asked.

"Because he seemed like a nice guy."

"Ted Bundy seemed like a nice guy too. And he murdered a helluva lot of women before they caught him."

"Well, Bundy didn't look like a serial killer either," Alex pointed out.

"What does a serial killer look like?" Phil asked.

"I don't know."

"Exactly," Phil said.

We stood there looking at Daniels' house.

"You figure he's inside?" Alex asked.

"It's a good place to start looking."

We actually started with the garage. We parked our car on the street, then walked up the driveway to Daniels' garage. Phil kept watch on the house to see if Daniels was looking out a window or a door at us, while Alex and I peered through a small window on the garage door to see what was inside.

There was a car.

A brown car.

A brown Toyota.

Not that it proved anything, but it was the same kind of car —a Toyota—that had tried to run me down.

Maybe Edgar Daniels liked Toyotas.

More importantly, the fact that the car was in the garage indicated that he was still inside the house. I said that to Alex and Phil.

"Let's go find out," Alex said.

The three of us walked back to the front of the house.

"Are we just going to knock on the goddamned door?" Phil asked.

"You got a better idea, Phil?"

"He might make a run for it."

"Is there a back door?"

"Yes, I saw one leading out onto a small porch. If he knows it's us knocking at his front door, he could possibly get away there."

"Okay, Phil, why don't you watch the back? Alex and I will go to the front door. That way we'll have him trapped on both sides."

"If he's in the house," Alex said.

"I'm betting he is."

"And if not?"

"Then we keep looking until we find him. He can't run forever. We know who he is now, we know who we're looking for. We'll get him."

"Just remember," Phil said, "the guy's a police officer. He's got a firearm in there. Maybe more than one. He could open fire at you two while you're standing there at the front door."

"We'll keep our heads down and try to make sure we don't get hit, Phil," I said.

"That's our plan?" Alex asked.

"That's our plan," I said. "Let's go."

Alex and I approached the front door of the house as Phil went around back.

We rang the bell.

There was no answer.

We knocked on the door.

No one opened it.

We began pounding on the door.

"Edgar Daniels, are you in there?" I shouted.

Still nothing.

"FBI here. Agents Cassidy, Del Vecchio and Girard. We need to talk with you right away."

There was just silence from inside.

"What do you think?" Alex asked me.

"Not good."

"We need to go in, Nikki. Even if we have to break down this door or go through a window."

Except everything changed then.

Because we heard a loud noise.

It was a gunshot.

A gunshot coming from inside the house.

FIFTY-SEVEN

Alex and I dove for cover away from the door at the sound of the gunshot. A few seconds later, Phil came running around from the back and joined us huddled by the front of Edgar Daniels' house.

"You heard that too?" I said to him.

"Damn straight."

"Was he shooting at one of us?"

"If he was, I'm glad he missed."

"We need to go in there right now," I said.

"Maybe we should call for backup first," Alex said.

"Go ahead and call. But I'm not waiting for Earnshaw or any of his people to show up."

Alex called our situation into the Huntsdale station on her phone, then we carefully made our way back onto the front porch. There was no more gunfire. No sounds of any kind were coming from the house.

Yes, I probably should have waited for the backup team from Earnshaw and the Huntsdale station to show up. That was certainly the by the book way to do this, just like Alex had talked about with Phil and me.

But I didn't always play it by the book.

And I wasn't going to now.

I wanted Edgar Daniels.

I was ready to knock the door down to get inside, but I didn't have to do that. The door was unlocked.

I carefully turned the knob, we took out our weapons and walked into the living room. It was empty. We all had guns pointed in front of us as we checked the living room area out thoroughly before proceeding.

"We're clear here," I said. "FBI," I yelled out again. "We are inside this house. And we are armed. Let us know if you are here."

No answer.

"We're about to search the rest of the house," I shouted again.

We moved down a hall from the living room to a bathroom.

Nothing there either.

Ahead was a bedroom. We made our way there, our guns still pointed ahead of us as we walked.

And that's where we found Daniels.

His body was lying on the bed. Blood covered his face, especially around his mouth. A gun—his service weapon—lay on the bed next to him, inches from his hand. As if he had dropped it after firing the weapon.

We searched the rest of the house then to make sure a gunman wasn't lurking somewhere. But we figured that was a waste of time at this point. It didn't seem like it was a gunman who had come into this house and shot Edgar Daniels.

Daniels had apparently killed himself, presumably because he found out from Earnshaw or someone else on the Huntsdale police force that we were closing in on him as the suspect in the murder of all those young girls. That was the gunshot sound we had heard. He knew we were out there at the door. He knew we'd found out all about him and the terrible deeds that he had done. And he knew he couldn't get away. So Edgar Daniels took the only way out that was possible for him.

"He ate his goddamned pistol," Phil grunted.

That was police lingo for when a police officer uses their service weapon to commit suicide. Usually, it was sad and tragic when that happened. But not with Edgar Daniels.

The bastard got what he deserved.

"Look at this," Alex suddenly said as she looked at a box—more of a trunk actually in size—on the floor next to Daniels' body lying on the bed. She put on plastic gloves to preserve any fingerprints that might be on the box or the handle, then opened it up.

Inside were pictures of young girls. I wasn't sure how many pictures were there, but I did see that three of them were pictures of Becky Benedict, Jessica Staley and Carolyn Garms. There were also other things in the box we could see even before examining the contents more closely. Articles of female clothing; locks of hair; pieces of jewelry; and even a book that looked like a journal or diary.

"It's a trophy box," Alex said.

"Yes," I agreed. "He kept all these things as trophies of the girls that he abducted and eventually murdered."

"What a sick son of a bitch."

"Let's see exactly what's in the box," I said.

FIFTY-EIGHT

The pictures of the other six girls we were looking at as victims were all inside the box found in Edgar Daniels' house. Along with the pictures of Becky Benedict, Jessica Staley and Carolyn Garms. There were photos of other girls too. More victims? Presumably, but we would have to check all of that out. We were back at the Huntsdale station house going through it all in as much detail as we could.

The scene back at Daniels' house after we discovered his body had been an uncomfortable one. Earnshaw and a contingent of officers from the Huntsdale force showed up shortly after we notified them of Daniels' death—an apparent suicide by gunshot wound. That was bad enough for Earnshaw, but then we told him how and why we wound up at the house to discover the body.

"Why didn't you come to me before you went there?" he wanted to know.

"We decided to check it out first," I said, then told him everything else we'd found out about Daniels. And, of course, about the souvenir box found in the bedroom along with his body.

"You should have told me about your suspicions of Daniels earlier, before you went to the house," Earnshaw said.

"We didn't want to say anything to you about him until we were sure."

"That's bullshit. You didn't want me to know what you were doing because you thought I'd try to stop you. That I'd tell you that you were all wrong about Daniels."

I understood why Earnshaw was so upset. First, we'd undermined his authority. And then, not only was he not the one to crack this case, the bad guy turned out to be someone on his force. And his friend. He never suspected anything until we figured it out. This was going to look bad for Earnshaw. Really bad when it all became public.

I didn't figure Stacy Harris was going to be too happy about this outcome either. Sure, the mayor knew I'd had questions about the local cops. But a killer—a mass killer of young girls—on the town's police force? And right after the Huntsdale District Attorney was exposed as a murderer too. This wasn't going to help the town's image very much. Or Stacy Harris's either.

Meanwhile, Big Mickey Franze confirmed that Daniels had died by suicide, not murder.

Or at least pretty much confirmed that.

"It definitely looks like a suicide," he said after doing the autopsy and other investigations on Daniels. "Everything about it says suicide. Including everything you found out about him leading up to finding the body. And the fact that you heard the gunshot from inside the house. If someone else shot him, where did that person go? There was no one you saw inside the house except Daniels. As the old saying goes, if it looks like a duck, walks like a duck... then it probably is a duck. I'm ruling this a suicide, Nikki. But..."

"But what, Mickey?"

"It's always difficult to be a hundred per cent sure. Could someone else have broken into the house before you got there? Shot Daniels in the mouth with his own gun? Left that gun next to him to make it look like he did it to himself? Planted paraffin from his hand on the gun to set up the suicide scene even more? Wiped his own prints off everything else so it looked like Daniels was alone when it happened? Somehow got out of the house without any of you seeing him? Not impossible. But not very likely either."

"So you think Edgar Daniels killed himself when he realized we were coming to arrest him?"

"I'm ruling it a suicide."

There was more inside Daniels' souvenir box besides the pictures of the dead girls.

A lot more.

The highlights were the personal items, apparently from the victims. We found a watch engraved on the back with the names of one of the girl's parents; a bracelet with another girl's initials on it; and the pieces of clothing and hair in there we would presumably be able to match with other victims. There were also receipts from hotels and restaurants and stores around the country over a period of years—similar to the time period and locations of girls that had disappeared and been murdered—that we should be able to match up easily with specific murder cases.

But there was one receipt we didn't have to wait to check, as it was pretty obvious.

It was from a restaurant in Zanesville, Ohio. The same place where Jessica Staley had stopped on her odyssey from Michigan until she was discovered dead in Huntsdale. The date on the receipt was the same as the day she had checked into the

Garden Island Motel. We always knew someone had been with her. Now we knew for sure who that was. Edgar Daniels.

But the thing I wanted to check out most from the souvenirs box was the book that appeared to be a journal.

Did Daniels keep a record of all his killings? Did it chronicle his entire twenty-year killing spree of girls throughout the country?

As it turned out, it didn't.

In fact, almost all the pages were blank.

There was only one entry, on a sheet of paper tucked underneath the opening page of the journal. It was typed, so we couldn't confirm it was Daniels' from handwriting. But he must have done it. There was no other rational explanation.

The entry read:

They know. They know who I am now. Maybe not all about me, but they will very soon. And then it will be over. This grand adventure is done.

I have been a god to these girls. Maybe not the God, but a god. They worshiped me, they followed me and—in the end— they died for me. Even then, I think they were happy. Happy that they could please me one last time by dying for me. Because they knew it was their only way out.

Now I find myself in the same situation.

It is time for me to go.

Time for me to leave this world too.

I am at peace with that.

I regret nothing.

I have carried out my mission.

The mission that I was destined to do for my entire life.

You may think it was murder. But I saved these girls. I gave them a brief moment of happiness in their dreary, depressing lives. And I loved them. Yes, as hard as people might find that to believe, I loved them all. All the girls.

Below that was his name.
And something else below that.

Littlelostgirls.com

"A website," Alex said.
"A website."

FIFTY-NINE

The Nowhere Men site had been shut down after Tommy Thompson's death by whoever ran it besides Thompson. We'd tried to use the FBI technology team to track down some of the other member handles and passwords from the site. But it didn't take us anywhere. Everyone had disguised themselves and their contact information with layers of protection so their real names, emails or other personal information couldn't be detected.

Still, the site was no longer functioning. The sick perverts who once inhabited The Nowhere Men site no longer had a place to watch or sell pictures and videos of young girls who had been abducted—and then murdered on live snuff videos.

Where had all of these men gone?

Our worst fears were confirmed.

They had simply moved to a new site.

Different place, but just as sick as The Nowhere Men had been.

Littlelostgirls.com. It seemed harmless enough on the face of it, perhaps a way to adopt and give a home to needy young girls. But, even before I saw the site, I knew what it was going to be about.

When I logged on to Littlelostgirls.com, I got this message:

THIS SITE IS FOR MEMBERS ONLY.

    IF YOU ARE NOT A MEMBER, PLEASE LOG OFF IMMEDIATELY.

    ONLY PEOPLE WITH APPROVED USERNAMES AND PASSWORDS MAY JOIN THIS SITE.

    PLEASE ENTER BOTH NOW TO CONTINUE.

I pressed "enter." The introductory screen disappeared and I was now on the log-in page. I typed in Edgar Daniels. Two words. That got me a "wrong username" message. I did it again as EdgarDaniels, all one word. Another rejection. Then I tried again with just "Edgar" and then just "Daniels." The last name "Daniels" worked—and I was accepted.

Of course, that was the easy part.

Now I was on the password page.

Which meant I somehow had to figure out Daniels' password.

When I'd first accessed The Nowhere Men site the last time I was here, the password I used to get in had shocked me. It was my father's name—Luke Cassidy. I never did find out—and probably never will—why my father's name was a password on the site. The only possible reason I could come up with was that my father had somehow found out about The Nowhere Men site, like I did, and had accessed it as part of his investigation before his death.

Just for the hell of it, I typed in my father's name again. But it didn't work. PASSWORD INVALID, the message said.

I tried to think about things Edgar Daniels might have used as a password.

First, I checked and found out his middle name was James. I

tried that. Another rejection. Then I thought about what I knew about Daniels. He was a police officer in Huntsdale. But before that he'd worked on the police force in Columbus. Sometimes people used locations like that as a password. I typed in both of them. No good.

I ran through a lot of possibilities in my head. It seemed pretty hopeless. Anything I tried would just be a guess.

Alex and Phil gave me some suggestions. I wasn't sure about trying them since I might only have limited attempts. But then someone—I can't remember if it was Alex or Phil—talked about how Daniels was a big Springsteen fan. They said he'd told them that one day, just like the first time I met him.

Why not? I tried Springsteen first. After that Bruce and The Boss and even "Born to Run." Then I remembered that his favorite Springsteen song was actually "Rosalita (Come Out Tonight)."

It seemed worth a try.

I typed in the name Rosalita.

I was expecting to see another INVALID PASSWORD message. But I didn't. Instead, the password log-in disappeared off my screen and was replaced by something identified as the "entry room." There was also a figure on the screen, sort of like in Second Life and on the original Nowhere Men site, that I could move around with the computer keys. The figure looked a bit like Edgar Daniels. But younger, better looking, in better physical shape. Which happened a lot in these virtual reality scenarios. People made themselves—or at least their on-screen figures—as good looking a version of themselves as they could.

I sat back in my chair, took a deep breath and then used the keys to maneuver the Daniels figure through the only door in the room. When I did that, a table of contents appeared on the screen. A menu of everything that was available for the sex perverts to scroll through and then get off on.

I scrolled through them quickly to see if the video I'd once seen of my sister Caitlin was on this site. It wasn't. That was a relief, at least. But I did see the names of three people I recognized.

Becky Benedict.

Jessica Staley.

Carolyn Garms.

There were pictures of all of them. Lots of pictures. Looking happy and pretty and full of life at first. Then the horrifying pictures of them after they were dead, bloody and battered—which presumably was all a turn-on for the people on this site. But there was more than just these horrible pictures. There was video too. Video of some of the girls in the moments leading up to their murders.

It was difficult to watch, but I took screenshots of everything as I did. Now that Daniels was dead, who knew how long the site would remain active. And how long I could use his credentials to log on like this. I needed to record as much evidence as I could from it right now. It might be my last chance before the site shut down—or, even more likely, transferred to another website—again.

I thought The Nowhere Men case was over when Tommy Thompson died.

But now I knew The Nowhere Men weren't gone at all.

I still had to find more Nowhere Men.

And stop them before they killed again.

SIXTY

"Nikki, Alex, Phil, great job!" Dave Blanton said from HQ.

"Thanks," Alex said.

"Right, Chief," Phil said.

I didn't say anything.

I was thinking about stuff. Stuff I didn't want to really think about. But I couldn't stop myself from doing it, no matter how hard I tried.

We were back on another Zoom call with Blanton from the war room we'd set up in the Huntsdale police station—getting ready to pack up and head back to Washington now that Edgar Daniels was dead. Everyone seemed glad about that. Everyone but me, that is. I'd been thinking about everything that happened. Thinking about it a lot since we'd left Daniels' house.

"I'm glad this case is over," Blanton said to us. "I don't mind telling you that. I was worried there for a while how this was going to all turn out."

"Is it?" I asked.

"Is it what?"

"Over?"

Alex and Phil both gave me funny looks.

"What are you talking about, Nikki? Daniels is dead. We found all the evidence against him in his house. Including his access to that sick website. Sure, there could be more suspects out there who worked with him and maybe with the D.A., Thompson, too before you brought him down. But we'll get them too, very soon. Daniels is the main guy. He killed Jessica Staley and Carolyn Garms and the other girls, all the way back to Becky Benedict. He admitted in the journal about stalking and killing all those female teenage victims. And he had souvenirs—clothes, jewelry, locks of hair—from the girls. It was all there waiting for us with his dead body. Nope, this case couldn't have worked out any more perfectly for us."

"Almost too perfect, isn't it?"

"C'mon, Nikki. Sometimes you have to let a case go and simply move on to the next one."

"I'll let this one go when I know the case is over."

"And you're not sure?"

"Not yet."

"You can work on chasing after all the computer site stuff with our people here once you get back."

"It's not just the Littlelostgirls.com website—or the extension of it likely being from The Nowhere Men—that bothers me."

"Then what are you talking about?"

"Something doesn't feel right."

"Such as?"

"I'm not sure."

"But..."

"I'm not certain Edgar Daniels—guilty as he seems in death —is the answer that we've been looking for."

"Why? What about all the evidence you found against him at the house? The stuff from the victims? The confession in the journal?"

"Let's say you're the killer, and you're looking for a scape-goat. A patsy to pin the blame on. Who do you pick for this? Someone who has a very questionable record with a history of sexual misbehavior involving young women. Someone who fits seemingly the profile of a man who might murder girls like Benedict or Staley. Someone who likely shouldn't even be a member of law enforcement anymore after everything he's done. Someone like Edgar Daniels. He makes the perfect patsy."

"For the real killer," Alex said.

"Exactly."

"But who is that then?" Blanton asked.

"Well, who hired Daniels to be on the Huntsdale police force despite his shady background?"

Suddenly, everyone realized who I was talking about.

Even if no one wanted to believe it.

"Chief Frank Earnshaw?" Alex asked.

"Why not?"

"My God, he's the police chief," Phil said.

"So? Tommy Thompson was the district attorney. Maybe they were working together, him and Earnshaw. I checked and found out Earnshaw got the job as chief here on a recommenda-tion from Thompson. Then Earnshaw hires Daniels as his deputy. It all begins to fit together when you take a hard look at it." I looked around the room at Alex and Phil again, and at Blanton on the Zoom screen. I could see they were all thinking about what I was saying here.

"It's worth checking Earnshaw out further," Alex said.

"How do we do that?" Blanton wanted to know.

"He'd be suspicious if I started asking questions," I said. "Probably Alex too because he knows we're friends."

"Let me do it," Phil said.

"Huh?"

"Earnshaw likes me. I get along better than you or Alex

with him. Maybe because I'm a man, and he's more comfortable dealing with that. You've seen that in our meetings with him. I'll try to check him out as best I can. See what I can find out about him. See where it all goes."

"I don't know," Blanton said. "Doing something like that with a local police official we're supposed to be cooperating with on a big murder case? That could get messy. If anything goes wrong, we could put ourselves in a very precarious situation."

"Don't worry, I can handle this," Phil Girard said.

Was Frank Earnshaw really the killer?

Was Earnshaw the man we were looking for who was responsible for all this, and not Daniels?

Had Earnshaw set up his former partner to take the fall if he thought we or anyone else was getting too close to the truth?

One way or another, we agreed to stay in Huntsdale to see if Phil Girard could find out the answers to these questions.

SIXTY-ONE

"You might be right, Nikki," Phil Girard said later. "It could well be Frank Earnshaw."

"Really?"

"It all makes sense when you put the evidence together."

We were sitting in Phil's hotel room. He'd asked Alex and me to meet him there. When we arrived, we saw papers and documents all around, and he was sitting in front of his computer screen. Typing furiously away on his keyboard, and clicking on screen with his mouse. He wasn't playing Wordle or checking for information about UFOs or the JFK assassination this time. Phil Girard was working. Working hard on the case.

"Look at what I found out," he said to us, pointing to the screen. "Remember this?"

It was a picture of the Becky Benedict crime scene, the trash bin where her body had been found more than twenty years ago.

"Okay," I said, "so what's the significance of the trash bin again?"

"Not the trash bin, Nikki. The other thing in the picture."

I looked at the screen again. The same building was still

there. The building with offices and a parking lot next to the trash bin.

"We're talking about the office building?"

"Yes."

"We checked that out, Alex and me and the Dorchester police, when we first went there. Couldn't find any connection between any of the businesses and the murder. Everyone we looked at from that building turned out to be clean."

"You missed someone. I'm not talking about a person who worked at one of the businesses there. I'm talking about someone else who worked in the building. Someone who worked security there. They had a security team in that building because a lot of the businesses inside dealt with big time financial stuff. I went back and checked the records for the security people on duty when Benedict's body was found outside. And one of them, the youngest, was a kid named Frank Earnshaw."

"Holy crap," Alex said.

"Yeah, that was my reaction too."

"Why wouldn't Earnshaw have told us he was there then and the connection to Becky Benedict's crime scene once it got linked to the Staley murder?" she asked.

Of course, I knew the most likely answer to that even before Alex uttered the words.

"He didn't want us to make the connection between him and Becky Benedict," I said.

"There's more too," Phil said.

He talked then about doing a deep dive into Frank Earnshaw's background after finding out this, and about discovering more disturbing stuff. Earnshaw's mother was a drug addict, his father constantly in and out of trouble with the law. Young Frank went through a tortuous childhood, until he was moved out to a foster home—a series of foster homes actually—where he had more unhappy experiences. It wasn't until he went out on his own and got the job working security at the building in Dorchester that he realized what he wanted to do. A career in law enforcement. He moved to a bigger security job, then to the Columbus police force and eventually on to Huntsdale as the police chief.

"Do you see the pattern here?" Phil asked us when he was finished. "Earnshaw had an unhappy home, an unhappy childhood. He ran away from it. Just like Jessica Staley and Becky Benedict did. Maybe that's what motivated him to go after girls like that once he escaped from his own unhappy home."

"But why?" I asked.

"There's never a logical reason for this kind of thing. But somehow I think he's reenacting his own experience with these girls. He wants to rescue them from their unhappy lives, the same kind of unhappy life he had. Maybe the fact that they're all young and pretty gives him some kind of a sexual thrill too. Who knows? But, after he's rescued them, he moves on to another girl."

"Because he's bored?" Alex asked.

"I think it's more about power. He was powerless when he was a teenager. But now he has power. The ultimate power. The power to decide how—and when—people live and die."

He was throwing a lot of information at us; I was having trouble processing it all. Even though everything he said made sense. It was horrifying if true, but it did make sense.

"What about the idea that the killer was some kind of a Charles Manson figure? A charismatic cult-like figure who could lure young girls to follow him? Frank Earnshaw couldn't charm anyone, much less a teenage girl."

"Neither could Edgar Daniels, if we're talking about nothing but charm. But they both had something in common that could convince a young girl she was safe with them. They were police officers. A troubled girl like Jessica Staley or Becky Benedict would never have felt they were in danger with a police officer. They might easily have followed him. Followed him until... until he killed them."

Phil looked back at his computer screen, then back at us. "Frank Earnshaw lied to us about Edgar Daniels too," he said.

"How? He told us they were partners."

"That's the lie. They weren't partners. Earnshaw and Daniels weren't even on the Columbus police force at the same time."

"Why would Earnshaw lie about that?'

"To explain why he would hire a guy with Daniels' record on his force. It sort of made sense when you believed they were partners, the way Earnshaw said. It makes no sense at all if they never worked with each other in Columbus."

"Unless Earnshaw wanted Daniels for help in whatever he might have been doing with young girls."

Phil nodded. "Or, even more likely, he wanted Daniels to take the fall if anything went wrong. Maybe Daniels knew nothing at all about what Earnshaw was doing."

"You think Edgar Daniels was only a patsy?" I asked.

"The perfect patsy. A cop with a record of inappropriate behavior with a teenage girl. Once Earnshaw thought we might be getting too close to the answers, he shoots Daniels, makes it look like suicide and leaves all the incriminating evidence with his body."

It was just a scenario at this point, we all knew that. But it was a damned logical scenario. It made a lot of sense. More sense than the idea of Edgar Daniels as the killer had made. People had always said that Phil Girard used to be a really smart FBI agent, and I was never quite sure I believed it. But now, on the verge of retirement, he might just have solved the biggest case of all our careers.

"So what the hell do we do now?" Alex asked, saying aloud what we were all thinking.

SIXTY-TWO

"This isn't enough," I told them.

"Nikki's right," Alex agreed. "We need more."

"Yeah, I know," Phil said. "We're close. Damn close. But we don't have a case against the guy. Not a case that could hold up in court. There's too much speculation. We've got a lot of pieces, and when you put them together in the right way they say Earnshaw is our guy. But separately, he can probably come up with plausible explanations for all these things. And a good defense attorney could get them thrown out pretty quickly if we don't have anything else but our gut instinct on this."

"We need some hard evidence," Alex said.

We talked about a lot of stuff then, tossing ideas back and forth about how to proceed on Earnshaw. And, in the end, we did come up with an idea. A pretty obvious one. The DNA.

"We know the DNA for the Benedict murder and also from the motel room where Jessica Staley stayed before she was killed were a match," I said. "We compare that DNA to Earnshaw's DNA. If it's a match, then that's the evidence we need."

"Except we don't have Earnshaw's DNA," Phil said.

"So we figure out a way to get it."

The federal DNA files we kept contained DNA from many criminals over the past twenty-five years or so since the DNA technology became known and used by law enforcement. Not all criminals were in the data bank though, and there was nothing from law enforcement officers like Earnshaw and Daniels. Even FBI agents like me don't have their DNA on record. It's not a perfect system. We'd need to get a sample of Earnshaw's DNA some other way.

"Well, we could ask him," Phil said. "But I guess that would alert him to what we were doing."

"Not a good idea." I laughed.

"Then we get it surreptitiously."

That was something that had become more popular in law enforcement in recent years. Getting someone's DNA without their knowledge you're doing it by getting it from a drinking glass or a cigarette or even out of a trash can. There were legal issues to doing this, of course. The evidence we got might be inadmissible. But at least we would know we were right about Earnshaw. Then we could focus on finding more evidence against him after that.

"It will take time," Phil said, "to get results back."

He was right about that.

"What is the DNA testing turnaround time right now?" I asked.

"The last I heard it was at least forty-eight to seventy-two hours to check out a sample. Could be longer, like up to fourteen days. We'd hopefully be able to expedite it a bit. But even then, we're talking about a couple of days before we know."

"Still better than nothing."

"I hate to wait that long," Phil said. "I mean, the guy could be looking for another victim right now. He's already said he was going to come after you, Nikki. The last one to die, remember? So what if we draw him out before that?"

"How?" But even before I asked the question, I knew the answer.

"By luring him out of hiding to attack the target he wants to kill," said Phil. "You'd have to be the bait in the trap, Nikki."

"Now wait a minute," Alex started to say. "That's crazy—"

"No, it's a good idea, Alex," I said. "It is me he's after next, he's made that clear in the communications we've seen. We've got to try to catch him before he can hurt anyone else. I'm not happy about it either, but it's probably the best shot we have at the guy."

In the end, we decided on both approaches. Someone would try to get Earnshaw's DNA and we'd compare that with the DNA found at the Becky Benedict crime scene and the Garden Island Motel in Zanesville.

But, in the meantime, we'd try to lure him into a trap with me as the bait. We just had to work out how we would do that.

"I have a way," I said. "We call him and say I'm at my father and sister's graves, and that I want him to meet me there right away, that I've found out the answers to the murders. The location should intrigue him. Assuming he's the guy we're after, he might well decide this is the best time to come after me, the location where he presumably followed me from in the car before trying to run me over in the parking lot."

"Except we'll be waiting for him," Alex said. "To stop him before he can do anything. Then we'll have him..."

"Only one of you can be there," I said. "The other should try to get his DNA first, then we lure him from there to the cemetery to meet with me. One way or another, that should be enough to get the evidence that we need."

"We need more agents for backup then," said Alex.

"I'll call in to get some backup from our bureau in Columbus," Phil said.

"Okay," Alex said. "Then you go get the DNA from Earnshaw—trick him with a glass or something to get it—and I'll stay at the cemetery with Nikki and the other agents from Columbus."

"No, let me do that, you meet Earnshaw."

"She's my partner, Phil."

"Hey, it's really important to get his DNA, Alex. He might not even show up at the cemetery. Or do anything if he does come. Then we'll have to figure out some lame story about why she asked him there. The DNA is something substantial we can work with, no matter what. I think you've got the best chance of getting that from him. Me and the other agents can make sure Nikki is safe. There'll be more than enough of us to protect her."

Alex reluctantly agreed.

I had a question before we set it all in motion. "What about Chief Nolan from Dorchester? He's still around. Even if he hasn't been involved in our investigation since the TMZ stuff. We have to tell him what we're doing, right?"

"I don't think we should tell him or anyone outside the bureau," Phil said.

"But he's been part of what we're doing.'

"So has Earnshaw supposedly."

"You don't trust Nolan?"

"Do you?"

I thought about the questions I'd had about Nolan in the past. About things from the Benedict investigation and his wife's death and his refusal to ever talk with me about that.

"I think Phil's right," Alex said. "Let's keep this an FBI operation. No local cops. Not Nolan or anyone else."

"If we can't trust Earnshaw as a local police chief, how do we know that we can trust Nolan?" Phil said.

SIXTY-THREE

Alex called Earnshaw and asked to meet with him at his office. She said she wanted to go over some evidence with him as soon as possible. She said it might be important, and she couldn't find me or Phil right now and needed to discuss it with someone. She said—as casually as she could—that she was bringing some coffee for both of them.

Originally, we had considered her meeting Earnshaw in a coffee shop or a bar, but it seemed less suspicious to simply meet him in his office like we usually did. Then she could figure out a way to take the paper coffee cup with her when she left to test it for his DNA residue.

Meanwhile, Phil got on the phone and made arrangements for an FBI backup team to join us at the cemetery later. The FBI had a big office in Columbus, less than an hour away. There was plenty of time for them to arrive here, get in position near my father and sister's graves and wait for Earnshaw to make his appearance.

I waited for it all to happen, trying to ignore as best I could my growing feeling of discomfort over what was going to go down soon. I didn't really like the idea of being used as bait.

Even though I knew it was something we had to do to nail Earnshaw.

Phil and Alex picked up on my uneasiness.

"Don't worry, Nikki, everything will be fine," Phil assured me. "I'll be there to back you up. The team from Columbus is on the way, and we won't show up until they're in place. We'll have plenty of firepower. All you have to do is confront Earnshaw, get him to admit to you he's the killer and then—when he tries to go after you—we move in and get the son of a bitch into custody."

"Hopefully."

"Definitely," Phil said.

"I wish I could be there," Alex said.

"Alex, it makes more sense for you to get Earnshaw to give you his DNA. That's our backup plan. In case Earnshaw doesn't show up at the cemetery when we tell him to meet Nikki there. Or he doesn't admit or do anything suspicious if he does. At least we'll then have his DNA to try for a match."

"I guess you're right, Phil."

"How is this going to work with Earnshaw?" I asked. "Do I call him and say I want to meet him at the cemetery? What exactly should I say about why I want to see him there right away?"

"I think I should make the call," Phil said. "We know he likes me better than you. He won't be suspicious of me."

"What will you say?"

"I'll tell him you've been acting crazy, saying all kinds of wild stuff about the murders. That you went to the cemetery to commune with the spirts of your father and sister, or something like that. And that you think you know now what really happened and who really did the murders. But she'll only talk to you about it, Chief Earnshaw."

Alex smiled. "That ought to pique his interest enough to find out whatever it is you know."

"And, when he gets there, I confront him about everything and hope he tries to make me his next victim—his last victim, as he put it—so we can arrest him."

"That's the plan," Phil said.

"It's a good plan," Alex said.

"Then let's do it," I told them.

A short time later, Phil and I were driving to the cemetery.

In the parking lot of the hotel, before we'd left, we'd run into Connor Nolan. He'd tried to talk to me, but I brushed him off and got into the car with Phil. I felt badly about cutting him out of this, but I had no choice. Whatever was going to happen between Connor and me would have to wait until this was all over.

During the ride to the cemetery, Phil made a call confirming that the agents from Columbus had arrived and were in position near the two graves, but out of sight for whenever Earnshaw arrived at the site. He also made the call to Earnshaw, going through the story we'd thought up about why Earnshaw needed to meet me there and find out about all the crazy theories and accusations I was suddenly making about the murders. He said after he hung up that Earnshaw had bought all of it hook, line, and sinker.

"He's on his way. He sounded upset. Which is all good."

We pulled into the cemetery and drove to the two graves. I looked around and saw the same things I saw whenever I'd come to this spot. The trees nearby, the pond, the ducks, and the leaves from the trees rustling in the evening breeze. It was starting to get dark now, but I could still see all this. It was comforting in a way. Just like it was comforting to be so close to my father and sister's graves at a moment like this. I wasn't sure if there was an afterlife. But, if there was, I wanted to believe they were out there somewhere still looking after me.

"How long do you think it will be before Earnshaw shows up?" I asked Phil as I started to get out of the car.

"Well, it might be a long wait."

"But you said he was in a hurry to find out what I was talking about. It's only a five-minute drive from the station house. And you talked to him longer than five minutes ago so..."

"Actually, I never did talk to Earnshaw."

"What?"

"And I didn't call for any FBI backup either."

He took his gun out of his holster now and pointed it at me.

"Just you and me here, Cassidy."

SIXTY-FOUR

I suddenly realized how wrong I had been about everything. It wasn't Earnshaw. It was Phil Girard.

"You," I said.

"Me." He smiled, gesturing for me to give him my weapon.

I did. I had no choice.

"Why?" I asked.

"It's not important. Let's just say I enjoy my work."

"You mean killing?"

"I've been doing this for a long time, Cassidy. You never knew it. No one knew that it was Phil Girard. I put on a pretty good act, huh?"

"But you've been an FBI agent for such a long time."

"And I've been killing people even longer."

It was all so frighteningly clear to me now. Frank Earnshaw was not coming to the cemetery to confront me. Girard had never called him, he'd lied about that. And there was no FBI team waiting in the nearby woods either. Girard had lied about that too. He'd lied about everything.

"What about Frank Earnshaw working at the office building

next to the trash bin where Becky Benedict was found?" I asked him.

"No, I made that up to make him a suspect and lure you out here."

I wasn't sure why it really mattered to me now, but I still wanted answers.

And I wanted to keep him talking for as long as possible. Just in case someone else showed up—or something else happened—that I could use as a distraction to get the gun away from him.

"Edgar Daniels?"

"Oh, that was a lie too. Daniels really was Earnshaw's partner. But he was perfect for me. The minute I met Edgar Daniels —and found out about his background, like you did—I knew I could use him as a diversion if anyone got too close to the truth. That's what I did when you started closing in. I even fired that shot we heard at his house when I was around back, so you'd assume he'd just committed suicide—even though I'd killed him and set up that suicide scene before we got there. But you were too smart for me. You figured out Daniels might be a patsy for the real killer. So I had to put Plan B into effect."

"Which is to kill me here."

"Hey, I could have done it that day in the parking lot. But I wanted it to be more dramatic. At the graves of your sister and father. You come back here and you wind up dead too. How great will that play out in the media?'

"Why me, Phil?" It seemed strange to call him by his first name, like we were still co-workers or friends. The man was about to murder me. But it came out of my mouth by habit without me even realizing it.

"Because you will be the final triumph for me. My last kill, as I put it. And the most dramatic and famous, thanks to all your heroic achievements and that kind of crap. Everyone will be talking about the killer who was so smart that he took out the star FBI agent hunting him. Of course, no one else will know that's me. But I'll know. I'll know I outsmarted you. I got the best of you. I won, Cassidy. That's all that really matters to me now. I am going to retire to Florida. Just like I've told everyone. And now I can look back fondly on everything I accomplished with you as my final trophy."

It was getting dark now. You could barely see the head-stones of my sister and father, and the trees and the pond around us. But I could hear the wind. The wind blowing through the trees. Sometimes, when I used to visit my family's graves, I would imagine it was their spirits in the wind reaching out to me; still looking out for me in some unexplained way from wherever they were. I sure wished that was true.

"Get out of the car," Phil said, gesturing to me with the gun in his hand.

"What's next?"

"You walk over to the gravestones of your damn father and sister. The ones you're always talking about. Now you're going to join them... for the last time."

"That's where it's going to happen?"

He nodded. "It seems appropriate. They'll find you on top of the graves. No one will be sure if you were killed or killed yourself there. Hell, Earnshaw might even go down for the murder if I want to make him the scapegoat. It's something to think about."

"What about Alex? She knows you were coming here with me."

"Alex won't be telling anyone anything."

I realized what he was saying. "You're going to kill Alex too?"

"I can't have any loose ends on this one. Now get moving."

I got out of the car and began walking toward the grave-stones. All I could think to do was to keep him talking. I wasn't sure what that would accomplish, but it was the only option I had. The longer I could keep him engaged in conversation, the longer I had to live.

"What about the website?" I asked. "The Nowhere Men website. I shut it down, but we found something just like it on Daniels' computer. You put it on there, right? Are you part of that website? Are there people from The Nowhere Men still operating with you?"

He laughed. "Never knew about them until I came out here with you when you were investigating your sister. No, I have nothing to do with them. Whether they're still out there doing the same thing as me, that makes no difference as far as I'm concerned. I work alone. I've always worked alone. I've been alone all my life."

That's when I understood something else. Or at least I was pretty sure I did. The story about Earnshaw coming from an unhappy home life and a string of dysfunctional foster homes. That story wasn't about Earnshaw.

"It was you, right? You were the person from an unhappy childhood. That's why you targeted young girls in similar circumstances. Promised to make them happy and they believed you. Until you killed them. But why? Why would you do something so horrible as murdering all those impressionable young girls?"

"Oh, I'm sure the bureau's profilers and shrinks could have a field day analyzing me if they ever got the chance. But that isn't going to happen. There's never a simple reason for why people do things like I've been doing. I've learned that, and so have you, from many years in the FBI. Let's just say it's something I need to do. I really have never had any choice in the matter. Like I don't have any choice now."

We were standing at the graves of my loved ones now. I listened again to the wind as it whistled through the trees around us. The leaves on the trees moved slowly, almost gracefully, in the breeze. I tried to focus on that beauty. It could be the last thing I would ever see.

And then I spotted something else.

In the trees closest to us.

A figure moving in the darkness.

"Drop the gun, Girard!" a familiar voice said.

It was Connor.

"Drop the gun right now!"

Girard didn't. Instead, he whirled around and fired in the direction of the trees.

There was a shot returned by Connor.

Then another.

Girard screamed and fell to the ground.

I moved toward him, hoping to get his gun away. But he got up and stumbled back to the car. He managed to get in the driver's seat, start the engine and roar off down the road leading out of the cemetery.

Connor came out of the woods now.

"You hit him," I said.

"How bad?"

"Bad, I think. He can't get far."

"I'll call Earnshaw and get out a bulletin on him and the car." He did that, then came over to me.

"How did you know?" I asked.

"I just felt something was wrong. You were weird and evasive after I asked you what you were doing. And then Girard seemed in such a hurry to get on with whatever it was. I'd never seen him that interested or in a hurry during all this time we'd been working together. So I got curious. I decided to follow you."

"I'm sure glad you did."

"Hey, I'm a cop, that's my job."

SIXTY-FIVE

They found Phil Girard's body a few days later. Or at least what they're pretty sure was his body.

A car plunged into the Ohio River from a bridge, about a hundred miles south of Huntsdale. The car had been stolen from an auto dealership. In the driver's seat was the body of a man. He was carrying a gun and an FBI badge that were believed to have belonged to Phil Girard.

There was also a gunshot wound in the body. No bullet. That had apparently gone through the wound and exited the body, so there was nothing to compare to the bullets from Connor Nolan's gun. The body itself was unidentifiable too. The car had smashed into some rocks when it hit the river, and it exploded into flames.

The body couldn't be positively ID'd for the time being because of that and the damage from the water too. It would take a while to determine from DNA or dental records if they matched. But the presumption—at least the unofficial ruling from the FBI and other law enforcement authorities until further tests were done on the remains—was that Phil Girard died in the river.

I wasn't as sure about that. It seemed a little too pat for me, and I wondered if maybe he had set it all up by shooting someone else and sending them in the car off that bridge to give him more time to get away. But Phil Girard was either dead, or he was hurt and in hiding and on the run. And I was alive. That was the important thing.

The scenario of what happened after the shooting in the cemetery went like this:

A badly wounded Girard—there was a trail of blood leading from the graves to where the car had been parked—drove a short distance then abandoned the car. He stole another, knowing we'd be chasing the rental, from a woman at gunpoint. He drove that south until he switched cars again, this time stealing one from an auto dealership not far from the Ohio River where the car and body were found. The assumption was he had lost so much blood by that point he finally lapsed into unconsciousness behind the wheel, lost control of the car on the bridge and drove it off the side into the waters below.

A theory on how Phil Girard became what he turned out to be—a cold-blooded killer of teenage girls operating behind the protection of an FBI shield—was more difficult to figure out.

Why did he do it?

No one really knew the answer to that question, probably even Phil Girard himself if he was around to ask.

We did confirm more stuff about Girard's background. It was him who had come from a broken home, like he tried to tell us about Earnshaw. It was Girard's mother who had been a drug addict, and his father who had been in and out of jail before he died. And, after digging more deeply into the father's death than authorities had at the time, FBI investigators were convinced that Girard had murdered his father. It was his first kill, they now believed.

But otherwise Girard's motives remained a mystery, like with many other serial killers.

Why did Ted Bundy do what he did?

Why did Son of Sam?

Why did goddamned Jack the Ripper kill all those women?

It apparently fulfilled some inner need, fantasy or compulsion for all of them, like it must have done for Phil Girard. That's really the only explanation that made any sense, even if it did seem difficult for a normal person to comprehend.

We found out later that Girard had used his access to law enforcement files to target the young girls he went after. Many of his victims turned out to be from homes where complaints of domestic violence had been filed with authorities at some point. Then as he traveled around the country in his role as an FBI agent he'd reach out to his victims.

No one will probably ever know for certain how many victims Phil Girard was responsible for in his years-long spree. The ones we'd pinpointed in recent times, plus Jessica Staley and Carolyn Garms, for sure—but probably many more. What we did know was that he had befriended these girls who were living in unhappy homes, and then used his status as an FBI agent to get them to trust him and go with him in hopes of finding a better life. And he would do that until—for all the reasons we'd never understand—he'd kill them and move on to another target.

I had no idea why Phil Girard had come after me. Maybe it had something to do with me solving my sister's murder the last time we'd been here. He'd been a part of that, he could have killed me then if he'd wanted to. But he didn't. Perhaps it was true that he'd decided I was going to be his "last kill." A final trophy he wanted to take with him into retirement in Florida or wherever he wound up after leaving the bureau.

Why? Why me? That was a secret that sadly Phil Girard was able to take with him to the grave—or wherever he was hiding now.

There was one surprise though.

Becky Benedict.

It turned out Girard hadn't killed Becky, even though he'd gone to great lengths to make it look like he had. We discovered that he had manipulated the DNA results from the motel to make it seem like they matched the DNA found with Benedict years earlier in the trash bin, even though it did not. It wasn't clear exactly how he did that, but Girard had been in the FBI for a long time, and he understood the machinations of the DNA lab very well. He used this knowledge to somehow manipulate the report to make it seem like Becky Benedict and Jessica Staley had been killed by the same person. That's why he had Staley register at the Zanesville motel using Becky Benedict's name too.

He'd also paid off Lester Eldridge, the sleazy owner of the motel, to feed us a phony story about Edgar Daniels being there with Jessica. Eldridge admitted that when we confronted him later.

Why did Girard want us to think that the same person killed the Benedict girl more than twenty years ago? I suppose it was part of whatever sick game he was playing with us; he wanted to complicate the trail even more.

So then who killed Becky Benedict?

We went back on the case and talked to all the earlier suspects again—the principal and teachers at her school; Donald Maris, her ex-boyfriend and now a Dorchester cop; the finance guy William Zachary who'd gotten so upset with us when we showed up at his house; even the other students and cheerleaders—looking for some clue after all this time. Finally, after a lot of questioning, we got one of them to break down and confess. It was William Zachary.

Becky had told him she was pregnant, and he was the father of the baby.

Then she'd demanded money from him.

He was a student at the Wharton Business School, and this —the scandal and the money she wanted to take care of the baby—would have ruined his future, he said.

So, in a rage, he'd brutally beaten her to death, hid her body for several days and finally left it in that dumpster.

When Daniel Gary Leighton falsely confessed to the murder a short time later, Zachary figured he was in the clear. And it stayed that way for more than twenty years until Alex and I showed up at his door. We thought he'd been upset about the federal probe into his financial business, but that wasn't it at all. We'd brought up Becky Benedict after all this time. And that's what upset him so much that day; he knew then that the nightmare from his teen years wasn't over.

So in the end I'd accomplished what I set out to do.

I'd solved Becky Benedict's murder for her mother.

I'd gotten her the closure she'd been looking for for so long.

SIXTY-SIX

I'd spent a long time—hours that seemed to stretch into days—being questioned by FBI officials about everything that had happened with Girard. This was an FBI agent—a respected, veteran member of the bureau—that I had exposed as a serial killer. It was a horrendous black eye for the FBI, one they would have to try to explain away somehow for a long time to come. And I was the messenger who had delivered the bad news. So I might have been seen as a hero in the media again, but not so much at HQ.

I went back to Dorchester after all the debriefing was over to see Connor Nolan. I hadn't really had a chance to talk much with him after the shoot-out in the cemetery. Only a few brief words of thanks before we'd been whisked away to different spots for questioning.

I found out later he'd returned home.

I was there to see him for a couple of reasons, I suppose. One, of course, was to express my gratitude to him for saving my life. But also I wanted to find out where he and I stood in our relationship—or if we even had a relationship.

The conversation didn't go well.

"There's a new effort being made to remove me as chief of police," he explained to me. "There were lots of questions—after the TMZ stuff and now this—about what I was doing in Huntsdale in the first place. The argument is that I neglected my official duties for personal reasons. That personal reason is you. At least that's what people in city government here are suggesting. Maybe they're right."

"You saved my life. And you killed a serial killer. Or at least put him out of commission so he probably won't murder anymore young girls, even if he is somehow still alive."

"But I didn't do the job they're paying me here to do." He shook his head sadly. "On top of that, your people nabbed William Zachary for the Becky Benedict murder after all this. They want to know why I wasn't the one who figured it out. Don't get me wrong. I'm glad he's behind bars and the case is finally solved. But I wish you would have involved me in that. Didn't you trust me enough to tell me what you were doing on Zachary, Nikki? That really left egg on my face too."

"Wasn't my call. It was handled by the people above me in the bureau."

"Maybe so. But you didn't trust me enough to tell me about your plans with Girard either. I had to do that on my own. Yes, it saved your life in the end, but we got lucky. If you'd only trusted me enough to tell me what you were doing then."

He was right. I should have told him. No matter what Phil Girard and Alex said to me when we were planning it.

But Connor didn't trust me either.

Not about everything.

I told him that now.

"Like what?" he asked.

"Your wife." I looked at the picture of his wife—his ex-wife, his dead ex-wife—that still sat prominently on his desk. "What happened when she died, Connor?"

"Do you mean did I kill her?'

"No, I don't think you killed her."

"Well, you think something happened between us when she died, don't you? Something that I did wrong? A lot of people think that, Nikki. They always have, and they probably always will."

"Then what did you do?"

"It's not what I did, Nikki. It's what I didn't do. I didn't save her." Then he finally told me the story about him and his wife's death. "Lauren was an alcoholic," he said. "A bad alcoholic. It destroyed our marriage. I loved her, and she loved me. But it was a toxic relationship because of the drinking. She would lie to me about being sober, then I'd find her drunk or discover bottles of alcohol she'd hidden around the house. Eventually, it became too much to deal with, and I left her."

"But then you tried to get back together again."

"Yes. We were trying to give it another go."

"And that's why you were at her place the night the fire happened?"

He nodded. "We'd just made love. And talked about getting re-married. We talked about a lot of other stuff too. What would have happened if she'd lived? I'm not sure because she was drunk that night. And so was I."

"You were drinking with her?" I thought again about the times I'd been with him in the bar where he'd avoided drinking any liquor. "Are you an alcoholic too?"

"No, not at all. But I was drinking that night. Drinking with Lauren. I wanted to be close to her again, I wanted to share my life with her again. I figured maybe if I shared her drinking—drank with her, instead of always complaining about it—it might bring us together. I know that doesn't make much sense. But I decided to match her drink for drink that night. Which is what I did until we both passed out."

"And that's when the fire started?"

"That's right. You see, Lauren was a chain-smoker as well as a drinker. I always warned her about falling asleep with a lit cigarette in her hand. Which is what she must have done that night. All I remember is that I woke up and saw flames everywhere. I staggered around in a drunken, confused daze, and somehow found myself outside. Then I realized Lauren was still inside the burning house. I tried to go back inside to get her, but it was too late. She was already dead."

"But that wasn't your fault."

"Wasn't it? If I'd been sober, I could have saved her."

"You can't be sure about that."

"I believed it when Lauren died, I believe it now, and I'll believe it for the rest of my life. I let my wife die. That's something I can never forget no matter who else I'm with. Even you, Nikki."

"And that's why you don't drink anymore."

"Yes."

"Because it reminds you of your wife."

"Let's just say alcohol brings back too may bad memories for me."

That left me with one big question I had to ask him.

The question about us and our future.

If there was going to be one.

"I think we should cool it for a while," he said. "Put everything on hold for now. I need to deal with my job situation here. Being linked with you even more than in the past... well, that's not going to help, Nikki."

He must have seen the look of disappointment on my face, even though I tried my best to hide it. He was right, of course. But I was still hoping he might answer me in a different way.

"You don't agree?" he asked.

"I do. I'm in the same situation as you. I might be a hero in the media, but I'm not exactly a hero these days with my bosses. My immediate boss is a big stickler for FBI protocol and always following the rules. I didn't do that here a lot of times, especially in my relationship with you. Sleeping with a local police chief isn't conducive to advance in the bureau. This is my career we're talking about here, too."

I stood up to leave.

I wanted to kiss him goodbye or something before I left Dorchester, but the door of his office was open, and I figured it wasn't a good idea for someone to catch us smooching again. Not a good idea for him or for me.

"Thank you again for saving my life," I said.

"Happy to do it." He smiled.

"This isn't really goodbye."

"Of course not."

"We'll stay in touch, right?"

"I hope so."

I shook hands with him, holding onto his hand for a long time before I finally let go.

Then I turned and walked out of his office, leaving him alone there with the picture of his dead wife.

SIXTY-SEVEN

"There's something about all this that still really bothers me," I said to Alex.

"You mean how we got fooled by Phil Girard? Yeah, that bothers me too. I mean, we worked with the guy on this case. He was part of our team. And then he turns out to be the guy we were looking for the whole time. That pisses me off too."

"No, I'm talking about the Becky Benedict case."

We were on the phone. Alex had gone back to Washington as soon as she could. She wanted to be with her family and her loved ones at home again. Me, I was still in Dorchester. I didn't really have any loved ones or a real home to rush back to. But that wasn't what was on my mind right now.

"Becky Benedict told people she was pregnant before she was murdered," I said.

"Right. That was the motive for killing her. Zachary told us that's why he flew into a rage and beat her to death. Because she was threatening him with the pregnancy. Using that to get money and attention out of him."

"Except she wasn't pregnant. There's nothing in the autopsy report that indicates she was carrying a baby. Even a baby in the early stages. I've gone over it again and again looking for something. Not a word."

"Maybe the coroner—or whoever did the autopsy—just missed it."

"Or maybe she was never pregnant at all."

"But she told Zachary she was."

"She told her cheerleader friend too. And maybe she told other people."

"Why would she do that?"

"To scare people—people like Zachary—enough so that she could get what she wanted from them."

"You mean money."

"Yes. And maybe something else too. Something to help her get out of her unhappy life. To help her get away from that house where she lived. We might have it all wrong about what really happened with this girl."

"Wait a minute—are you saying you think Zachary didn't really do it?"

"No, he killed her. He knew too many facts about the case when he finally gave it up to investigators. I believe his confession. Zachary will be convicted, and he'll go to jail for a long time. I'm certain about that."

"Then what's bothering you? Why are you still poking around in Dorchester about Becky Benedict?"

"Becky Benedict wasn't the only person who died here back then."

I went to see Stan Upshaw, the former Dorchester police chief who had handled the original Becky Benedict murder investigation twenty years ago.

"Sure, I heard talk about a pregnancy, just like you," he told me. "Hell, I'm sure we wound up talking to a lot of the same people. But the pregnancy turned out to be not true. At least not as far as we could determine. There was nothing in the autopsy report to indicate she'd been pregnant."

"Did that bother you?"

"Of course, it bothered me. But then this Leighton guy confessed to the crime, and the investigation was over. So whether she was pregnant or not—and, as far as we knew, she wasn't—had nothing to do with her getting killed the way she did."

"What about now? Do you still have some questions about the case like I have questions about the case, Chief Upshaw?"

We were sitting on the back porch of his house. Next to the roses and hyacinths and other plants that he tended to so diligently in his retirement. Inside in his living room were all the awards and commendations from his days on the force. He'd had a good career, a good life. That's what he told me the last time I was here. But he was still a cop. And you never lose a cop's instincts no matter how long you've been away from the job.

"It bothers me," he said. "It bothers me a lot."

"Any ideas."

"I have one idea. Got no proof for it. It's only a hunch. Something about the case that bothered me back then—at least until that Leighton fellow confessed and we shut down the investigation."

"Go ahead."

"The father."

"Becky's father?"

"Yes."

"The one who died not long after she did."

"Right. I got the feeling... well, I got the feeling that something was going on inside that house."

"Sexual?"

"Maybe."

"You think the father was having sexual relations with Becky?"

"He was defensive, nervous and evasive about everything when I talked to him after her murder. Especially when I asked about the pregnancy rumors. I had a feeling he was hiding something. Maybe she had told him she was pregnant. Maybe she did it to scare him. Maybe he believed her, and he thought it was his baby. If Leighton hadn't confessed back then, he might have been a suspect in his daughter's death. But now—with Zachary—we know the father didn't do it. Anyway, he's been dead for a long time. He died right after the girl died."

"Do you think the mother had any idea what was going on between her husband and Becky?"

"She must have known," Upshaw said.

The house where Becky Benedict had lived looked the same as it had the last time I was there. But I knew things were different now. Everything was different.

I rang the bell and knocked on the door. Inside I could hear a television playing. I pushed on the front door. It was open. I went inside. I'd called ahead to let Mrs. Benedict know I was coming, so I figured she was here somewhere.

The house felt empty. Empty of any real life. On a mantel was the picture of Becky I'd seen before; wearing her cheerleader outfit and smiling happily for the camera.

I called out to Mrs. Benedict.

"I'm upstairs in Becky's bedroom," she said.

I made my way through the house and up to the room that had been Becky's. The room that Mrs. Benedict had kept intact all these years. Like she was waiting for something. I thought she had been imagining that Becky—or her spirit—might return to her there somehow. But it was something else she had been waiting for. Closure. Final closure for her daughter.

That's where I found her, packing Becky's stuff—all the belongings that she'd kept intact for twenty years—into cardboard boxes.

"What are you doing?" I asked, even though I was pretty sure I knew the answer.

"Saying goodbye to Becky."

I looked in the boxes. They were filled with Becky's clothes, her books, and the rest of her things from the bedroom. "What are you going to do with all this?" I asked.

"I'll donate her clothes to charity, Goodwill or places like that. Give her books to a library. Then get rid of the rest the best I can. Maybe throw it away if I have to."

"After all these years?"

"It's time," she said. She told me that she was planning on selling the house. Moving to a new town. Starting life over. There were too many memories here for her, she said. Becky, and her dead husband too.

That gave me the opportunity to say what I wanted to her. "Tell me about your husband," I said. "How exactly did he die?"

"He had a fatal heart attack. You know that. I told you the first time we met."

"What caused his heart attack?"

"Excuse me?"

"It wasn't from natural causes, was it?"

"I don't know what you're talking about."

"Mrs. Benedict, were you aware that your husband was sexually abusing your daughter in this house? Probably had been doing it for a long time."

It was still a guess on my part, of course. But I could tell right away from the look on her face that I was right. It wasn't a look of surprise or shock, but more one of resignation to the truth she knew was coming. The truth about her daughter and her husband which she had hidden for so many years.

"Not when it happened, I didn't know then," she said

slowly. "It was later, after Becky was dead. That's when I put the pieces together. Hints she had given me, without specifically saying anything, and the way she often seemed uncomfortable around her father. After her death, I confronted him and he finally admitted it. But he said he would deny it if I ever told anyone, and that Becky could never confirm it because she was dead.

"I even wondered for a while if he might have been the one who killed her, killed his daughter to keep her quiet. But I never really believed that. And then the Leighton person confessed, and the case was over. Except for me and my husband. I couldn't live with him anymore. Every time I looked at him, all I could think of was what he'd done to Becky. And then…"

"I'm pretty sure what you did next," I told her. "You killed your husband. Your grief and guilt over Becky became so overwhelming that you figured out a way to murder him without anyone suspecting anything. Maybe with poison or some other drug—but you were able to make it look like he had a heart attack. Everyone believed you. He died of a broken heart over his daughter, you always told people. And no one ever questioned that, did they? Until now."

She didn't admit it, but she didn't deny it either.

"Are you going to arrest me?" was all she said when I was finished.

"I have no evidence to arrest you."

"But you do think I killed my husband?"

"Yes, but I can't prove that."

She sighed. "So what happens now?"

"Nothing. You sell the house. You leave Dorchester. And you try to somehow put your daughter and your husband behind you. If you can ever do that. I'm not so sure you can, Mrs. Benedict."

I started to leave her.

"Thank you for catching the person who really did kill

Becky," she said to me. "I didn't think there was much hope of doing that. But you did it, you got the man. I'm very grateful to you."

There wasn't much more for me to say to this woman.

Eleanor Benedict had asked me to get closure for Becky's murder.

I had accomplished that.

Now all she had left was to hope for some kind of closure for herself.

SIXTY-EIGHT

I've always had trouble letting go of a big case. I spend so much time investigating, immersing myself in the case, working on it 24/7 until I get the answers—like I finally did in this one. And then it's just gone.

I feel a real sense of emptiness at times like this. Almost like a bereavement. That's how I felt about the cases of Becky Benedict, Jessica Staley, Carolyn Garms and all the rest right now. Phil Girard was gone, Edgar Daniels dead, William Zachary in jail, Eleanor Benedict moving away, and it looked like I wouldn't have to deal with Frank Earnshaw anymore. It was time to go back to Washington and move on with my life there.

Or so I thought until I got a call from a woman named Maureen Wilcox. At first, I didn't recognize the name. But then it came back to me. She was the woman I'd met who was living in the house where I'd grown up in Huntsdale.

"Agent Cassidy," she said, "something happened here that I think you should know about. A woman came to the door of my house. She told me that she used to live here."

I was confused. "Of course, Ms. Wilcox," I said. "That was me. Don't you remember?"

"No, not you. It was another woman. She looked a little like you. But different too. And she had a different name."

"What name?"

"She said she was Caitlin Cassidy."

A LETTER FROM DANA

I want to say a huge thank you for choosing to read *Last One to Die*. If you did enjoy it, and want to keep up to date with all my latest releases, just sign up at the following link. Your email address will never be shared and you can unsubscribe at any time.

www.bookouture.com/dana-perry

This is the second book I've written featuring Nikki Cassidy, a woman FBI agent who specializes in cases of abducted or murdered teenage girls. This is more than just a job, it's a passion for Nikki—who is haunted by the loss of her sister to a killer, years earlier. The two towns where the book is set, Huntsdale in southern Ohio and Dorchester near Pennsylvania, are fictional places—as are all the people I write about in them. But I grew up in Ohio and I live now not far from Philadelphia, so I think they're both pretty realistic as small towns where bad things sometimes happen. As for the Nikki Cassidy character, I love writing about her—and there's more Nikki coming soon!

I hope you loved *Last One to Die* and if you did I would be very grateful if you could write a review. I'd love to hear what you think, and it makes such a difference helping new readers to discover one of my books for the first time.

I love hearing from my readers—you can get in touch with me on social media or through my website.

Thanks,

Dana Perry

www.rgbelsky.com

 facebook.com/DanaPerryAuthor
x.com/DanaPerryAuthor

PUBLISHING TEAM

Turning a manuscript into a book requires the efforts of many people. The publishing team at Bookouture would like to acknowledge everyone who contributed to this publication.

Audio
Alba Proko
Sinead O'Connor
Melissa Tran

Commercial
Lauren Morrissette
Jil Thielen
Imogen Allport

Data and analysis
Mark Alder
Mohamed Bussuri

Cover design
Jo Thomson

Editorial
Helen Jenner
Ria Clare

Milton Keynes UK
Ingram Content Group UK Ltd.
UKHW012011280324
440101UK00004B/360